STAKED OUT FOR DEATH!

Penkin tied the Baroness' hands and ankles to the stakes, making it impossible for her to break free. He peeled the hotsuit off, using his sharply bladed knife to cut the fabric.

The gnome Viktor was dancing about. "Please," he begged. "She looks so beautiful lying there in the snow. Just once, can't I have a woman like that?"

'All right, Viktor," Penkin said gruffly. "But be quick about it. I'll keep a watch for the wolves."

But suddenly they heard the unmistakable wail of the approaching wolves. And when the wolves encircled the naked Baroness, they watched her with ears pricked forward and lips drawn back over white fangs in the horrible semblance of a smile....

OPERATION DOOMSDAY
is an original POCKET BOOK edition.

OPERATION DOOMSDAY

by
Paul Kenyon

PUBLISHED BY POCKET BOOKS NEW YORK

OPERATION DOOMSDAY

POCKET BOOK edition published August, 1974

L

This original POCKET BOOK edition is printed from brand-new plates made from newly set, clear, easy-to-read type. POCKET BOOK editions are published by POCKET BOOKS, a division of Simon & Schuster, Inc., 630 Fifth Avenue, New York, N.Y. 10020. Trademarks registered in the United States and other countries.

OPERATION DOOMSDAY

Chapter 1

There were about thirty men scattered through the vast gray cavern of Mission Control, sitting wherever they could find chairs among the empty rows of dead consoles. Most of them were NASA brass. The rest were sober, business-suited men with that Washington look.

A bright point of light appeared on the left edge of the enormous display screen at the front of the room. The light drifted toward center screen as the remote camera operator adjusted his alignment.

"Is that it?" said the young doctor from the Center for Disease Control.

"That's it," said NASA's deputy director. "The Russians are putting it down in the Taurus-Littrow region, just about where our computer projection said they would."

The spark of light grew, still centered. The bleak horizon, looking like lumpy oatmeal, appeared as the remote lens, a quarter-million miles distant, tracked the spark downward.

"The picture's coming from the camera they left mounted on the lunar rover?" said the man from Defense.

"That's right," the deputy director said.

"I thought it was supposed to be dead."

"That's what we told the public."

The thirty VIPs leaned forward as the spidery outline of the Russian lander took shape against the stars. The spark had grown into a blossom of flame. The lunar landscape rushed toward it. The flare died abruptly, and the Russian lander dropped the last few feet, sending up a slow-motion cloud of debris. The lander sat there, squat and ugly, while the dust settled slowly around it.

"Smack in the middle of the Apollo 17 landing site," someone said unnecessarily.

1

The camera operator swung the distant lens in a slow circle so the VIPs could see the litter left behind by Cernan and Schmitt: the boxy form of the solar wind spectrometer, the tilting grid of the laser reflector, the extended panels of the gravimeter. The camera paused for a moment when it came to the ungainly bug that was the American lunar module's spent landing stage. The Russian lander had come down barely a hundred yards away from it.

After a while a hatch opened in the side of the Russian lander. It unfolded into a ramp. There was movement inside; light glinted off something metallic.

A preposterous vehicle rolled down the ramp. It resembled a washtub on eight old fashioned wire wheels. There was a pair of TV cameras on movable stalks, looking like lobster eyes, and a set of mechanical claws.

"Another Lunokhod," somebody murmured.

"I don't like this," said the CDC man.

"It can't do any harm if they take a look," said the FDA man reasonably. "It's not as if they were going to send samples back to earth, the way they did with Luna 16 and 20."

The Lunokhod scuttled around the site, sniffing at the American equipment like an inquisitive cockroach. It paused at the solar wind spectrometer, its lobster claws quivering.

"By God, if they knock that over, we ought to lodge a diplomatic protest!" the deputy director said through clenched teeth.

But the Lunokhod backed off carefully. A ripple of relieved laughter swept through the room.

"What the hell is it doing now?" the CDC man said.

The Lunokhod was picking up small pieces of litter in its claws: a geological hammer dropped by Schmitt, the damaged fiberglass fender that Cernan had accidentally ripped off the moon rover back in 1972. It held the souvenirs up to its TV eyes for a closeup view, then stowed them in a compartment that opened up in the washtub.

The FDA man stirred uneasily. "What'd it do that for?"

he said. "Why didn't they just drop it when they were through looking?"

The Lunokhod had discovered the TV camera mounted on the moon rover. It rolled up for a closer look. On the big screen, the thirty men in Houston could see the Lunokhod's own TV eyes swivel directly toward them, giving an uncanny illusion of an intelligent creature staring at them.

"I wonder if it's the same driver who operated Lunokhod 1 and 2," the deputy director said. "According to a Russian joke, he's a Moscow cabbie."

As they watched, the Lunokhod raised its lobster claws at them in a brief, unmistakable obscene gesture.

"Insolent bastard!" someone said.

The Lunokhod backed away again and began diligently collecting rock samples on the fringes of the area. Manipulating a small shovel with great skill in its pincers, it transferred the samples to a row of capsules mounted on a rack on the washtub. As each cylinder was filled, the Lunokhod sealed it, twisting a knob that evidently flooded the capsule with an inert gas.

The CDC doctor gripped the arms of his chair. "Did you see that?" he said in a strained voice. "It filled that last capsule with those pearly rocks that look like feldspar."

"Relax," the FDA representative said. "It's probably just going to take the samples back to some kind of automated laboratory aboard the lander—send the results of the analysis back to earth by telemetry."

"That's right," the deputy director said soothingly. "Those Lunokhods are designed to stay up there and explore. The first one operated for ten months before the batteries gave out."

"Then why the gas?" the CDC man said. "The moon's a vacuum anyway. You don't *need* an inert atmosphere to protect biological samples from contamination."

The two doctors looked at one another in wordless surmise. The big room had suddenly become very quiet.

Everybody stuck it out for the next eighteen hours, while the Lunokhod continued its sampling operations.

None of the thirty men left the third floor Mission Operations Control Room, except for brief visits to the john. Food, coffee and cigarettes were sent in. A few of the onlookers catnapped in their chairs.

By that time they were all rumpled and bleary-eyed. Even the Washington men had lost their impersonal tidyness. The man from Defense was snoring, his head on the console apron in front of him. His assistant shook him to wake him up in time for the next development.

"What's happening?" he yawned.

The Lunokhod was rolling purposefully toward the Russian lander, its mesh wheels leaving tracks in the gray porridge of the valley.

"I think it's going to . . ." The assistant trailed off, and stared at the screen.

The Lunokhod rolled up the ramp. It paused for a moment at the top, then disappeared into the square blackness of the opening. The hatch closed.

A ring of clamps around the skirt of the lander fell away. A fiery belt appeared at the craft's waist, and grew wider.

"There's an ascent stage," the deputy director whispered.

The young doctor from CDC was clutching him by the sleeve. "You said the Lunokhods *stay* on the moon and explore!"

The deputy director looked at him bleakly. "The Russians are showing us another space spectacular. *This* Lunokhod's going to return to earth."

The ascent stage popped out of the spindly legged base like an egg jumping out of an egg cup. A cloud of moon dust boiled upward, and then the Russian craft was rising above it, heading for home. In Houston, the remote camera operator followed it until it was a pinprick among the stars.

"Oh my God!" the CDC man said, burying his face in his hands. "What are we going to do now?"

The deputy director was already picking up the scrambler phone. The man from Defense, his face white as ashes, was at his elbow.

"Put me through to the President," the deputy director said.

While he waited, some of the VIPs tried to leave the Control Room. They found their way blocked by armed guards at the doors.

"Mr. President," the deputy director said, "this is Houston." His voice broke. "It's happened. It'll be here in approximately sixty hours." His voice dropped to a whisper. "Doomstone."

The President had ordered everybody out of the room on the second floor of the Pentagon except for the senior Presidential translator—the Army colonel who was currently in command of the Hot Line.

He'd brought only two officials with him: the Secretary of Defense and the director of the National Security Agency. The NSA director—like the President and the Secretary—had been routed out of bed in the middle of the night. But unlike his two superiors, he looked spruce and chipper. Heading an intelligence operation bigger and more secret than the CIA tends to make a man unflappable.

"What time is it in Moscow?" the President said.

The Hot Line commander glanced at his watch and made a calculation. "Nine oh four in the morning, Mr. President," he said.

"Then they're not getting the Premier out of bed?"

"No sir. He's an early riser. He's generally at his desk by eight-thirty."

The President looked haggard. He hadn't taken time to shave. "Then what's taking him so long?"

The colonel cleared his throat. "It should only be a few more minutes, Mr. President. They'll have had to get him out of his office in the Kremlin, and then he'd have to walk across to the other side of Red Sqare to the party headquarters building, where they keep the Hot Line terminal."

The teleprinter began to chatter. Instantly, the colonel was bending over the printout, reading the Cyrillic characters as they appeared. He began translating almost immediately.

"To the President of the United States of America. From the General Secretary of the Communist Party of the Union of Soviet Socialist Republics. Your message headed Urgent, Code Omega, received. The Premier, and the chief science advisor for the Soviet Union, are present at this end, as you requested. We are prepared to receive the vital information you indicate you wish to transmit. Please proceed."

The President took a deep breath and began talking.

The colonel moved to the English-language keyboard. His fingers flew over the keys, tapping out the message as fast as the President could dictate. It would be translated into Russian at the other end—standard operating procedure in a world where a slight misunderstanding over a word or phrase could lead to thermonuclear war.

The electronically scrambled signals streamed into outer space from the big directional antenna on the roof of NSA's nine-story Operations Building Annex at Fort Meade, Maryland. They were picked up by Intelsat 4, in a parking orbit over the Atlantic, and bounced to Russia's Molniya I communications satellite. The old Hot Line cable system, routed through Stockholm and Helsinki, had been phased out ever since Washington and Moscow had begun to worry about possible cable sabotage by Scandinavian extremists.

The colonel hadn't been prepared for the content of the message the President was feeding him for transmission. He was a professional, and his hands never faltered on the keys. But when he finished, his face was white.

He looked mutely at the President. "Is it true, sir?" he said, breaking protocol.

"It's true all right, Colonel," the President said.

"What do we do now?" said the Secretary of Defense.

"We wait," the President said. "They'll have to talk it over."

They waited for an hour and a half. The President paced, looking at his watch from time to time. There was no conversation. Twice during that time, the President picked up the secure phone and gave instructions to waiting aides outside. Once there was a discreet tapping at the door, and he admitted a sleepy, unshaven White House assistant who handed him a thick folder with a President's Eyes Only stamp on the cover.

The Cyrillic teleprinter began its machine gun rattle. Everybody in the room instinctively jumped. The colonel was the first to recover. Before the carriage had jumped to the second line, he was at an adjoining keyboard, craning his neck to read the emerging message, typing his translation by touch.

When he finished, his face was even whiter. Wordlessly, he ripped off a length of stiff paper and handed it to the President.

The President read the message and handed it to the Secretary of Defense and the NSA director.

"It's no use," he said. "He didn't believe me."

The Secretary of Defense looked at his watch. "The Russian capsule should touch down in approximately fifty-four hours. Couldn't you at least talk them into bringing it down in a remote area?"

The President grimaced. "I can try. I don't think it'll do much good."

"If they open that capsule, it's all over. For them and for us."

The President said, "The Russians want a shot at some moon rocks too." He gestured toward the translated message. "They seem to think Doomstone is a ploy to undercut Soviet space prestige, now that our own lunar program is finished."

The Secretary of Defense sat down. His hands were visibly trembling. "God help us all."

The President turned to his NSA director. "What are our options, General?" he said quietly.

"There's only one option, Mr. President," NSA said. "Operation Doomsday."

The President nodded. He turned to the Secretary of Defense. "It's your responsibility to get Doomsday rolling. The machinery's ready. It's existed ever since the Houston Disaster of 1972."

The Secretary got up and left without a word, taking the thick file folder with him. The President looked meaningfully at the Hot Line colonel. He got up and left too.

"Is this room secure?" the President said.

"I had a team from the COMSEC section check it out just before you arrived."

"You understand we're going to have to use Coin on this one?"

"I understand, Mr. President."

"It may destroy Coin's effectiveness as an agent. Your superspy is going to have to attend the Doomstone briefings. His cover may be blown."

NSA smiled thinly. "Maybe not, Mr. President. I think we can trust Coin to find a way to keep his identity secret. Our friends at the CIA are still going crazy, trying to crack Coin's cover."

The President laughed in spite of himself. "General, I realize that *I'm* prohibited from knowing Coin's identity —I signed that particular presidential directive myself. And I appreciate how you've outfoxed CIA. But don't tell me *you* don't know who your own agent is."

"I don't *want* to know, Mr. President. I'm just the man who passes on the assignments. And about a million and a quarter worth of operating funds." He looked at his watch. "I better get down to the cookie factory and turn the Key."

The President nodded. "You do that. We're running out of time."

It was three o'clock in the morning when John Farnsworth got the call. He was watching a late movie on TV —he hadn't been able to sleep, and he was sitting in front of the set with three fingers of Scotch, neat.

Farnsworth was a lean, confident man in his fifties, with the commanding good looks you often see in distinguished military men or the chief executives of large corporations. Even insomnia and a rumpled bathrobe couldn't take away his air of authority and good breeding. He had a lean, civilized face with a firm mouth and penetrating eyes, steel-gray hair and a clipped mustache.

The show on TV was an old Western. Randolph Scott was standing poised on a dusty street, his hand hovering above his holster, facing down the bad man. He opened his mouth to speak.

"Key, do you read me?" the TV set said. Randolph Scott's lips continued to move, out of synch. "Repeat, Key, do you read me? Please acknowledge."

Farnsworth snapped to attention. He put down the Scotch and crossed the darkened living room to the television. It was a big color set, a little bulkier than ordinary. He reached around back and found the *vertical hold* knob. He pressed it instead of twisting it, punching in the code of the day.

Two hundred miles away, in a windowless steel and concrete building on the outskirts of Washington, a giant IBM 7090 computer received Farnsworth's signal from the MESTAR (Message Storage and Relay) satellite that had bounced it. A couple of nanoseconds later it signaled its peripheral processors that it had located the person known as Key. Obediently, the computer peripherals stopped their electronic searching for Key at his office, country home, in his two automobiles and his private aircraft.

The NSA communications officer on duty turned to the Director. "He's ready, General. You can go ahead."

The NSA Director looked amused. "That damned computer knows who Key is, and we don't."

"It knows *where* Key is," the communications officer corrected. "It doesn't know *who* he is. And the 'where' is just an electronic address programmed into the computer. He could be anywhere on this planet."

"Security," the Director sighed. "All right, Andrews, leave me alone with this electronic monster." When the communications officer was out of earshot, he shoved a cassette into the optical scanner. He bent over the scrambler microphone and began talking.

In his New York apartment, Farnsworth watched Randolph Scott and the dusty Western street fade from his television screen. Now there was a picture of an absurd little vehicle that looked like a washtub on eight wire-mesh wheels.

The TV set spoke with the voice of the Director of the National Security Agency. "You're looking at the Soviet *Lunokhod IV*. Approximately six hours ago it took off from the moon with a load of rocks from the old Apollo 17 landing site."

Farnsworth nodded automatically. Absently, his hand reached for the Scotch.

The TV screen was showing a closeup of a capsule strapped to the Lunokhod's back. Stenciled on it was a Russian word that looked like *KaMeHb* and the number 6.

The voice went on. "We've got to stop the Russians from opening that capsule." The voice choked. "If they do, it means the end of life on earth."

Farnsworth arrested his hand. He frowned. The Director wasn't usually given to making melodramatic statements.

"So that you can understand what's at stake, I'm going to show you some films that were taken in Houston in 1972. . . ."

On the screen there was an opening shot of the exterior of a building. An establishing shot. The camera zoomed to a closeup of a plaque reading *Building 37, Lunar Receiving Laboratory*. Then it showed some scientists in white smocks and surgical masks feeding a container through an airlock into a sealed, glass-walled chamber. One of the scientists stuck his hands into a pair of glove-like waldos. Inside the sealed chamber, a pair of mechanical hands began to unscrew the container.

Then the horror began.

The briefing took an hour. When it was over, Farnsworth picked up the glass of Scotch and drained it in one gulp. He was sweating.

He recovered quickly. In Farnsworth's trade, you had to have steady nerves. If you didn't, you didn't live very long.

What part of the world was Coin in at the moment? Farnsworth walked over to the TV set again. This time he punched a digital code into the *brightness* knob.

An electronic signal pulsed through a roof antenna. It

spurted into space and tickled a relay in the MESTAR satellite that was currently hanging three hundred miles over the Atlantic. MESTAR talked to one of its brothers. For a fraction of a second, millions of electronic fingers probed the outstretched body of Europe. One of the fingers felt something: a pea-sized transponder hidden in a very special wristwatch.

On Farnsworth's TV screen, a map of Europe took shape. An arrow of light appeared, pointing at a spot on the Riviera.

Monaco. Coin was in Monaco.

Farnsworth snapped his fingers. Of course! It was the day of the Grand Prix. Coin would be racing.

Farnsworth remembered the pictures from Houston. Grimly he leaned forward and punched his instructions into the set for transmission to MESTAR.

Grand Prix or not, this couldn't wait. The world was in a race, too. A race against doom.

Chapter 2

"Son of a bitch!" growled the Baroness Penelope St. John-Orsini.

She glared savagely at her skinned knuckles. Then, her exquisite jaw set with determination, she picked up the heavy crescent wrench again and attacked the stubborn nut with redoubled ferocity.

"It's frozen," said the big, bent-nosed man standing behind her. He looked like a cigar-store Indian in mechanic's coveralls. "You'll never get it off without a hacksaw."

"The hell I won't!" said the Baroness.

The cords stood out on her long graceful neck. Her body strained like a bow. Her stunning face, with its enormous green eyes and sculptured cheekbones, contorted with effort.

The spectators gathered around the pit watched the little drama with interest. One of them, a French journalist, raised her Rollei and snapped a picture.

Even with a smudged face and grease on her white coveralls, the Baroness was a knockout. She looked like a *Vogue* cover—and had been: a dozen times so far. And her bat-winged red Ferrari, with its rumored modifications, was the talk of this year's Grand Prix racing circuits.

The spectators leaned forward as the Baroness put her magnificent shoulders into the effort. There was a tiny squeal of tortured metal.

"Goddamn!" the Baroness yelled. The wrench slipped, taking more skin off her knuckles. But the nut had turned a minute fraction.

Grinning broadly, she finished unscrewing the nut with thumb and finger, and tossed it carelessly into the big Indian's hand.

"There you are, Joe," she said. "You and Paul can lift the engine out now. And hurry, darling. It's almost starting time."

"Crazy!" Joe Skytop rumbled. "We're out of our mother minds, changing engines an hour before a race. You've never tested it."

"Tom Sumo says it'll work, and that's good enough for me," said the Baroness.

Sumo smiled, looking embarrassed. He was a boyish, frail-looking man with Japanese features. But if you looked closely at his hands, you could see the hard, stiff edges of a karate master. What you couldn't see was the nimbleness of touch that contributed to his wizardry at anything mechanical or electronic.

Paul was already fitting the hooks of a block and tackle to the engine. He was a slim, elegant black man who wore his mechanic's coveralls like a fashion plate. And he was. He was one of the top male models in the Baroness' organization, International Models, Inc. He was also an ex-street fighter and guerrilla warfare expert.

"Right on, Baroness," Paul said, a smile creasing his handsome mahogany face. The engine swung up and over, and he and Skytop wrestled it into the cradle.

The spectators nudged one another, buzzing with curiosity. The French journalist was bending over for a low-angle shot with her Rollei. Skytop pinched her bottom, and she yelped with indignation. *"Allez vous-en!"* she snapped. The spectators laughed.

It was a fine day in Monaco. The crowded tiers of buildings gleamed in bright sunlight, against a sky as deep and rich as blue beryl, and you could smell the salty tang of the Mediterranean even through the gas fumes of the pits. People were already crowding the barriers along the winding course and the terrace of the Hôtel de Paris, waiting for the race to begin.

The clustered onlookers surrounding the Baroness' pit gave way as a tall, lean, square-jawed man in racing gear pushed through them. "Hullo, Baroness," he drawled. "Having engine trouble, are you?"

The Baroness was wriggling out of her baggy coveralls, the generous curves of her body molded by a skin-tight white Nomex outfit with an azure stripe down the arms and legs, and the Orsini family crest emblazoned above her left breast.

"Good morning, Basil," she said with dangerous sweetness. "No, I'm not having any trouble. I just thought I'd throw the other engine away. I've already used it twice."

The French journalist scrambled for a picture of the two of them talking. The tall man was Basil Quarles, the fabulous driver who had already carried away honors at the South African and Spanish Grands Prix. The press was having a field day, playing up the rivalry between Quarles and the equally fabulous Baroness Orsini on the track, and their rumored tempestuous affair off it.

Quarles squatted beside Paul for a look at the new engine. It was a twelve-cylinder job with a complex arrangement of tubes replacing the carburetor venturi.

"Looks like a plumber's nightmare," he said. "How're you going to keep those two homemade turbochargers from interfering with one another?"

"I've got a little homemade computer about the size of a poker chip built into it, Basil darling."

"Hmm . . ." Quarles' manner was casual, but he looked

the Baroness' car over with meticulous care. Like most Formula 1 racing cars, it had a flattened devilfish shape, with wide rear tires like beer kegs. But the delta-shaped front fins looked as if they belonged on a jet plane, and the big rear wing was a graceful batwing equipped with what looked like independently maneuverable vanes.

". . . I suppose you have a little computer controlling those, too," he said.

"As a matter of fact I do, darling. It tells the wing which wheel needs the most weight on it at any given time."

"It'll never get off the ground, Baroness. Or . . ." He laughed. ". . . it jolly well *will* get off the ground and take you out of the race."

"We'll see, darling."

He hesitated. "Is it true that you've invested $200,000 of your own money to modify that freaking thing?"

"Word does get around, doesn't it?"

"We're an incestuous group, here on the Grand Prix circuit." His expression grew serious. "But darling, you haven't a chance—little computers or not. The French Matra team has the whole bloody government aerospace and missile industry behind them. They pulled engineers off the Concorde program for this year's Matra entry."

"*You* beat them in Spain last month."

He grinned. "That's different. *I've* got balls."

"And *I've* got ovaries, darling. We women get just as much mileage out of them, you know. Where the hormones, there moan I."

He laughed. "Very good. Speaking of hormones . . ."

She pursed her lips ironically. "And since the Grand Prix circus is so, how did you put it, *incestuous* . . . Basil, darling, whatever in the world can you be trying to work up to?"

"Why not, Penny? We might as well. The press is giving us credit for it anyway."

He hooked a thumb at the French journalist, who was trying frantically to get past Skytop's broad shoulders for a closeup picture of Quarles and the Baroness.

Penelope gave Basil an enigmatic smile. "I'll treat you like a sister, darling."

"How shall I take that, Penny?"

"Ask me after the race."

"Are you trying to bribe me to lose?"

"I'm trying to bribe you to win, darling. Or do your best to win, at any rate."

"Ovaries against balls, is it?"

"Ovaries against balls."

He stuck out a big hand. "It's a bet." They shook hands solemnly.

The French journalist had dropped to her knees, and was clicking away with her camera from between Skytop's legs. The big Indian reached down and hauled on the collar of her khaki fatigues. She ended up with her neck clamped firmly between his thighs, looking like a prisoner in the stocks.

"Cochon!" she screamed. *"Au secours!"* She dropped her camera and beat ineffectually at Skytop's treelike legs.

The Baroness laughed. "Let her up, Joe. She can take all the pictures she wants . . . of the car."

The journalist picked herself up and began dusting herself off indignantly. She retrieved her Rollei, but didn't try for any more closeups of the two drivers.

Over in the grandstands, the spectators were stirring. Princess Grace and Rainier, with their three children, were entering the royal box, surrounded by members of the palace guard in their white uniforms. The band began to play the Monegasque anthem.

"I'd better get over and see to fueling my car," Basil said, looking over his shoulder. "We'll be forming up for the drivers' parade soon." He cocked his head at the Baroness' Ferrari. "Good luck, Baroness. I hope you get that thing assembled before the race starts."

Paul made a final adjustment with a wrench and looked up. "All set, Baroness," he said.

Penelope climbed into the narrow cockpit and strapped herself in. Her long legs stretched out almost level from the thin pad that passed for a seat. Her head was no more than three feet above the ground.

She twisted the ignition. The new engine let out a powerful roar. She listened to it critically. It sounded fine. Her foot on the brake, she took it through all the gears, letting out the clutch for each one. There was no sticking of the gearshift, and it seemed to engage properly for each one.

"It'll do," she said. Tom Sumo beamed proudly. Paul came over, wiping his hands on an oil rag.

"Cream 'em, Baroness," he said.

She fretted restlessly during the parade of drivers, impatient for the ceremonial nonsense to be over and the race to begin. But nobody in the stands could have guessed at her impatience. She always gave them a good show. She was the legendary Baroness Orsini—model, multi-millionairess and jet set beauty whose doings you read about in the gossip columns and glossy international magazines, risking her life and good looks on Europe's most dangerous racing circuit. Some of them doubtless were reminding themselves that her second husband, the dashing young Baron Reynaldo St. John-Orsini, had died in a flaming crash on this same circuit during the Monaco Grand Prix a couple of years ago.

The Baroness flashed her dazzling smile at the crowds, keeping her protective helmet in her lap until the last minute, so they could see her famous features and mop of glossy black hair.

When she inched her car past the royal box, Princess Grace gave her a small correct smile and an imperceptible nod, not wanting to seem to favor her above the other drivers. The Baroness gave the Princess a tiny nod back. Her family had known the Kellys back in Philadelphia— it was hard to avoid them when you had one of the Main Line's most socially prominent names. Penelope Worthington—that's what she'd been then: a grave little girl of twelve, when Grace made headlines by marrying the Prince. Penelope's father, Arthur Worthington, had considered the Kellys to be *arrivistes* and *nouveau riche*. "But Grace is a nice girl," he'd said. "I hope this thing with this Rainier fellow works out."

She was on the starting grid now, her eyes on the flagman. Around her, the other cars were revving up. The engine noise was deafening, and she was surrounded by choking clouds of gasoline fumes. In the car to her left, Basil Quarles caught her eye and waved to her with a grin. His lips formed the word, "Balls." She gave him the finger and mouthed a silent "Ovaries" back at him. She wondered if the gesture had been noticed in the royal box. Princess Grace would have been shocked.

The starter dropped the red and white flag, and the Baroness let her Ferrari loose. She shot forward in a haze of tire smoke. Stewart's Tyrell Ford was in the lead, followed closely by Barry's triple-winged Lotus. The Baroness urged her car uphill in third, toward the first fast corner. Her tach said 9000 rpm. She slid easily past the French Matra, a slow starter despite its jet-plane nose.

Her wheels clipped the curb at Ste Devote at ninety-five miles per hour—the only way to get into position for the steep climb toward Casino Square. Then she was pushing the Ferrari at top acceleration, shifting to fourth gear halfway up the hill.

She risked a quick backward glance. Basil was crowding her, his goggled face turned into a weird, widened mask by the wind that was forcing its way through his lips. She wondered what her own face looked like at the moment. The sting of the airstream was like a rare, exhilarating tonic.

And then she was whizzing over the crest of the hill, instinctively giving the brakes the precise touch needed to steady the car for the next curve. The car was very light now, and the big bat-wings spread automatically to push her rear wheels into the road. The Baroness felt a flash of triumph. Her gamble had worked! The computer-controlled vanes were doing what Tom Sumo had hoped they would.

There was a flag marshal, waving a blue flag at her. Someone was coming up fast behind her! It was Jacky Ickx. She could see his homely-sexy, bent-nosed profile as he passed her at 120. He always reminded her of Jean-Paul Belmondo. She cursed. He had taken the one slot in that low wall of racing cars stretching across the road ahead.

Just before Casino Square there was a break in the lineup as Jacky pulled ahead again. The Baroness gunned her car into the slot, crowding the cars on either side. She felt the familiar thrill that comes from gambling with death; a momentary loss of control by any of the drivers would mean flaming disaster.

Now she could sense the blurred façade of the Hôtel de Paris at her left, and she'd managed to get over to clip the curb again. The cars ahead of her had their wheels off the ground: it was another spot where the cars became light. But the bat-wings worked again as she went over the hump by the gardens. She flew past the row of nightclubs, gaining steadily.

She braked heavily at the next sharp corner, shifting to second. Her whole body snapped forward, straining against the straps. She goosed it down the hill toward the hairpin curve ahead.

Somehow Basil was ahead of her. He gave her the finger as he passed, taking one hand off the wheel like a damn fool. She laughed aloud, amused in spite of herself. She had to brake hard at the hairpin, once more dropping to second gear. She'd catch him again on the straightaway further ahead.

She hurtled under the railway bridge, and her front tires suddenly touched the curb beside the seawall. She wrestled with the wheel, feeling the strain in her shoulders and chest, getting back onto the road. This was the place where Reynaldo had died. Unbidden, the mental image came to her: his red Ferrari slamming into stone, breaking apart like a badly made toy, bursting into flame while she watched. They'd had two good years; it all was good —the sex, the excitement, the pulse-quickening danger of the sports that she and Reynaldo sampled together. And then the blackened mummy they'd pried from the wreckage, and the huge villa in Florence for her to rattle around in after that.

She hadn't rattled very long. Another set of mental images came to her: the bland-faced CIA man who'd summoned her to the Embassy and appealed to her as an American citizen to do courier chores; the border officials who'd looked through her well-thumbed passport and passed her through with a smile, dazzled by her wealth and beauty and connections; the discreet, powerful man in Washington she'd inveigled into creating the elite, secret espionage organization she headed, buried somewhere in the budget of the National Security Agency; the long year of incognito training at Army and CIA and NSA bases that had turned her into the deadly, efficient agent known as Coin.

And the rest of it: the parties and the lovers and the excitement of the fashion and film worlds and the dangerous sports like skydiving and auto racing that Reynaldo had introduced her to, and which she continued to practice almost as a religion.

Especially the auto racing. She was going to win this one for Reynaldo! Death had cheated him of the Grand Prix. She was going to collect the debt.

She was flashing out of the Tunnel now, the sudden bright light blinding her. She consulted the precise photograph in her memory to avoid hitting the curb—this was where so many drivers clobbered the exit barrier—and then she was going like a bat out of hell down the fastest part of the course. 165 mph. She laughed aloud with the sheer joy of the speed and danger.

The little car shot ahead in top gear, a flat spearhead skimming the paving stones. The Baroness was a part of it. The engine noise deafened her; the wind clawed at her face and tried to tear off her helmet. The machine was her and she was the machine: a hurtling bomb of steel and rubber and flesh, throbbing with power, made for this suspended moment of blind speed.

She whizzed past one car, then another. The waterfront was a sparkling blur in the corner of her eye. How many cars were still ahead of her? There was a bright glitter of metal a quarter-mile ahead. A Lotus Ford—it must be Brazil's Fittipaldi. The Lotus whipped round the sharp curve of Tobacconist's Corner and disappeared from sight. Penelope made an instant decision not to shift down for the corner. She'd have to rely on brakes and the downward push of the bat-wings. Her foot was all the way down to the floor. She was doing 175 mph at 15,000 rpm. Her spine was slammed into the backrest.

She hit the brakes hard just before the corner, then released them almost immediately before the ramp. The big keg-like rear tires left the ground. She would have flipped end-over-end then if it hadn't been for the authority of the big wings, pushing them firmly back onto the pavement. She was safely past the pits now, heading toward the new danger of the Gasworks Hairpin. There was an irregular salmon-colored streak at her left: the faces of the people lining the rail. Behind them was a solid cliff of high-rise buildings, seeming to wheel majestically against the mountains beyond as she flew past.

She whipped around the corner, and there was a flutter of yellow ahead: a flag marshal frantically giving the danger signal. There it was: the crumpled wreckage of a McLaren against the barrier, a column of greasy smoke rising from it. Flames licked round the cockpit. She could see a dangling arm and a helmeted head hanging over the side.

Basil! It was Basil Quarles!

In the same frozen instant, she could see the little figures of fire marshals in helmets and masks, pounding toward the accident. There was the scream of an ambulance siren. But Basil's uniform was already on fire.

Ahead of the wreck she could see Fittipaldi's Lotus streaking past the finish line, on its way around the second lap. Behind her was a staggered line of more cars, coming up fast, fighting to pass one another.

Tears of frustration stung her eyes. It was so unfair! She was almost ahead of the pack now. The new motor and the computer-controlled vanes were working. She'd have been far out front by the end of the second lap, with no one able to catch her. The Grand Prix trophy was within her grasp.

But Basil was burning!

With a sob, she wrenched the wheel left and hit the brakes hard. The little Ferrari stood on its nose, the bat-wings fighting to slam the rear end down flat again. The car bucked crazily. The restraining straps bit into her chest and shoulders. In a bare twenty meters she slowed a hundred miles an hour. She was still going fast when her left tires hit the barrier.

The left front wheel came off then, and the bat-wing tore loose with a scream of tortured metal. The underbelly of the Ferrari scraped the roadway, inches from her tender bottom. Weaving like a maniac, her teeth feeling as if they'd been jarred loose, she came to a stop directly behind the burning Lotus.

Her car was a mess. A quarter-million dollars worth of crumpled tattered metal. But there was no time to think about that. She was jammed against the steering wheel, the crumpled cockpit telescoped backward. She tore loose the wrench that was taped to the wheel for just such an emergency, and, with a tug and a deft spin, unscrewed the nut. The wheel came off.

She unstrapped the restraining harness and squeezed herself out of the cockpit. Throwing an arm across her face to ward off the flames, she plunged through a wall of heat toward Basil. He was unconscious, but still breathing. Little flames crawled across his coveralls: he'd been sprayed with burning fuel. She managed to undo his safety harness, but when she tried to pull him loose, she found that his lower body was jammed fast between the bent floor plates and the steering wheel. She got the wheel loose with the help of the hex wrench that Basil had taped there and tried again. He was still stuck.

She beat at the flames. It was no use. He was still trapped in that damned tin bathtub of a car. She needed a pry bar.

The roll bar! If she could somehow get it loose! She poked her head into the cloud of foul smoke enveloping the rear of the car and found the nuts—there were three of them on either side, a total of six holding on the arch of metal. Dear God, if Basil's wrench were the right size . . . but it was too much to hope for. Or was it? She slipped the wrench over the first nut and it fit! Working fast, her gloves scorched by the hot metal, she got the roll bar off. She had a stout, U-shaped length of metal in her hands.

Her own suit was beginning to smoulder. But there was no time to worry about that now. She inserted one end of the U into the cockpit, at the place where the panels bulged inward. Grasping the other end firmly in her strong hands, she pulled. Nothing happened. She put all her weight into it. The metal gave a little. But it wasn't enough.

Holding onto the end of the U, she put the soles of her boots against the side of the car and leaned outward. The magnificent model's body was deceptive. Penelope was tall, with lots of leverage in those long limbs. Under the lush feminine curves was a superb musculature. She heaved with bone-cracking force. For a moment she hung there, braced against the car, her body bent at right angles, while little feathers of fire licked over her shoulder blades like a pair of wings. The fire crept down the tight Nomex jumpsuit. She ignored it. The metal plates began to bend. Her body was almost horizontal now, standing out from the side of the burning car like a jib. And then the roll bar came free, tumbling her onto the oil-slick pavement.

She sprang to her feet and lurched toward the cockpit again. She'd managed to widen the gap by several inches. She slipped her arms under Basil's and locked her hands across his chest. She pulled. His body slid upward, fabric tearing on the jagged metal.

His eyes flew open then. "Careful, love," he said. "See you don't rip my cock off."

"Shut up, you bastard!" she said, her eyes stung by smoke.

"We're going to need it, you know," he said, and lapsed into unconsciousness again.

He was heavy, but she heaved him over her shoulders and staggered a safe distance from the burning car with him. Her own Ferrari was on fire now, too, from the flames that had leaped across the gap. She smiled wryly. A quarter of a million dollars, she thought; you'd better be damned good in bed, my friend, to make up for that!

She dropped him unceremoniously on the ground and flung herself full length on top of him to smother the

flames that were engulfing his chest like a fiery bib. She
could feel their hot breath on her breasts. She locked her
arms and legs around Basil and rolled the two of them
over and over.

His eyes opened again. "I say, Penny!" he wheezed.
"This is rather fun, what?"

She grunted, heaving at his limp body, tumbling like a
single two-backed creature until the rest of the flames
were out. Then she collapsed, panting, her cheek nestled
in the hollow of his shoulder.

The photographers got there before the fire marshals
did.

"Merveilleux!" said a gold-spectacled young man in
jeans and battle jacket, pointing a Nikon at them. *"C'est
très épicé."*

"Say something for ABC, Baroness," said a puffy, pale
American, poking a microphone at her. He had a Sony
recorder slung over his shoulder.

"Bravest thing I've ever seen," said a gangling man
who was balancing a 16mm Beaulieu movie camera on
his shoulder. He began shooting footage immediately.

Helplessly, Penelope watched the other cars whiz by,
on their way around the second lap, streaking past the
wreckage like a swarm of giant bees.

The fire marshals came puffing up then, bulky in their
asbestos suits and masks, spraying them with foam.

"Hey, bugger off, will you?" Basil choked, sitting up.
"The bloody fire's already out!"

Penelope helped him to a standing position. The ambulance had arrived and two orderlies were hurrying toward them with a stretcher.

"Get that fucking thing away from me," he said, pushing weakly at the white sleeves.

A fussy little man with a doctor's bag was poking at
Basil. *"Etes-vous bien?"* he said.

"He's got burns on his hands and forehead," Penelope
said. "And he's probably concussed."

"Take a look at her, you bloody sod," Basil growled.
"Can't you see she's bleeding?"

The doctor turned to Penelope. "You have cut your cheek," he said accusingly. "And your hand is burned."

Penelope touched her face. Her fingers came away bloody, but she hadn't felt anything worse than a flap of skin and the sting of an abrasion. She flexed her hands. They were a little scorched from the hot metal, but it was nothing serious. They were beginning to swell. But none of the burning fuel had fallen on exposed flesh, thank God!

"Get him to the hospital," she said brusquely. "I'm all right."

Basil was feeling himself all over, very carefully. "No broken bones," he said. He looked at his hands. "I've done worse than that falling asleep at the beach."

The little doctor was close to tears. "But Monsieur Quarles, those are gasoline burns. And you may have internal injuries. You must go to the hospital."

Basil swayed. Penelope caught him and he managed to remain upright, leaning against her. "The hell I will! I've got something more important to do." In the end he let the doctor clean up the worst cuts and scrapes, spray an antiseptic ointment on the burns and plaster him with gauze patches. The doctor worked quickly, shaking his head and clucking. He refused to go until Penelope allowed him to tape a square of gauze on her cheek and treat her hands with burn ointment.

The reporters were jostling around them, interfering with the orderlies and the marshals. They'd managed to douse the flames on the two wrecked cars. A column of sickly smoke was still straggling upward. There was a yellow flag man around the bend now, cautioning the remaining cars that they couldn't pass one another on the hairpin.

Skytop, Paul and Sumo were pushing their way through the crowd. The big Cherokee knocked journalists aside like tenpins. Trailing him, she noticed, was the same big-assed lady reporter with the Rollei.

"Are you all right, Baroness?" Skytop said. He looked at the bandage on her face. "Christ! We're supposed to shoot a beachwear feature for *Bazaar* the day after tomorrow!"

Skytop was one of the hottest fashion photographers around, despite his rough-and-ready appearance and his rougher manners. International Models, Inc. couldn't exist without him. It made a good cover for his other activities in behalf of the Baroness.

"Don't worry about it, Chief," she said. "It's nothing that a little masking lotion won't cover."

He surveyed her torn and blackened jumpsuit.

"Any bruises under there?"

"Probably. It feels like it. We'll worry about it later."

Sumo was close to tears, looking at the smoldering wreck of the bat-winged Ferrari. "You would have won!" he said.

"We've got four weeks till the Francorchamps race, Tommy," she said gently. "Time enough to modify the other Ferrari."

Paul shot a venomous look at Basil. "You should have let the joker burn."

"That's enough," she said sharply.

Basil tottered. "He's right, y'know, Baroness," he said. His knees began to buckle.

Skytop was at Basil's side in a flash, hooking an arm the size of an oak branch around his ribs. Basil was a big, heavy man, but Skytop held him as if he were nothing but a rag doll.

"What do you want to do with him?" Skytop said.

"Take him to my suite at the Hôtel de Paris," she said. "We'll look him over there."

The surrounding journalists buzzed, and stepped up the rate of their picture taking. Skytop scowled at them.

They shoved their way through the crush, Paul and Sumo clearing the way, and Skytop bringing up the rear, supporting Basil Quarles. *"Assez!"* Paul said sharply. *"Il est blessé!"*

The journalists parted. With some amusement, Penelope saw that the big-assed lady reporter was still trailing them, making sheep's eyes at Skytop.

Sumo had the van pulled just outside the barrier, waiting for them. He held the door open for her. Before getting in, Penelope turned toward the track for a last look.

The bright little racing cars were zooming past the line, on another lap. Jackie Stewart's Tyrell Ford was in the lead, but Jack Brabham was coming up behind him fast.

She could see Grace and the Prince, standing stiffly in the reviewing box, wearing dark glasses and looking starched and uncomfortable. The silver trophy cup was waiting on a stand by Rainier's elbow. Penelope sighed. It had almost been hers.

Chapter 3

Back at the Hôtel de Paris, she sent Sumo out for a kit of medical supplies, then dismissed the three of them. Skytop had stripped Basil and put him in a hot tub.

"He's tough," the big Cherokee said, pausing at the door. "The bastard doesn't deserve any tender loving care. He made you lose the race. Take care of yourself, Baroness. Your skin's more important. *He's* not going to be posing in a bikini on the Côte d'Azur day after tomorrow."

"I'll take a good soak and inspect the damage," she laughed. "Now get out of here."

When she returned to the bathroom, Basil was soaping his back gingerly with a sponge.

"Ow!" he complained. "Feels like a barbecued beef back there!"

"Let me take a look," she said. There was a livid burned area the size of an outstretched hand.

"I'd better do that," she said, taking the sponge.

She swabbed away at it carefully, washing out the little embedded black flecks. It was oozing a little. Basil drew in his breath sharply, but otherwise made no sound. The burning petrol must have eaten through the fabric of his coveralls at that spot.

His hands were awkward paws in mittens of pink adhesive, with the fingers sticking out. The little doctor had done a good job on them.

There were more pieces of sticking plaster dotted over his arms and torso, along with a crazyquilt pattern of abrasions and purple bruises that the doctor hadn't thought bad enough to dress. She scrubbed his abused body gently, taking away the crusted blood and the soot and grime of the race.

"You're a mess, Basil darling," she said, rumpling his hair. She leaned over the tub and kissed him on the mouth.

"Don't forget to sponge between my legs, old thing," he said.

She looked into the soapy water. His pole was standing rigidly above the surface, casting a periscope eye at the ceiling.

"Impossible man!" she laughed. "How can you think about sex in your condition?" She reached between his legs and gave him a quick scrub.

"It's my solace. Takes my mind off my wounds. Besides, you promised, didn't you? Ovaries against balls."

"You didn't give me much of a race."

"The race isn't over." He grasped her wrist with his taped hands and put her hand on his stem. It was a nice fit, like the rubber sheathed gearshift of her Ferrari.

"We'll see. I'm going to change your dressings."

She helped him out of the tub, dripping, and dried him off. He tried to slip a hand inside the terrycloth robe that had replaced her ruined driving outfit, but she took his arm firmly and placed it around her shoulder. With an arm around his bruised ribs, her hip braced against his, she let him lean on her all the way to the bedroom. She eased him down onto the mattress. He lay on his back, his big, lean, competent frame livid with bruises against the white sheets.

"Take off that silly robe," he said.

"I'm all grime and oil. I'll have a bath first. You can lie there and contemplate your navel."

"It's not my ruddy navel I'll be contemplating." His stem pointed toward the ceiling at a forty-five degree angle, as livid as his bruises.

She laughed. "If you're not strong enough to stand on your own feet, you're certainly not strong enough for sex."

Wincing, he heaved himself up on one elbow. "Fortunately it's something I can do lying down."

"Try to nap, darling. Gather strength while I'm bathing."

In the tub, she surveyed the damage. Bruises. God, they were sore! Scraped knees and elbows. A gash down the forearm she hadn't noticed; the soap and water set it bleeding again. Those seared hands. They'd be a week or more healing, and in the meantime they were stiff. A lovely purple badge on the underside of her left breast, where she must have struck it against the edge of the cockpit. The penetrating warmth of the water felt good.

She shampooed the rubber dust and oil out of her hair and combed it out straight. It was thick and black, sweeping past those spectacular cheekbones and falling past her shoulders to her breasts. She fanned it out and blew hot air at it with the little hand dryer. She looked at her face critically in the steamy mirror. The enormous jade-green eyes stared back at her. The abraded cheek didn't look too awful now, with the dirt and dead skin out of it. She decided not to replace the gauze pad. She opened the medical kit that Sumo had fetched for her, and smeared ointment on it. She sprayed antiseptic on the gash on her arm, and rubbed more ointment on her hands.

Then, carrying the kit, she strode naked to the bedroom. Basil was lying on his back, his penis still pointing upward.

"Hullo," he said. "Is that the duty nurse? I love your outfit, Sister."

"Shut up and lie back. You're not doing a thing until I see to those burns and scrapes."

"Lie back, is it? Very well. What's that I see? There's a small part of me that refuses to take orders!"

She laughed. "Basil, you silly ape, stay still while I get this ointment on you!"

"Greasy stuff, isn't it?"

"Hold still!"

"How come you're wearing your watch? It spoils your outfit."

"I'm going to take your pulse."

She took his wrist in her long slender fingers. He craned his neck and took a peek.

"Where are the hands?"

"It's an electronic watch, darling. With a liquid crystal display."

She pressed the stem. Numbers flashed across the miniature screen. 11:01:55. Five o'clock in the morning in New York. John Farnsworth wouldn't be hearing about her accident for another two hours, when he got up and switched on the morning news. She'd get a worried transatlantic call from him then. She smiled. John was a nice old fusspot. She corrected herself. A nice *deadly* old fusspot. She remembered what he could do with a knife, a gun or those strong bony fingers.

"Am I alive, love?" Basil said.

The last two digits kept changing as she watched, flashing the seconds. She counted under her breath.

"You're alive, darling," she said. "A little *too* alive. Your pulse is racing."

"Is it any wonder?" He ran his eyes down her naked body and reached for a breast. He ran the ball of his thumb across her nipple. It surged erect almost instantly. He squeezed the breast. The adhesive and gauze was rough against the tender flesh.

"Careful, darling. That's the bruised one."

He laughed. "We're a pair, aren't we?"

"We'll manage."

She finished up by spraying anesthetic on his torn and raw elbows, taping thick gauze pads over them.

He burst into laughter. "One of the male's most important accessory organs, the elbow."

She rolled him a joint from the little silver box by the bedside, and took a couple of long drags herself before passing it over. It was good stuff, and it didn't take very long. There was a nice floating sensation, and all her aches and pains were outside her body, where she could inspect them without feeling them.

Basil was feeling that way too. "A balm for the embalmed," he said, a smile wreathing his face.

"A balm for the bombed embalmed," she said, running an oily hand down his chest and belly, and grasping his tumid shaft.

"That's not anesthetic?" he said, alarmed.

"No, darling, it's antiseptic."

She rubbed some of the jellied stuff on his penis, making it slick. He reciprocated by thrusting a bandaged mitt between her legs. A blunt finger probed.

"We shan't need any lubrication, love," he said. "I see you're doing quite well on your own."

She groaned with a sudden rush of pleasure. He probed deeper, the taped knuckles scraping against her outer labia. She put a warning hand on his wrist.

He withdrew his hand and held it up to the light. He stared critically at his extended middle finger. "You need about a quart."

Unaccountably, she burst into tears. It was the pot, exaggerating the swing of her moods.

Basil put a clumsy hand around her shoulders. "I know what you must be thinking, Penny," he said. "When you pulled me out of those flames, I was remembering poor Reynaldo too. Wonderful chap! Superb driver!"

She turned to him fiercely. "I couldn't get there in time to save Reynaldo. Saving you paid off part of the debt. Winning would have paid off more. Now don't make me regret it. Don't be tedious."

She flung herself across his body, heedless of the twinges of pain she was causing them both, and fastened her lips on his. They kissed thirstily, and Penelope signaled his lips with her tongue. He opened them obediently and her tongue darted between them, exploring. His breath was harsh from the grass, his tongue hot and muscular. He had his mitt between her legs again, cradling her raised mons with the heel of his hand.

Basil was right. She was well lubricated already. Her loins had flowered, oozing anticipation, even before he'd touched her. She knew what had done it. It was the race. It had always been that way with Reynaldo: the hot excitement, the danger, the thrill of high speed, the hours of living crowded into split seconds, had brought them both to fever pitch on race days. And today, the crash; the brush with death that had told every cell of her body that life was more precious. She had a lot of adrenalin to use up.

She took his penis in her hand and felt him shudder all over. She caressed it lovingly, feeling the pulsing warmth in her fist. Her thumb pressed into the bulbous tip. There was a single sticky drop there, a jewel of intent. She ran the ball of her thumb around the acorn tip. He groaned.

His own thumb was on her clitoris, teasing it outward in a lazy, voluptuous stroke. Her legs vibrated. There was a tingling shock at the base of her spine. He dipped a finger inside her, then another. Thank goodness the doctor had left them unbandaged! The fingers explored the hot slippery cavern of her vagina with a circular motion. She felt something else. The fingers were spreading. He was making a V sign. The sensation was indescribably delectable. She shivered.

He twisted the fingers around a half circle. They slid easily within the oiled core of her.

His thumb grew busier. The knurl of her clitoris was distended to bursting. Her entire body felt flushed.

Panting, she raised herself on one elbow, still gripping his tool. Her breasts dangled in front of his face. He craned his neck and sampled them with his mouth. Her fingers tightened convulsively on his cock.

"Aaah . . ." he gasped. He went rigid for a moment, then mastered himself with a helpful squeeze from Penelope.

He'd found the raised cone of a nipple now. His lips were around it, tight as a rubber ring. He moved it in and out of his mouth, the tip of his tongue caressing its peak. Penelope's vision blurred.

Her hand, trailing behind her, manipulated his swollen prong. She put it through four gears. His body vibrated like a racing car.

"This can't go on, love," he wheezed. "We're not even at the starting grid."

She was reluctant to abuse his burned back by getting on him with all her weight. "How are your elbows?" she gasped.

"Bloody sore."

She eased him to a half sitting position against the headboard, putting two of the Hôtel de Paris bolsters behind his neck and at the small of his back. She clambered on top of his thighs, her legs splayed out in a vee, resting on the headboard at either side of his hips. It was a little like sitting in a racing car. His long rod stuck up in front of her like a gearshift. She eased back a little and bent it forward so that its knob rested against her cleft. She moved it up and down against her clitoris, tears of ecstasy running down her face.

The crowd roared. The voices surged in through the big glass windows of Penelope's suite, from the terrace below where the quality was watching the race. More of the rich and the famous were leaning out their own windows, enlivening the façade of the Hôtel de Paris, taking pictures and placing bets with their friends.

Penelope leaned over and turned on the television set next to the bed.

Basil was making blind, automatic pelvic motions, trying to push his way all the way inside her. She held him steady.

"Elle est dans le fossé!" came the excited voice of the announcer.

"Not yet, darling," the Baroness said.

She lifted her bottom a little and dipped the end of his mast just inside her crevasse. She moved the spongy head around the edges, not letting it penetrate too far yet, rubbing it against her clitoris at each circuit.

Basil gave a hoarse bellow. His body strained. She continued to hold firmly onto his shaft.

"Tenez à droite! Tenez à droite!" the announcer shouted. Out of the corner of her eye, Penelope could see the bright little cars flashing across the screen.

"For pity's sake, darling!" Basil moaned. "I'm at the end of my tether!"

She pushed forward. He parted his legs enough to let

her drop to a proper alignment, his hands on her hips to position her. His swollen baton slithered effortlessly inside her, all the way. At once she hooked her toes into the bars of the headboard for leverage and began riding his stick.

Basil gasped in rhythm to her movements. Penelope, breathing harshly, felt the taped hands on her hips, the long stem waggling inside her in reciprocating motion, like a piston.

"Matra au milieu," the announcer said. The little cars zoomed at the periphery of her vision.

She raised herself up and down, feeling the hot piston slide in and out, her eyes fixed on the instrument panel of his chest with its blind male paps like switches. He heaved in time to her thrusts, contributing an interesting sidewise wobble. His pubic ridge massaged her distended vestibule as he worked away inside. It was total ecstasy.

Outside, the crowd gasped. *"Faites attention!"* the announcer said.

A big warm wet sensation was starting to take shape inside her. She pumped away more quickly. With Basil bracing her hips, she leaned all the way backward, her long black hair trailing on his toes, her breasts splashed across her torso like eggs, quivering with her exertions. The position brought his billy hard against the forward edge of her scabbard. She squirmed with delight.

He stretched his hands towards her and she took them. He pulled her forward again. Her breasts swung forward and bumped his bony chest. He put a brawny pair of arms around her and worked away some more, pushing at the base of her spine with a big gauze-padded hand. She bit his neck.

"Deuxième vitesse ici," the announcer said. On the color screen, the little cars growled and buzzed.

It was coming closer now, a huge, intolerably delicious sensation. Penelope moved the piston of flesh in longer strokes inside her. A hot little bubble burst. She clamped down on the others that were struggling to rise through the thick fluid of her ecstasy, willing them to wait, to combine into that one enormous red bubble that would

fill the universe of her senses. She gripped Basil's shoulders for dear life, feeling his body shuddering against her
breasts and belly. A roaring filled her ears: the engine
noises and the crowd and the vast rumbling of her nerves
and brain. Basil thrust frantically into her, faster and
faster, panting.

The bubbles grew and combined. The urgency was too
much to bear. She pushed him into her as far as she
could and held him there, her teeth clenched. On the
screen the cars were crossing the finish line. The big red
bubble grew distended and burst. It flooded her insides
with a hot blessedness. She gave a great shuddering cry.
The sweet convulsion seemed to go on forever. It was a
big one, one of the biggest. She came down slowly from
it, in diminishing tremors. Her entire body was flushed
and covered with moisture. She gave a little wriggle, and
there was a whole little string of new explosions.

She arched her spine and stretched, Basil's cock still
hard inside her. He was lying back like a dead man, his
mouth hanging open, gasping for air. His face was the
color of brick. Gradually it subsided toward normal.

"*C'est fini,*" the announcer was saying. "*Le vain-
queur . . .*"

"What in heaven's name did you do to me, Baroness?"
Basil said.

"I gave you a race, darling."

"Who won?"

"I think we crossed the finish line together."

She lifted herself off his stem, cupping a hand under
herself to catch his spilled juices. On the television, the
announcer was reviewing the day's events, talking about
the accident that had taken Basil Quarles and the Baroness Penelope St. John-Orsini out of the race.

She strode naked to the big windows and looked out
through the curtains. People were spilling out onto the
roadway now, crowding around the spent little cars. There
was activity in the reviewing box; she could see a cluster
of officials around Grace's powder-blue suit and Rainier's
correctly dark one. The band was playing again.

She turned to Basil. "How do you feel?"

"Bit sore, that's all."

"Sorry about the accident?"

"Best thing that ever happened to me. Baroness . . ."

"Yes?"

"Think we might try for a second round?"

She was about to say yes when the answer came for her.

There was a tingling sensation in her wrist, and she knew that, somewhere in space, floating hundreds of miles above Europe, MESTAR had hurled an electronic thunderbolt at her.

She sighed. They picked the most *inconvenient* moments.

"What about it?" Basil said.

She pressed the stem of her watch. A luminous tracing appeared on the tiny blank screen.

It was a picture.

A picture of a human skull.

Penelope stared at it, startled. There never had been anything like *that* before. The most urgent code was Code Sigma: a crooked M lying on its side. And that one was reserved for impending nuclear war or similar disasters involving possible death to millions.

And then she remembered. The skull signal had been programmed into MESTAR's electronic brain as an expression of the ultimate disaster. The unthinkable. The passing of all life on earth. They'd briefed her on it once, long ago, just in passing. And they'd been apologetic. It was silly, of course, they'd said, but just in case of the theoretical possibility . . .

And here it was. Not theoretical any longer.

"Well?" Basil said.

She pressed the stem to wipe the little screen. Planes of polarization rotated. MESTAR's electronic trigger scattered light across the face of her wristwatch. Letters and numbers appeared.

DD49

DC5

M

Doomsday was only 49 hours away. She was required

in Washington in five hours. In masquerade. Not with a cover story. With an uncrackable disguise. That meant that Coin was going to be exposed to view.

Washington was over 4000 miles away. She had to get there in five hours. It was going to take a bit of doing.

"Sorry, darling," she told Basil. "I've got an appointment."

Ten minutes later, she was driving like a demon toward the airport at Nice. Her private Learjet 25C was hangared there; she'd flown it from Rome for the race. Not that it would do her any good. With a cruising speed of 507 mph, it would take her almost eight hours to get to Washington, even if there were time to install the special fuel tanks for extra range.

No, she couldn't use the Learjet.

She had to go supersonic.

There was a Concorde 02 at Nice. She'd seen it on the runway the previous day. She made a few telephone calls from the drawing room while Basil snored away.

"*C'est impossible!*" the Minister had sputtered.

But nothing was impossible for the Baroness Penelope St. John-Orsini. She'd made a few more calls. When she was finished, the Concorde was hers. She was probably going to have to sleep with two French cabinet ministers and an official of *Aerospatiale*. But for the time being, she had her wings.

Dan Wharton met her at the gate. "Paul and Sumo are in the plane, checking it out," he said. "It was already fueled, waiting for takeoff. They had to cancel out a VIP charter flight of a hundred passengers. They're milling around, making phone calls to their governments. There's going to be a few diplomatic incidents." He looked at her with his gray eyes. "How in *hell* did you do it?"

Wharton was a big, rugged man with sandy hair and a broken nose. He had a face like a granite outcropping and a body like a bear. His hands became gentle only when he was stripping an automatic weapon or setting a plastic explosive charge. He was the Baroness' armorer, among other things. He also happened to be a member of the Social Register. They hadn't disowned him yet.

"Get in," she said.

He clambered into the Triumph Spitfire's passenger seat, and she drove it down the runway.

The Concorde was waiting for her, a big bird with a bent beak—the swing-down nose section they'd designed into it. The illusion of a giant hawk was uncanny. She shivered. She was going to have to fly that thing.

There was a knot of officials from *Aerospatiale* and British Aircraft Corporation clustered under the wing, looking worried. One of them stepped forward: a Britisher with a ruddy mustache.

"Baroness?" he said.

"I'm in a hurry," she said. "Am I cleared for takeoff?"

He frowned. "This is absolutely unprecedented," he said. "This aircraft is one of the first production models. It hasn't been flown commercially yet. The consortium..."

"Yes, yes," she said impatiently. "I've already been through all that."

He frowned again. "You're qualified for jets, I'm told."

"You're *not* going to ask to see my pilot's license, darling?"

The consortium man flushed. "Supersonic flight is quite another thing."

"I've flown the SR-71, darling," she said sweetly. "That's the one the United States calls the Blackbird. One of the privileges one has when one has friends in Washington. It flies at above Mach Three. I understand that your sweet little bird flies at about Mach Two point Two."

A little sweating Frenchman stepped forward. *"Le bang sonique . . ."* he began.

"Darling, I know all about *le bang sonique,*" she said, pushing past the clustered officials, Wharton at her heels.

Another official stepped in front of her. "Baroness," he said unctuously, "we have managed to provide you with a flight crew at short notice—co-pilot, navigator, flight engineer. . . ."

"I've my own crew, thank you."

His lip trembled. "Madame, that is a fifty-million-dollar aircraft!"

She patted his cheek. "If anything happens, I'll write you a check."

She gave them a wave and a dazzling smile before she closed the door in their faces. They scrambled in panic when she cut in the afterburners. Some maintenance man had the wit to wheel the steps away, and she slapped the throttles all the way up.

When they were in the air, wheeling over the blue Mediterranean, Sumo lowered his headphones and turned to her.

"The Concorde's banned from National Airport in Washington, you know," he said. "No supersonic flights."

"Call John Farnsworth through the scrambler, Tommy. You can bounce a signal off MESTAR IV." She looked at her watch, telling time again. "Tell John he has three and a half hours to get us landing permission."

Sumo nodded happily and started to unpack the special electronic equipment he'd brought abroad with him.

The Baroness turned to Wharton. "Why don't you go back to the cabin and see what you can find us for lunch, Dan?"

He poked his head back in a few minutes later. "One hundred and twelve servings of *blanquette de veau,* still warming up, from Le Grand Véfour in Paris."

She laughed. "Fetch four of them, will you, darling? And some chilled wine."

Sumo was tapping out his signal. "John's going to have fits," he said. "And so is the FAA."

"Tell him we'll come in subsonic," she said. "If there's any trouble, a call to the FAA from the White House ought to do it."

She eased the throttles forward. The big airliner shuddered for a moment as it approached Mach One. Through the windscreen she could see the Concorde's beak, no longer bent, but thrust forward for supersonic flight.

They were over Gibraltar. The gray Atlantic stretched endlessly ahead of her. With a shiver of joy, the Baroness crashed through the sound barrier.

Chapter 4

They'd rerouted all other incoming traffic at Washington National Airport and cleared the north runway for her. She came in low over the Potomac, her tail tucked under, the swing nose pointed down for a subsonic approach. The Baroness could see the cluster of service vehicles waiting at the runway's southeast end, and the barriers keeping away the crowd of curious onlookers. The arrival of a Concorde was something special.

"What time is it, Tommy?" the Baroness said.

"Nine forty-five in the morning, Washington time," Sumo said.

She skimmed low over the vehicles and touched down with a gentle bounce. The big bent-nosed bird skidded as she hit the brakes; they hadn't left her much room. She taxied to the far end of the runway and waited.

A long gray limousine with opaqued windows detached itself from the group of vehicles and drove down the runway toward her. It moved heavily, as if it were carrying a lot of armor plate. A jeep full of Marines with automatic weapons followed it.

The man who got out of the limousine and stood waiting under the wing was not John Farnsworth. It couldn't have been. John Farnsworth was lean and trim. This fellow had a disgusting paunch. John Farnsworth had a handsome, distinguished-looking face with an aristocratic beak of a nose. This fellow was puffy and sallow, with a bulbous snout and wide nostrils. John Farnsworth had a clipped gray military mustache. The man who waited for her on the runway had a bare, if somewhat thick, upper lip.

"Slob," was Paul's verdict.

The slob who was John Farnsworth stood waiting, hands on his hips, for the agent named Coin to emerge.

He was obviously one of the crude outside operative types whom the ivy league gentlemen at CIA and NSA turned their noses up at. You could even see the unforgivable bulge of a large caliber revolver at his waistband.

The Baroness opened the hatch and let down the ladder.

"Stay with the plane," the Baroness told her crew.

The person who climbed down the ladder was a thick-bodied man in a double-breasted suit. He was fairly tall —just short of six feet. He had wide shoulders and meaty forearms. He had a flat, rather brutal, face, and he needed a shave.

"Where's the briefing?" he said in a rough bass voice.

"Fort Meade," the slob said. "You're right on time, Coin."

They climbed together into the back seat of the limousine, after giving the Marines orders to keep everyone away from the plane. It was possible to see out the opaqued windows from the inside. The slob pushed a button, and a thick glass partition went up between them and the driver. It was opaqued too.

"Amazing!" John Farnsworth said. "How did you do it, Penny?"

The other man said: "It's a body mask, John. Shoulders to crotch, with padded arms. It gives just like flesh, in case anyone grabs me by the arm or pokes me in the chest while they're talking."

"But the face . . ."

"Plastic flesh. Applied layer by layer over my own facial contours." She rubbed her whiskers. "The beard's a nice touch, don't you think? If CIA's got an observer at the briefing, I'm going to let him watch me shave it off in the men's room."

"Speaking of men's rooms . . ."

The Baroness gave a deep rumbling laugh. "The body mask comes equipped with some realistic plumbing, John. I'll take a break with the rest of the boys."

"Let me see your hands."

She held out her hands. They were thick-fingered with black hair curling down to the knuckles.

"More plastic flesh?"

"That's right," she said.

"And the voice?"

"There are two flat discs taped to my throat under the plastic flesh." She laughed again. "You may have noticed that I have a *very* thick neck—positively bull-like. I'm talking silently, of course. They pick up the vibrations from my larynx, like a throat mike. There's a small computer in this rig that alters the vibrations—lowers the pitch and gives them male characteristics. The sound comes out a little loudspeaker under my necktie. Think anyone'll notice that I don't make a breeze when I talk?"

"*I* didn't." He wrinkled his nose. "The garlic rather puts one off."

"Part of my uncouth image. It keeps witches and CIA men at a distance."

It was Farnsworth's turn to laugh. "I saw the last CIA report on you. It describes Coin as a tall, handsome, fair-haired man. Apparently they got a description of Eric on that Moscow caper. This will *really* throw them."

"Well, I'm still tall. Three-inch soles in these brogans, and a fake instep so the soles won't look thick."

He shook his head in wonderment. "How in the world did you whip all that up in less than five hours?"

"Sumo and I have been working on the body mask and the voice alteration device for months. We had to rip out some of the passenger stereo equipment on the Concorde to finish up the voice adapter, though. Incidentally, you haven't done too badly yourself."

"Standard disguise kit from Fort Meade's special effects department," he said deprecatingly.

She looked out the window. They were already on the Baltimore-Washington expressway, heading northeast. The flat Maryland countryside stretched outside.

"We haven't much time, John. Perhaps you'd better tell me what this is all about."

"It's big, Penny. You're a last resort. They don't expect you to succeed. They're throwing you into the game because you're the only other card this country has to play.

But their real money's on something they call Project Doomsday."

"Project Doomsday?"

"It's under the direction of the Secretary of Defense. That'll show you where we're at. A huge national effort is being mobilized, cost and civil liberties be damned. Billions of dollars in unauthorized funds will be siphoned off to pay for it. Anybody finds out too much—or asks too many questions—finds himself under house arrest. That includes senators and Supreme Court justices. The news media will print what they're told, or else. All to prevent any public panic that might interfere with Project Doomsday. It's Armageddon, Penny."

"And what *is* Project Doomsday, John?"

"All-out mobilization. A vast program to try to save a few thousand selected people to start life on earth again . . . afterward."

"Afterward? . . ." Her eyes, masked by muddy brown contact lenses, swung toward him. "It's really all that serious, then?"

"This morning they started herding cattle and other domestic animals into pressurized underground caverns with air filtration systems. They're going to send plant seeds into orbit as insurance, to be brought down later. There's a rumor that they're even going to shoot a couple of Adams and Eves into orbit to wait out the next couple of weeks. But most of the worthy ones will go underground, in the sealed caves, along with our government leaders. The computers are already picking out the punch cards of the lucky few potential survivors. They won't be told about it until the last moment, of course. Then they'll be put under military arrest and escorted to the caves."

"What in God's name brought this all about, John?"

Farnsworth clasped his hands over his foam rubber paunch. "You've heard about the latest Russian space spectacular?"

"Yes. They landed a Lunokhod. It collected some rock samples. They're returning the samples to earth. So what? They've done it before. Not with a Lunokhod, of course."

"But that's the point."

"What do you mean?"

"The previous Russian samples came from soil that had been sterilized by the landing rockets. But Lunokhods rove. This one roved to a place that had been contaminated by man."

"The Apollo 17 landing site?"

"Yes."

"What do you mean—contaminated?"

Farnsworth looked suddenly old, even behind his make-up. "It seems that one of our astronauts had a virus."

The Marine guard at the gatehouse opened the car door and gave them a hard, unfriendly look. He inspected their iridescent green ID badges and took his time over the papers that Farnsworth showed him.

"All right, gentlemen," he said finally. "You're to go directly to the auditorium in the main building. Your car stays here. You'll have an escort to take you there."

The outer gate closed. There were buzzes and flashing lights from some kind of electronic apparatus. When the device was satisfied, a gate opened in the second of the three fences. This one was made of five-strand electrified wire. There was another security check. Then a gate in the inner fence opened and two armed Marine sentries fell in step behind them.

"They're nervous today," the Baroness said in her deep male voice. She squared her shoulders and strode forward, taking long masculine steps. The hard shell of the body mask flattened her breasts uncomfortably. She was carrying a hell of a lot of weight around, with the special shoes and the battery pack for the computer-operated voice adaptor. But she managed to make all her body movements look easy and natural. Natural for a big, thick-bodied man with a face like a wrestler's and a build like an ape's.

The NSA Building had no windows. It was a steel and concrete structure laid out like a huge A, with a boxy nine-story annex nestled between the jutting arms. They walked across a couple of acres of asphalt parking lots to get to it, the Marine guards treading at their heels.

Inside was an enormous corridor, almost a thousand feet long and wider than a city block. It was lined with a watchful army of Marine sentries, protecting the rows of doors along both sides.

The place made CIA headquarters look like a dollhouse.

The auditorium was filling up when they arrived. The door was locked behind them. There were a couple of hundred people scattered among the seats or wandering around. The air conditioning was struggling with an overload of cigarette smoke. It was a noisy hubbub, with small knots of men talking excitedly to one another.

Penelope and Farnsworth took seats near the rear. A few men nearby looked at them curiously, then turned away to continue their conversation.

"Isn't that Dr. Lionel Barth, the Nobel Prize winner?" Penelope said.

She pointed her whiskered chin at a frail, ascetic man with a shock of white hair.

"You're right. He became embroiled in a germ warfare controversy four years after winning the prize. The academic community found out that he'd accepted a research project from the Fort Detrick biological warfare laboratory. His fellow biologists disowned him. Tried to have his Nobel Prize rescinded."

"Interesting."

"More than interesting. The man he's talking to is Hans Kolbe, the epidemiologist. Between the two of them, they probably know more about plagues and pandemics than anybody on earth."

A lean military-looking man in sports jacket and slacks was working his way down the aisle toward them, pausing to exchange words with various people along the way. He was the most powerful intelligence executive in the world, Farnsworth's and Penelope's putative employer, the director of the National Security Agency.

"Hello, Key," he said to Farnsworth when he got to them. "The last time I saw you, you had red hair, freckles and a case of galloping hyperthyroidism." He peered at Farnsworth's badge number. "You *are* Key, aren't you?"

Farnsworth slouched, still playing slob. "You ought to know, General. One of your gate guards planted an FM body tag on me when I was being frisked."

The Director gave him a bland stare. *"Everybody* here today is wearing a body tag. We're going to keep track of them all until the crisis is over."

Penelope said, "There are too many people here for security. You're going to have to lock up the blabber-mouths."

The Director turned shrewd eyes on her. "You must be Coin."

Penelope watched his eyes. There was no sudden widening of the irises that might indicate that he had recognized the nature of her disguise.

"I must be," she said.

"I never thought the day would come when I'd meet you."

"You still haven't," she said.

"I just came over to warn you that we've got CIA in the room. They know you're here. They're going to try to get a line on you."

"We'll take care of it," Penelope said.

He nodded and passed on to another group of people. The auditorium was about filled up. A solid-looking man in a dark business suit stepped to the podium. It was the President's national security advisor.

"Gentlemen, ladies," he said into the microphone. "Will you kindly take your seats. We're about to begin."

People moved and found places. The chatter of voices gradually died down. Penelope noted that all of the auditorium doors had been locked. Uniformed Marines stood along the walls and blocked the aisles.

The President's Man rapped for attention. "All of you are here because you have a need to know about Project Doomsday. Some of you will play important parts in it. I need not emphasize that your silence and discretion are strictly enjoined."

His face assumed a pained, mournful expression. "For the time being, I'm afraid, your constitutional guarantees are suspended. We hope and pray that this extraordinary state of affairs will last only a few days. But in the meantime, I can assure you that the penalties for any infractions of security will be swift and severe." He peered over the tops of his horn rims. "There will be no exceptions. None."

A mutter of indignant voices was heard.

The President's Man nodded meaningfully, and three men stood up to let the audience see them. Penelope recognized the majority and minority leaders of the House and the minority leader of the Senate. The Senate majority leader was conspicuously absent.

Farnsworth leaned toward Penelope. "The big boys have decided not to make a fuss. They must have scared hell out of them."

The briefing was begun by a space agency official. He showed them slides and films of the Russian lander and the activities of the Lunokhod. There was a fuzzy closeup, blown up from a TV image, of the Lunokhod scooping up samples of whitish crystals and filling a capsule strapped to a rack.

"The crystals in that particular capsule are mostly feldspar," the space agency man said. "For the benefit of non-mineralogists in the audience, it's popularly known as moonstone."

A slide flashed on the screen. It was a stunning color picture of a kaleidoscope of crystals.

"It's a fairly common mineral here on earth," he went on, "and the opalescent variety is highly valued as a jewel. It's also a fairly common mineral on the moon." He made a weak joke. "So, appropriately enough, the moon seems to be full of moonstones."

Another slide appeared. More crystals.

"This is a sample from the first lunar rocks brought back by Armstrong, Aldrin and Collins. We found that the feldspar crystals were mixed with brightly colored pyroxene grains in the lunar basalt. There's nothing quite like it here on earth. For one thing, it's hot. Rich in radioactive elements."

There was a closeup of a geiger counter reading on the screen.

"It's also rich," the space official went on, "in potassium, rare earth elements and phosphorus."

His face suddenly twisted. "And that's why we're in trouble." He stopped, unable to go on.

The President's Man put a hand on his shoulder. "Dr. Payne has seen his friends die," he said softly. "I think we're ready for the next section of the briefing."

The next briefer was Dr. Barth. The whispy Nobel winner stepped to the podium and waited for the noise to subside. He cleared his throat.

"We began to suspect that the moon might hold some —dangers—after the Apollo 12 flight. Conrad and Bean brought back, among other things, the television camera that Surveyor 3 had left behind in 1967." He paused for effect. "We discovered that the camera insulation was contaminated with streptococcus mitus. These germs are normally present in the human nose and throat. I assume that the technician who installed the camera in the spacecraft breathed on it."

He looked round the auditorium. "These particular streptococci had survived 950 days on the lunar surface. Almost three years. They'd been exposed to vacuum, cold, heat, intense sterilizing ultraviolet radiation. But they flourished, surviving on nutrients found in the plastic insulation. They adapted."

Somebody raised his hand. "But Dr. Barth, it was after Apollo 12 that NASA *ended* its strict quarantine procedures for returning astronauts. Why is that?"

"We were overconfident. We simply ended the practice of bringing back samples from sites that had been contaminated by previous landings."

There was a hubbub. Several academic types got to their feet and tried to speak. Dr. Barth waited until they'd quieted down, then continued.

"We learned our lesson after Apollo 17." His voice shook. "We're now going to have films of what we've since come to call the Houston Disaster. The public was never informed of it. More than a hundred deaths were hushed up—and you can imagine the effort that went into *that!* Since that time, the emergency mobilization plan known as Project Doomsday has existed. Only a handful of people has known about it . . . until today."

The lights in the auditorium dimmed further, and a movie appeared on the big screen. Penelope found herself looking at scenes taken in the Lunar Receiving Laboratory at Houston. Behind airtight glass, mechanical hands were busy with the moon rock samples, preparing microtome slices, performing mineralogical tests, adding minute pinches of ground-up rock to culture dishes to see if anything grew.

"Something went wrong," a new voice said out of the darkness. "There must have been a leak in the air seal."

On the screen, one of the white-coated technicians suddenly looked puzzled. He put a hand to his chest and felt it. Then he shrugged and went back to work.

"It happened with incredible swiftness," the voice said. "At this point, the technicians had been working on the samples for only an hour or two. The site of infection in this case was the most accessible—the lungs. We've since found that the microorganism involved can gain entry anywhere—the mucosa of the eyes, nose, anus, sex organs. Cuts and scratches. Or simply eat its way through the skin. Once established, it multiplies with unbelievable rapidity."

On the screen, there was a cut indicating a brief passage of time. The technician staggered and began gagging.

"We were filming the usual documentary footage," the voice said. "We caught it all—till the camera died."

You could see the technician's face turning purplish. His hands clawed the air. He fell to the floor, unable to breathe. Other white-coated figures went to his aid. The camera followed the action.

A strange thing was happening to the technician's body. It was growing flatter, as if, within the clothes, the tissues were slumping like jelly. A cavity suddenly appeared in the chest, like a footprint stamped in slushy snow. The face collapsed and began to run like melted wax.

Penelope gripped her arm rests. "There's no disease process that works that fast," she whispered.

The technicians around the body were looking frightened. They moved away from it. Other men began clutching at themselves—their throats, their eyes, their groins. One man stared in horror at his abdomen, which was ballooning like a pregnant woman's. The balloon burst and his guts spilled out. He stared stupidly at them, lurching, his feet getting tangled before he collapsed writhing to the floor.

Here and there in the auditorium, people were being sick. There was a confused babble of everyone talking at once.

Some of the technicians were beating at the sealed doors. One of them evidently had triggered an alarm.

The cameraman focused on a face seen through the outer glass port. It was staring at the hell inside, transfixed with horror. A man whose entire skin was oozing a thick fluid was hammering on the port.

"The entire Receiving Laboratory is divided into concentric zones of negative pressure," the voice said. "The opposite of a modern hospital operating room. Air presses in, not out. No microorganism is supposed to be able to escape."

The face at the port suddenly developed a runny nose.

"But it did. The Moonstone Virus broke through into Zone Two, then Zone Three. Thank God we were able to confine it within the building itself!"

There was a scene showing a ring of chemical fire surrounding the entire vast installation. Within the ring, men in sealed airsuits with fishbowl helmets and respirators were spraying the walls and applying some sort of sealant from pressurized tanks. The sealant hardened into a glistening coat over the walls and windows.

"We got the cooperation of the Atomic Energy Commission in disposing of the bodies—what was left of them," the voice said.

On the screen, men in space suits were directing robot handlers that looked like miniature tracked vehicles with claw arms. The robots were loading their horrible burdens, encased in body-size plastic bags, into airtight vans.

"The vans were escorted by armed convoy to the site in Colorado," another voice broke in over the loudspeaker. It was the President's Man again.

Penelope watched the screen. Mobile cranes were lowering the vans on steel cables into what looked like a mine shaft. The robot handlers, encased in plastic shrouds, were dumped in after them.

"The shaft is a mile deep," the President's Man said. "The AEC had dug it previously for an underground nuclear experiment."

Farnsworth leaned over toward Penelope. "You remember that? Project Plowboy. It was a scheme to extract natural gas from underground sources by setting off a hydrogen bomb. The AEC awarded a contract to a private corporation called General Tectonics. The ecologists raised hell. Said it might trigger earthquakes, contaminate water supplies with radioactivity—even contaminate the oil-bearing shale above the gas pockets. They got up a study showing that the whole thing wasn't economically feasible anyway. There was a lot of public pressure. The whole thing had to be called off."

Penelope wrinkled her brow under the plastic flesh. "Yes. And then they suddenly announced they were going ahead anyway. Now we know why."

The screen showed men in shielded lead suits lowering something that looked like a length of sewer pipe into a small shaft parallel to the big one. It was about eight inches in diameter and some thirty feet long.

It was the hydrogen bomb.

The next scene was taken from a distance, through a telephoto lens. The entire surface of the earth suddenly bulged. The flat Colorado desert turned into a shallow dome that must have been a half-mile across. There was a network of cracks. A thin spume of glowing vapor shot high into the air.

"There was a radioactive leak," the President's Man said sorrowfully. "The environmentalists gave the Administration a hard time. The Russians complained that we'd violated the nuclear test ban."

The lights went on. The President's Man stood there, blinking. He looked around the audience.

"But," he continued, "the moon virus was destroyed.

Every trace of it. Until the Russians went back to the same site and got another sample."

A hand went up. It was the chairman of the Joint Congressional Science and Astronautics Committee.

"Can I ask a question?" he said. "Since we're being frank today? Is that the reason manned lunar exploration was curtailed after Apollo 17?"

"Yes," the President's Man said. He looked uncomfortable.

The Senator shook his head. "I'll be damned. They trotted out a lot of budgetary reasons. They never even told *me!*"

Another hand went up. "You've been describing the disease agent as a virus," he said belligerently. "Every first-year biology student knows you can't grow viruses in a culture medium. Bacteria, yes. But viruses can only multiply in living cells."

Dr. Barth stood up, his face weary. "It's a virus. Or something of that order. Maybe a viroid, like the one that causes potato spindle tuber disease. No protein envelope. Possibly no more than a single molecule of free DNA."

"But how can you tell?" the man persisted. "If every trace of this—disease agent—was destroyed, as we just heard. Is this another government lie? Are you secretly working on something as dangerous as this in some government laboratory?"

"We've made computer models based on all available data," Dr. Barth explained patiently. "We reconstructed what we believe to be a mathematical analogue of the moon virus shortly after the Houston Disaster. We've been carrying on intensive research on it ever since."

"But . . ."

"Mathematical equations and computer programs can't infect anybody," Dr. Barth said dryly.

Another hand shot up. "What information about the virus have you developed, Dr. Barth?"

Dr. Barth faced the new questioner gratefully. "We believe it evolved from an ordinary adenovirus. One of our astronauts sneezed. There's a lot of radiation on the moon. By some fantastic chance, a particle of radiation may have knocked a single hydrogen atom out of kilter. We theorize that it was one of the hydrogen bonds between an adenine-thymine base pair. But it was enough."

"The audience may not be familiar with the chemistry of DNA," the President's Man broke in.

"I'll put it in layman's language," Dr. Barth said. "What we've got is a renegade molecule. It probably attacked its own protein coat—the protective skin that all viruses have. It raids everything in its environment for the stuff it needs to assemble replicas of itself. Everything. Ordinary viruses take over the genetic machinery of a living cell. They steal the cell's free-floating nucleotides to make viruses instead of new cells. But the moon virus finds what it needs anywhere." He paused. "And that's why—the previous gentleman to the contrary—those samples of lunar rocks, with their potassium and phosphorus and the energy and warmth of the radioactivity to help cook the stew along, are able to act as a culture medium."

Hans Kolbe, the epidemiologist, took Dr. Barth's place. He was a large man with a round face, dressed in a rumpled blue suit.

"Once the virus encounters living tissue," he said, "a new phase takes place. It's like a man on a starvation diet who's suddenly been invited to a feast. It explodes into a riot of reproduction. It increases by geometric progression—every eight seconds, according to our computer model."

There was a buzz from the scientific members of the audience.

"Just so you all can understand what that means," Kolbe said, blinking behind his thick glasses, "a single molecule of this renegade DNA, once it invades a 150-pound man, can change 150 pounds of man into 150 pounds of virus in something like three hours."

This time it was the laymen in the audience who buzzed.

"Of course," Kolbe went on dryly, "the man is dead after only a few ounces or pounds of himself has been converted to virus, depending on what vital organ systems the virus happens to attack. But the virus keeps feeding, and releasing itself into the atmosphere."

A man stood up, looking shaky. "So if the Russians open that capsule and let the virus loose, it will spread itself around the world. How long will it take, Dr. Kolbe?"

"We estimate," Kolbe said, "that with favorable wind currents and animal vectors such as birds and insects, every speck of organic matter on this planet could convert itself into moon virus within fifty days."

Penelope shuddered, remembering the jellied masses at the Lunar Receiving lab in Houston.

"I'm going to the men's room, John," she said.

She stood up. No one noticed. Here and there throughout the auditorium, other men and women were getting up to go through the doors that led to the rest rooms. The briefing had become technical. And some of the audience were looking queasy.

"He's getting up too," Farnsworth said.

"I know. I spotted him a few minutes ago. He's been watching us. I think he's been taking pictures with a Minox."

"Be careful, Coin."

She rubbed her shovel chin. "Careful? I'm going to take a shave and a leak."

She lumbered down the aisle, a heavy-set man in a double-breasted suit. The weight wasn't an illusion. She was carrying fifty extra pounds in molded plastic and electronic equipment under the body mask. Her superb musculature and the pep pills made it possible for her to move without apparent effort. But she was going to pay a price in fatigue and sore muscles when she finally shucked the rig off.

The CIA man—if that's what he was—followed her down the aisle a little too closely. He was eager. She toyed with the idea that he might be a Russian or Chinese plant. It was possible. The Russians had sleeper agents in the CIA, FBI, DIA, just as the U.S. had double agents working for the KGB and the GRU. She smiled thinly under her false face, remembering the Chinese-American Annapolis graduate, a few years back, who had actually managed to become special assistant to K'ang Sheng, then director of Peking's spy network.

The passage to the men's room was cordoned off with ropes. Marine sentries were stationed on both sides to make sure that people didn't stray. There was another guard outside the rest room door.

Inside, a half-dozen men were lined up at the urinals. A few more were at the sinks, washing hands, combing hair, splashing water into bleary faces.

She stepped up to one of the urinals and unzipped her fly. The motorman's friend installed in the body mask had been adapted from the space suit plumbing that NASA had designed for possible female astronauts. But the external genitalia had been sculpted by a noted artist and molded realistically in plastic.

Somebody stepped up to the urinal next to her. It was her CIA tail. He pressed close to the porcelain fixture, pretending to tinkle, while he leaned over sideways until their shoulders touched. Penelope was amused. If she hadn't known better, she would have assumed he was a homosexual.

There was a tingling on her midriff from one of the sensors taped to her skin. The CIA man was using some kind of microwave generator. She moved her elbow and encountered something bulky and hard under his jacket. He didn't notice the gesture.

She zipped up her trousers and went over to the sinks to wash her hands. The situation was unfortunate. She'd expected the CIA to assume that Coin was disguised. Even brilliantly disguised. But a disguised man. When they got around to analyzing the microwave configuration, it would show that under the body mask was a woman.

She reached into her side jacket pocket and took out a razor and a little tube of shaving cream. She could see the CIA man in the mirror. He was loitering over near the far wall, keeping her under surveillance.

She studied his face in the mirror. He was a tall, fair man with wheat-colored hair, very midwestern American. But the shape of the skull was a little too brachycephalic.

And there was something about the eyelids. Could they once have had epicanthic folds, altered by surgery? The Russians did such things at the mock American village near Kiev, where they trained their agents to think, act and look like authentic small-town Americans.

The Baroness sighed. She hoped the CIA man was a double agent. It would make it easier to do what she was going to have to do.

She took a swipe at her plastic jowls with the razor. The nylon whiskers came off smoothly, leaving a realistic-looking freshly shaven cheek. It was a good show. Too bad the CIA man wouldn't live to appreciate it.

He was taking more pictures with the Minox. It was under his necktie, the lens operating through a stupid-looking glass stickpin. No doubt he also had a specimen box in his pocket, to collect any whisker samples she might leave behind in the drain.

She dawdled over her shaving, waiting until the lavatory emptied out. She and the blond man were alone. She didn't know for how long. A minute, five minutes. It would have to be very quick.

The blond man was coming over. He stopped at the sink next to hers, though all the others were unused. There was another tingle on her abdomen as one of the sensors taped there went off. This one was an infrared camera detector. The CIA man was monitoring her body heat, getting an image on special film. The body mask would give off a different pattern from the normal human carcass. And there would be two telltale round patches where her breasts were.

She turned to the CIA man and smiled. The voice alteration device that changed her speech to a gravelly baritone was switched off.

"Do you have a cigarette, lover?" she said in her sexiest contralto.

The CIA man looked startled. His eyes widened in sudden surprise.

While he gawked, she brought her hand up in a side-wise swipe, the edge held stiff and flat and straight.

His reflexes were good. He knew the right defensive move. His arm flashed up to protect his throat. The striking edge of the Baroness' hand crunched into his wrist instead of his throat. There was a dry snapping sound as the CIA man's ulna broke in two.

His face had gone white with pain. But he was a pro. He moved back out of reach, his left hand dangling uselessly. His other hand was already scrambling for a weapon inside his jacket.

But the Baroness' reflexes were quicker. Her foot began to move, almost automatically, in the split second when it became apparent that his arm was going to intercept her death blow. Her entire body spun like a top, pivoting on the ball of one foot, the other leg held stiffly out at an angle.

Her heavy brogan with its steel plate in the sole smashed into his outer thigh. It had the speed and force of a sledgehammer blow. His femur broke like a stick of kindling wood. He crashed heavily to the tile floor.

He was a tough customer. His good hand was out of the jacket now with a gun it it. It was an official Browning .380 automatic with a very unofficial silencer on it.

There was a pop and a hiss and a streak of warmth past Penelope's ear. She dove, landing heavily on top of him with all the extra weight of her plastic shell and its equipment. Her right hand shot out and imprisoned his wrist. The momentum carried his gun hand to the floor, where it was instantly pinned by Penelope's knee. He flopped like a gasping fish, the broken wrist and thigh bones grating, while she got her two thumbs into his throat. They were broad, square thumbs with dirty nails and hair curling down to the joint. But inside them were Penelope's own strong elegant thumbs—thumbs that despite their slender grace could crack walnuts.

Now they cracked a human larynx. Her fingers hooked at the sides of his neck, she pressed sharply inward with her thumbs and felt the box of cartilage crunch and collapse into the top of his wind pipe. She kept her grip until he stopped thrashing. It took about a minute.

She got to her feet and looked for the bullet. It had gone up into the ceiling plaster above the sink. The hole wasn't conspicuous.

The whole episode had taken far too long. It was a miracle that no one had entered. She dragged the body over to the row of pay toilets. She didn't have a dime. She fished in the CIA man's pocket and found one.

The Baroness propped the corpse in a sitting position on the toilet lid. The feet, visible under the door, were placed normally. There was no blood anywhere. She found the little infrared detector in his jacket lining and removed the exposed plates. She pocketed the tapes from his microwave generator. There was a third, unfamiliar device—possibly ultrasound—that had an FM transmitter instead of a recording device. She didn't think he'd had time to use it; that was probably what he'd been about to do at the sinks. She smashed it under her heel anyway.

She clicked the door of the booth shut and left him sitting there. The little red flag read Occupied. She hoped it would remain Occupied for a long time.

A couple of dark-suited men came into the men's room just as she was leaving. They were talking about the briefing.

"Dictatorship," one of them said. "That's what they're talking about in there, dictatorship."

"The question's academic," the other said. "This country will cease to exist in fifty days, after the Russians crack that capsule. So will the world. At least this way, maybe a few people will survive to start the human race all over again. Maybe."

They walked over to the urinals together. "At least all of us here today are in the goddamn survival lottery," the first man said, opening his fly.

The briefing was still going on when Penelope re-entered the auditorium. An earnest young man was using maps to explain how the interstate highway system could be used to transport people and materials to the underground survival centers without alerting the general populace.

She slid into the seat beside John Farnsworth. "We'd better go," she said.

They got up together and went quickly to the Marine officer at the rear door. Farnsworth whispered a few words to him. The officer nodded and spoke into his walkie-talkie. He listened, looking surprised.

"All right, gentlemen," he said. "You can proceed to the Director's office. I'll have to send a man with you."

The Director was waiting for them. "Heard enough?" he said.

"How long does the government think it can keep this Doomsday thing under wraps?" Farnsworth said.

"A couple of weeks, maybe. There'll be rumors, of course. But we'll leave the press alone. We won't step on any toes until the virus gets out of Russia into Europe. Then we close our borders."

"But *we* have—" Penelope looked at her watch "—less than forty-eight hours to snatch that capsule away from the Russians. Right?"

The Director stared at her soberly. "We've bought you a little extra time. The President's been on the Hot Line again. The Russians still don't believe us. But they've agreed to play it safe."

"From what I heard in there, there's no *way* to play it safe."

The Director nodded. "There isn't. But they'll delay cracking the capsule until they work out what they be-lieve will be adequate decontamination procedures. That's a few more days or a week."

"And?"

"And they've changed the rocket's course. They're not going to bring it down in Kazakhstan as planned. They're bringing it down in a remote area above the Arctic Circle instead."

"Where?"

"They have a . . . certain facility on the Kanin Pen-insula, bordering the Barents Sea. They think they can adapt it into a special, strict quarantine, lunar receiving laboratory."

"What kind of facility?"

He gave her a bleak look. "It's a germ warfare laboratory."

They were back on the Baltimore-Washington Expressway, heading south, when the bug went off. It was one of the upholstery buttons in the back seat. The Marine who parked the limousine must have planted it.

"We found a dead man in the lavatory," it buzzed in the Director's voice. "You wouldn't happen to know anything about that, would you, Coin?"

"Check him out," Penelope said.

"We know about him. A CIA plant."

"Check him out some more. I wouldn't be surprised if this plant has Russian roots."

Farnsworth said, "What are you going to do?"

The bug hummed. "There'll be a highway accident after the briefing. The body will be found in the wreckage. Crushed larynx and other injuries, poor devil."

Penelope said, "Goodby, General." She plucked the button out of the upholstery and crushed it between her fingers.

Chapter 5

Chu Fei got out of the car and told the driver not to wait. The driver, a lumpy peasant from Szechwan, nodded and pulled across to the official car stand across the street for his midday nap.

Chu was a wiry, ascetic-looking man in his thirties, with cropped hair and a long, careful face. He wore a nondescript wrinkled blue tunic with a tight collar and a discreet badge bearing the Mao quotation, "Serve the People."

He nodded briskly to the two PLA soldiers guarding the steps of the building, their AK-47 machine guns held negligently in the crooks of their arms. The plaque at the side of the door said *No. 15 Bow String Alley.* A vertical red sign identified the building as the Social Affairs Department.

If Chu had had a sense of humor, he might have smiled at the sign. The Social Affairs Department was a polite euphemism for the powerful central bureau that controlled both internal security and foreign intelligence operations for the People's Republic of China.

He mounted the broad stone steps to the third floor headquarters for the International Liaison Department. The soldier on duty recognized him and passed him through without comment.

The door at the end of the corridor was unmarked. A buxom girl with braids and a bulging tunic sat at a little table just outside.

"Comrade Liu is expecting you," she said.

He nodded and went inside. The room was a pale institutional green, badly in need of paint. The furnishings were Spartan—some old filing cabinets, a few uncomfortable chairs, the obligatory portrait of Mao on the wall. He sat down in the visitor's chair, lit a cigarette and waited.

The man behind the desk finished making notations on a stack of reports and looked up. He was gaunt, almost emaciated, with skin like dry parchment. Liu's health, Chu knew, had been ruined forty years before when he contracted a case of liver fluke during the Long March with Mao. He was one of the few old comrades of Mao to have survived the intervening years.

"You're a northerner, I believe, Comrade Chu," Liu Hung-Fu said.

"Yes, Comrade. I was born in Foshan."

"Good. Then you should be used to cold. And Russians."

Chu's pulse quickened. A new assignment! An important one! He fought to keep his face impassive.

Liu was shuffling through a *jen yuan* dossier "And you have served as chief security officer for the Ten Beautiful Thoughts Biological Research Institute at Tsinghai?"

"Yes, Comrade."

The Ten Beautiful Thoughts Institute was the major biological warfare facility for the People's Republic. It had been one of Chu's most important jobs.

"Good," Liu said. "Then you know about germs."

"I know how carefully they must be handled. And how dangerous they can be. It was necessary, for me to carry out my duties for the People's Republic."

Liu put down the dossier. His unhealthy, yellowish eyeballs fixed on Chu's face. "Comrade Chu," he said, "the Social Affairs Department has a new assignment for you. The most important assignment you will ever have. It has been authorized by Party Central, *tang chung yang,* at the express suggestion of the Chairman himself."

"I am ready to serve, Comrade."

"Good." Liu got painfully to his feet and shuffled over to a wall map. "Were you aware that the Russians landed an unmanned rocket on the moon two days ago?"

"No, Comrade." Chu wrinkled his brow. What was this about?

"They are sending back a load of *yueh shih.* Moon-stones."

Chu remained silent, waiting.

Liu picked up a pointer and indicated a spot on the map. It was in Northern Russia, bordering the Barents Sea, due east of Finland and the Kola Peninsula. A small finger of land protruded into the ocean, well above the Arctic Circle.

"The Russians will land their rocket here, instead of their usual landing site in Kazakhstan. They agreed to do this after the most urgent representations from the Americans."

Chu pricked up his ears. This was getting interesting.

"The President of the United States himself spoke to the Russian leaders." His lip curled. "I can only describe his demeanor as that of a begging dog. He told the Russians a fantastic story. The Russians don't believe a word of it. Or so they say."

It was more than interesting. So the Social Affairs Department was now able to listen in to Hot Line calls between Washington and Moscow! Chinese electronic technology had come a long way since the technological break with Russia in 1960.

"The Russians don't believe them," Liu went on. "But we do."

Chu was unable to keep the eagerness out of his voice. "What did the Americans say, Comrade Liu?" he said.

Liu tapped the map again. "Do you know what is here?" he said.

"No, Comrade."

"This is where the Russians have their germ warfare laboratory. Like our own Institute at Tsinhai."

Chu was puzzled. "But what has this to do with moonstones?"

"The stones are contaminated with a new germ. One that never existed on earth before. The Americans are terrified of it. They say it cannot be controlled—that it eats through solid walls. And that if it gets loose, it will mean the end of the world."

Chu smiled. "Obviously the Americans are simply trying to keep the Russians from getting their hands on it. They must be working with this moon germ in their own laboratories."

"That is exactly what the Chairman and Party Central think."

"I would venture to guess that the Americans went to great lengths to manufacture false evidence that would convince the Russians that the germ was too dangerous to handle."

"You are correct, Comrade. You are an astute man. You are resourceful. Your record is impressive. That is why you have been chosen to lead the expedition."

"Expedition?"

"You will take a picked military force into the Arctic and land it here, in Cheshkaya Bay on the eastern shore of the Kanin Peninsula." He tapped the map for emphasis. "You will proceed inland. It is a remote area. There are few people—just nomadic savages under the nominal control of the Russians. You will kill everyone you encounter to keep them from betraying your presence. The Russians maintain the usual security force at their biological laboratory. You know about such things. You will be authorized to requisition any materials and men you need to overwhelm them swiftly. You must find the moon rocks and escape with them to the Arctic before Moscow can react."

Chu sat, stunned. "Anything is possible, Comrade, but . . ."

"You are correct," Liu said stonily. "Consider Mao's words on the Foolish Old Man Who Moved The Mountain. Anything is possible with sincere effort and the power of Mao's thoughts, is it not so?"

Chu was sweating. "I will do my best, Comrade Liu."

"Good." Liu became brisk. "Preparations have already begun. You and your force will be airlifted to an ice floe in the Arctic, well beyond Russia's security perimeter. A freighter with false Norwegian registry is already on its way there. It will sail you close enough to the Russian shore for you to float the rest of the way in on a small floe that will not alert Russian coastal radar. We are providing muffled propulsion units to push the ice without being detected by sonar."

Chu thought it over. It might just work.

"One other thing, Comrade Chu."

"Yes, Comrade."

"There must be no suspicion that the People's Republic of China is involved. We cannot afford a military confrontation with Russia. Not now, in the light of their détente with the Americans." He paused and smiled, showing brown stumps of teeth. "But perhaps we can destroy that détente."

"But how, Comrade Liu?"

Liu kept smiling. "We will see to it that the Russians blame the theft of the moon rocks on the Americans."

"We go in like this," the Baroness said.

She was sitting cross-legged on the reindeer fur rug, the map unfurled in front of her, facing the others. She looked utterly and enchantingly feminine in the soft fawn cashmere pullover from Givenchy and the skintight ski pants. The embroidered wool cap she'd worn that morning on the slopes was pushed back, pixie-like, letting her rich black hair fall down to enclose her cheeks.

"Just like that?" Skytop said. He sounded dubious.

"Just like that."

They were gathered in a semicircle around her: Skytop and Sumo and Wharton and Eric, with Inga a little off to the side, sprawled like a blonde Valkyrie on the floor between the two enormous white Russian wolfhounds.

"And the Russians just sorta tip their hats to us when we cross the Finnish border?" the big Cherokee persisted.

The Baroness laughed. She stabbed her finger at the map, toward the place where the Kola Peninsula faced eastward like a horse's head with Norway for its mane.

"Nobody worries about Lapps," she said, "not even the Russians. They're still classified as a native people. The spring migration is about to begin. They'll be crossing all the borders—into Sweden, Norway and into their grazing grounds on Russian territory on the Kola Peninsula."

"We don't look much like Lapps," Eric said. He was a long, lean, yellow-haired man in a black turtleneck, with a face that was a little too handsome. He was the top male model for the Baroness' firm, International Models, Inc. He was also one of her most resourceful agents.

"You and Inga are Swedish ethnologists," the Baroness said. "You're specialists in Finno-Ugric languages. You've been assigned by the Swedish Academy to follow a Lapp tribe on its travels and make a report on the economy of the reindeer herds. It's all been fixed up. If anybody checks up at the Academy, the right files and dossiers are there. And the Finnish government is cooperating."

Wharton whistled. "That was fast. It must have taken some doing."

"John Farnsworth arranged it, with a little assist from Washington. If the Finns knew what we were really about, there'd be hell to pay."

"Hey, Eric," Skytop said, "do you really talk those whatchacallit languages?"

Eric looked up soberly. "My father taught me Norwegian. And my mother taught me Swedish. And I can get along in a couple of the Lapp dialects. No one will catch

on. There are so many dialects that a Lapp from Jaemt-
land can't understand a Lapp from Karesuando."

"What about me?" Sumo said. "I can't pass as a Swede.
Neither can Chief."

The Baroness laughed again. "No, but the two of you
can pass as Lapps of Mongolian or Samoyed stock.
There's a lot of intermarriage. Just keep your mouths
shut."

"That won't be easy for Joe Skytop," Inga said dryly.
She ruffled the fur of one of the borzois.

Wharton was studying the map. "Okay," he said. "We
follow the reindeer herds to their grazing grounds on the
eastern shore of the Kola Peninsula. The Russians don't
bother us because we're a familiar sight this time of year.
And there's nothing that strategic on the Kola Peninsula.
But we've still got to cross forty miles of open sea to get
to the Kanin Peninsula. And that *is* strategic. The germ
warfare laboratory's there. The shore is guarded by radar,
and the Russians make regular overflights across the
Mezen Bay." He spread his hands helplessly. "Anything
—even rubber boats—is sure to be spotted."

"Tommy," the Baroness said.

Sumo got up and crossed the rough plank floor of the
hunting lodge to a stack of wooden crates against the
chinked log wall. He picked up a small pry bar and forced
open a lid.

"We cross underwater, in these," he said.

He drew out something that looked like an oversize
white plastic laundry bag. There was a rigid ring around
the mouth, topped by an irregular block of foam that
looked like ice.

"Man, I'm from Oklahoma!" Skytop bellowed. "I'm not
getting my ass frozen in that thing!"

"Can we survive in those?" Wharton said.

"They've been tested by the Navy in the Antarctic,"
Sumo said. "There's a multi-layer foam lining with air
space for insulation. There's a network of heating wires,
battery-powered. Works like electric socks at a football
game. We'll be warm as toast."

"What happens if you spring a leak?" Eric said. .

"You die. In about four minutes. Arctic salt water reads at about 28 degrees Fahrenheit."

Skytop shivered.

Sumo pried open another crate and took out something that looked like a boomerang with four bullet-shaped fans protruding from its trailing edge. The whole assembly was less than four feet from tip to tip, and looked as if it couldn't weigh more than a few pounds.

"This is what pulls us along," he said. "Remote controlled. We bob around just below the surface behind it in single file, on a long nylon line. We can do about ten knots. Cross the bay in four hours."

"How did Key get that up here so fast?" Wharton said.

The Baroness stretched and wriggled her toes in their thermal socks. "He has a lot of friends in Finland. He has a lot of friends everywhere. This lodge belongs to a Finnish industrialist. He thinks one of John's friends is having a honeymoon here."

"What else did John send up?"

The Baroness got up and joined Sumo. She took the pry bar from him and opened another crate. She took out a soft floppy package about the size of a knapsack.

"Guess what this is?" she said.

He furrowed his brow. "I haven't a clue."

She laughed with delight. "A snowmobile!"

"Looks more like a giant beanbag," Wharton said. "What are all those lumps?"

"Some of the rigid parts," Penelope said. "The engine, front ski assembly, tiller and so forth."

"But how . . . ?"

"You pull this ring. It releases a plastic foam that becomes rigid in a couple of minutes. It was developed by NASA for instant shelters on the moon. There's an earthbound version the construction industry is experimenting with. The foam forces its way between these tailored layers of fabric, takes its shape and hardens. Presto—instant snowmobile."

"That little lump can't be the motor. It's about the size of two coffee cans."

"Another space agency invention. Runs on liquid hydrogen and oxygen heated in a titanium combustion chamber by a flashlight-size laser assembly. We'll be sitting on a bomb, but it has a range of a couple of hundred miles before the hydrogen runs out. Enough to get us out—fast!"

Inga shuddered. The two wolfhounds, responding to her mood, whined.

"With a capsule of moon virus," Inga said. "I do not like that, Baroness. Suppose there is an accident?"

Penelope said, "We don't take the virus with us. Too dangerous. We destroy it on the spot."

"But how? They had to set off an underground nuclear explosion to dispose of the Houston virus. A hydrogen bomb!"

Even Skytop looked worried. "Yeah. We don't dare crack the capsule. And it's not the kind of thing you pour gasoline on and set afire."

"Tommy," the Baroness said.

Sumo was already opening another crate. He removed an accordion-like disarray of louvered panels. Like some oriental conjurer, he spread it out into a large metal box the size of a child's coffin. There was a cylindrical housing at one end.

"This will do in place of a hydrogen bomb," the Baroness said.

"What is it?" Inga said.

"A laser autoclave."

"A sterilizer? But is it good enough to . . ."

Penelope said, "The AEC released it to us from their hydrogen fusion research program. And added a few tricks stolen from the Plasma Physics Institute in Munich. It's top secret."

Sumo looked like a child with a new toy. "We enclose the capsule in the box. We focus a laser pulse on a frozen pellet of deuterium and tritium—heavy hydrogen. There's a thermonuclear reaction for a fraction of a second. It should be enough."

"A fraction of a second, man!" Skytop growled. "That doesn't seem like much."

"How long do you think a nuclear explosion takes?" Sumo said.

The Baroness cut firmly across the conversation. "The temperature inside the autoclave will reach something like fifty million degrees centigrade," she said flatly. "That's hotter than the surface of the sun."

"Everything vaporizes," Sumo said. "The virus, the autoclave and a forty-foot circle of the Kanin Peninsula."

The others looked at the autoclave, a hint of awe showing in their faces. The Baroness walked over to the window and looked outside. The Finnish landscape was bleak. The lodge was some 600 miles north of Helsinki, well above the Arctic Circle, bordering a frozen lake. It was remote even by Finnish standards, far above the winter sports center at Rovaniemi. Outside the window was a pale expanse of snow and washed-out sky, broken sparsely by the scraggly Arctic vegetation. Somewhere across that expanse was the Russian border, marked only by posts driven into the tundra.

She'd be crossing it soon. If only the damned Lapps would get here!

She paced impatiently in her stocking feet, her mind busy with the logistics of it. She tossed her head and whirled on Dan Wharton.

"What ordnance are we carrying?" she snapped.

Wharton spoke slowly and thoughtfully, refusing to be fazed by her impatience. He was used to her moods, including her high-strung eagerness just before a mission. And he was hopelessly in love with her. He had no realistic expectation of ever doing anything about it; he was chamberlain to her queen, and he knew it. Besides, you don't complicate your emotions when your lives depend on working as a close-knit team. But his worship of the Baroness remained deep inside his guts, a hard indigestible lump whose pain he cherished.

"We're using the Israeli *Galil* assault rifle," Wharton said. "Nine pounds. You can fire it with one hand. 650 rounds a minute. It also fires antitank rockets, two-inch mortars and signal flares. It works after being dunked in sand, snow, mud or water. Collapsible bipod and stock.

The bipod converts to wire clippers. There's even a built-in bottle opener."

Skytop lifted his great head. "Bottle opener? Come on!"

Wharton grinned. "The Israeli soldiers had the same habit you do—opening beer bottles with ammunition magazines."

"What else have you got, Dan?" the Baroness said.

"Sleepy gas. Plastic explosive. And some cutting edges."

"Memory plastic?"

He nodded. "I had it made up into a few things that we could conceal in our gear. Belts, straps and so forth. Here's straps for all our wristwatches. Hold a match under one of 'em and you've got a four-inch knife with a sharp point and a serrated edge for cutting."

The watchbands looked like fine leather. But when heat was applied to them, the neo-methylmethacrylate co-polymer they were made of "remembered" that it had been cast in the rigid form of a knife. The edges flowed and became sharp; the blade straightened.

"That looks like a dog collar," the Baroness said, pointing to a longer strap.

"It is. No reason Igor and Stasya can't carry some of the ordnance."

He whistled the two borzois over to him. "Good boy," he said, patting them on their long, narrow primitive heads. He fastened the collars around their necks. Igor grinned, showing the wicked wolf-killing teeth.

"Man, like those animals don't need a *knife!*" Skytop said. Everybody laughed.

"What about our Arctic gear?" the Baroness said.

Wharton said, "Same stuff we've used before. Those skintight skivvies developed by the space agency. Wired, with a small battery pack for high winds and emergencies. But we can conserve the batteries. That insulation was made for outer space. The Arctic shouldn't give it any trouble. And I've got us those insulated pup tents that fold to pocket size, with telescoping plastic rods. High-energy rations. The works."

The Baroness continued her restless prowling. "Then

we're all set. Except for our traveling companions. What *is* taking them so long?" She glanced uneasily at her watch. "Key said he'd fixed it all up with the Ethnological Institute. They were supposed to be here by midday."

"Relax, Baroness," Eric said. "You can't hurry Lapps. It's calving time. Maybe they took time off to hunt a stray reindeer. They're crossing all the way over from Swedish Lapland."

Sumo was inserting an earplug, raising an antenna. "I'll see if I can raise Paul or Fiona in Helsinki. Maybe they've had word from Key."

He began fiddling with his dials. The Baroness sighed. She sat cross-legged on the big stone hearth and began cleaning her tiny gold-plated Bernardelli VB automatic for the third time that day. Wharton and Skytop went to work packing the gear.

Inga was over by the window, looking across the tundra, her blonde hair dazzling in the Arctic sunlight. She pressed her face against the glass.

"They're here!" she burst out. "Come quick, take a look!"

Chapter 6

There was a fantastic sight outside the window. It was a convention of northern elves, small wiry men with triangular faces, wearing bright elaborately embroidered tunics and tight leggings. They were grinning at Inga through the glass, gesturing with mittened hands, their breath making frost patterns on the windowpanes.

More of them were swarming toward the lodge, trotting beside crude wooden sledges pulled by reindeer. More reindeer, hundreds of them, were streaming over the tundra, herded by little boys muffled in scarves and peaked embroidered caps.

They wouldn't come in. The Baroness and the others

crowded outside in the zero cold and immediately were surrounded by the Lapps.

"*Burist!*" came a chorus of voices. "*Buore baive!*"

"*Boure baive* yourself," Skytop thundered. The little men came barely to his chest. He smiled encouragingly at them, a rock protruding from a sea of vivid embroidery and bobbing red pompons.

Penelope greeted them one by one, using up her few words of Lapp dialect and switching to Finnish. They seemed delighted with her efforts. They smiled and nodded at her, none of them coming above her chin.

"*Onko taalla ketaan, joka puhuu Englantia?*" Penelope said. "Is there anyone here who speaks English?"

The Lapps looked at one another. "Vana," someone said. The cry was taken up. "Vana, Vana!"

A lean, intense man pushed his way through the crowd. He was tall for a Lapp—almost as tall as Penelope herself. She couldn't think of him as a small man. He projected an instant aura of force and masculinity.

"I am Vana," he said in a grave, controlled voice. "Welcome to our *sita.*"

Penelope looked him over. The triangular face, with its sharp cheekbones and pointed chin, didn't look at all elfin on him. He looked rather handsome and devilish. His eyes were blue, not brown—evidence of Scandinavian blood in his nomad veins. Like most of the other men, he carried a long wooden staff and wore a knife at his belt. His costume was banded with the same colorful embroidery. But slung over it was a wolfskin pelt.

She looked at his leggings. More wolfskin. Not reindeer fur, like the others were wearing.

"We thank you for allowing us to join your tribe," she said, flashing him her warmest smile.

He looked uncomfortable. "We have had people travel with us before. Studying our ways, studying the distribution of the reindeer herds. We are honored to offer our hospitality."

"You speak excellent English, Vana," the Baroness said.

"I went to school in Kautokeino," he said.

Another Lapp had elbowed his way into the group. "Vana also speaks German and Norwegian," he said.

"This is Aslak, my brother," Vana said.

Aslak was tall, too. Not as tall as Vana, but he had a good six inches on most of the other Lapps. He gave Penelope a crinkly faced smile. His eyes were blue, too.

Penelope introduced the others. The Lapps were openly in awe of Skytop. "He is like the Grandfather of the Hill," one of the nomads said, craning his neck to look up into Skytop's face.

"He means the Chief looks like a bear," Eric said. "That's what the Lapps call them."

"The bear is sacred to us," Vana said. He closed his mouth immediately, as if he had said too much.

Wharton and Sumo had been busy dragging gear out into the snow. It didn't look like too much equipment for six people. The collapsible snowmobiles amounted to an extra knapsack apiece, and the guns and explosives and the specialized Arctic gear could have passed for bedrolls and duffle bags. Everything was wrapped in reindeer skins, like the Lapps' own possessions.

There was only one package that seemed heavy. The flat bundle containing the laser autoclave. Sumo stayed close to it, never letting it out of arm's reach.

Vana and his people helped load the fur-wrapped bundles on sledges. The sledges were made of wood and leather, with wooden runners curving upward toward a bowed front. Vana and Aslak helped them hitch up the reindeer, big antlered bucks who waited patiently while the leather harnesses were attached. Penelope wondered where the legend of Santa and his elves had come from; the bundles stacked against the backboards of the sleighs looked no different from the reindeer skin packages the Lapps themselves were transporting.

The Lapps looked puzzled when Penelope and the others came out of the lodge again after changing to colorful embroidered tunics and hats. Most of the Swedish and Norwegian and Finnish government people they'd encountered wore nondescript winter gear. Penelope looked critically at her team. It would probably do; a

Russian peering through binoculars from a distance wouldn't be able to tell much about scale, as long as Skytop and Wharton and Eric stayed a reasonable distance from the smaller Lapps while on the move.

But the Lapps forgot their puzzlement when Inga came out leading the two enormous white borzois. They crowded around like children, pure delight showing in their elvish features.

"Wolfhounds," Aslak said approvingly. "We have seen them work. This is good."

The Lapps' own dogs resembled spitz: smaller animals that yapped at the two borzois and circled them at a wary distance.

Vana said, "The wolves have been bad this year. Worse than usual. They are wild with hunger. They have grown bold beyond belief. They are carrying off the calves. It will be worse when we cross into Russia. Perhaps you will let your dogs hunt the wolf with us."

Penelope could see the savage excitement in his eyes. She felt an answering excitement. This man was a hunter. The hunter in herself recognized the predator in him, that fierce, pitiless force that was her own mainspring. And he was feeling it in her, she could tell. A spark passed between them. She showed Vana her strong white teeth in a primitive grin.

"Yes, Vana," she told him. "We'll hunt the wolf with you."

Gorev finished transcribing the code groups and took off his earphones. He switched off the short wave receiver and closed the desk drawer on it. He yawned, stretched and crossed the office to the wall safe, scowling as usual at the simple, cleanly functional furniture. He preferred the comfortable clutter of the Moscow offices; the Finnish headquarters always seemed bare to him.

Gorev was a small dark untidy man with a potbelly the size of a Georgian melon. Six years of being stationed in Helsinki and stuffing himself with smörgasbord and piirakka and Karelian hotpot had put it there.

The safe was behind a cheap framed lithograph of

Sibelius. Gorev belched, and twisted the dial. The code pad, a one-time "gamma," was stuffed carelessly in the barrel of the Czech Omnipol automatic he kept hidden there.

He fished the gamma out with his fingernails. It was no larger than a postage stamp, its tissue-thin pages rolled up into an eraser-size tube. He brought it back to his desk. With a sigh, he got out a magnifying glass and set to work.

He glanced at the first five numbers of the transcribed message—the indicator group—and used them to locate the right page of the pad. He tore out the flimsy scrap of paper and smoothed it under his fingers.

He wrinkled his forehead, recalling the key phrase that was known only to him and his agent above the Arctic Circle. Ignorant savage, he thought contemptuously. But he'd been useful.

A cheap Balkan cigarette dangling from his lip, Gorev added the numbers derived from the phrase to the five-digit groups on the code pad. He traced the coordinates swiftly with a pencil, writing down the resulting letters one by one.

He scowled when he was finished. More problems. It would all come to nothing, as usual, he was sure, but whatever happened, he was sure to miss his dinner at the *Holvi* that evening.

He touched the end of his cigarette to the code page. The nitrated cellulose paper disappeared in an instantaneous flash. He put the rest of the pad back in the gun barrel and closed the safe on it.

Karp was sitting at his desk in the inner office, reading a chess manual. He slipped it under a pile of folders when Gorev came in and picked up a report. He looked up. "Yes, Comrade," he said sternly.

Gorev passed him the message. "Six people are crossing over to the Kola Peninsula with the Lapps," he said. "They're supposed to be Swedes. But they're talking mostly English."

Karp studied the paper, his thin lips compressed. He was spare and lean and functional, like the Finnish furniture that Gorev detested. He had a long, close-cropped skull with little ears plastered close to it, and a thin straight nose. His jacket was off, but the white starched shirt and necktie looked just as uncomfortable. Karp kept himself and his office very neat. It drove Gorev crazy, working for him.

"Most educated Swedes speak English," Karp said infuriatingly. "Some of them prefer it."

"Yes, Comrade," Gorev said. "But in view of the latest alert from Moscow, asking that we be on the look-out for any activities that might bear on the biological warfare laboratory on Cape Kanin, perhaps we should bring it to their attention."

Karp pursed his lips. "The Kola Peninsula is a big place. Moscow is not concerned about the wanderings of a primitive tribe. And it is separated from the Kanin Peninsula by forty miles of open water, scanned by radar."

"But . . ."

Karp went on. "If I wire Moscow, they will alert Penkin. Penkin is a madman. He will go wild. He will disrupt the activities of the laboratory, instituting unnecessary security measures. The last time he received a false alert, he put two scientists and a scientific administrator under arrest. He went so far as to abuse them. There were complaints. And we were blamed."

Gorev began to relax. He had done his duty. Nobody could say he hadn't. He had pointed out the importance of the message. But Karp, *k'shastyu*, was cautious. It was the one good trait that went with his finicky nature. It looked as if he'd be able to keep his date at the *Holvi* after all.

"No," Karp said with finality. "We will not wire Moscow tonight."

Gorev beamed. He could already taste the marvelous *lihapullia* and the *kiiseli* they served at the *Holvi*. And afterward . . . that goddesslike red-haired girl he'd met that afternoon at the Havis Amanda Fountain.

"We will look into it ourselves," Karp said. "If it is nothing, our report will say so. And if they are American spies, *then* we will warn Penkin. Or kill them ourselves."

"But how . . ." Gorev wrenched his mind from the

fantasy he was having about the red-haired girl. Fiona, her name was. She was British—Scotch or something. She was in Helsinki for a holiday. Dying to pick up a man. She thought Russians were exotic. He'd had his hand under her *blooska,* and she hadn't said anything. She'd smiled, in fact. And she'd said yes immediately when he'd invited her to the *Holvi.*

Karp consulted his watch. "There's a flight to Ivalo in an hour. We can be there in four hours. We can rent snowmobiles and cold weather gear at the airport."

Gorev's face fell. Even if Fiona were still in Helsinki when he got back, she'd be sure to have picked up someone else. A hot *devooshka* like that didn't stay lonely for very long.

"Relax, Gorev," Karp said with a sadistic smile. "You're going to have a winter holiday. At the State's expense."

Penelope moved at an easy trot beside the sledge, her hand resting on the side rail. Ahead of her, in a loose triangular formation, were the reindeer, hundreds and hundreds of them, flowing across the dazzling landscape in eerie silence, their hoofbeats muffled by the snow. Only the children, the old, the ill and the pregnant were riding in the sledges; the Lapps were sparing the draft reindeer for now, reserving their strength for the hauling of goods, not people. It had been a long, hard winter. The animals' ribs were showing.

At the point of the triangle was the most important reindeer of the herd, the one they called Follower. Vana had explained it to her. "He follows a man leading a haltered reindeer of his own free will. This sets an example for the other reindeer."

But there were stragglers. The Lapp herdsmen were continually rounding up strays and driving them back to the main body with their long staffs, aided by the yelping dogs. Joe Skytop was helping. Looking like some huge overstuffed rag doll in his gay skirted tunic and red leg wrappings, with his tall embroidered cap bobbing, the big Cherokee lumbered after strays with surprising agility, flapping his arms and yelping like a cowpuncher at a rodeo.

She could see the others, passable enough at a distance in their Lapp costumes, scattered throughout the migrating horde. Sumo was small enough to look authentic, but even Wharton and Eric, with their size and light hair, might have gotten by as Lapps with an admixture of Scandinavian blood.

But Skytop was definitely a problem. She had just about made up her mind to tell him to stop being helpful and make himself less conspicuous in the middle of the formation, when she became aware of someone loping along besides her.

It was Vana's brother, Aslak.

"You look like a true Lapp in your *kofte* and *skallers,*" he grinned at her. "Only too tall."

"Thank you," she said. "You speak good English, Aslak."

"I went to school in Kautokeino, also," he said.

"And did you study German as well?"

He grimaced. "No. I had other interests. Vana is the scholar."

"Vana is a very accomplished man. Is he the leader of this *sita?*"

Unexpectedly, he laughed. "Vana? No, Vana wouldn't be interested. He is not . . . steady . . . enough. He would rather kill the bear and hunt the wolf."

"Well, that seems like a useful occupation. Protecting the herd."

"Oh, our people are grateful," he said in an odd tone. "Vana is famous all through Lapland. Vana the wolf hunter. They tell stories about him in four languages and the *djavul* knows how many dialects."

"He must be an exceptional shot," Penelope said. She remembered the gleaming Tikka rifles she'd seen among the sledges, lovingly polished and kept ready to hand by their owners.

"Vana doesn't use a gun," Aslak said. "He hunts wolf the traditional way—with no other weapon than his staff and knife."

A thrill of excitement went through Penelope. Vana was indeed living up to her expectations.

"How is it done?" she said.

Aslak chuffed along in silence beside her for some time before answering. Finally he spoke, again with that odd tone in his voice.

"The trick is to hit the wolf hard on the muzzle with the staff, then finish him off with the knife. But you must not let the wolf catch the staff in his teeth. For then the wolf will quickly have the man on the ground. And if that happens, the man must kill the wolf quickly. Otherwise he will be too badly mangled to return to the camp."

Penelope visualized Vana killing one of the big Arctic wolves with his primitive weapons. They were powerful creatures, weighing up to 175 pounds—heavier than a man like Vana. It would be impossible to keep on your feet if those big paws hit you on the chest.

She felt a flush of excitement, warming her face despite the below-zero temperature. Vana was quite a man, not like the types you encountered in so-called civilization.

Aslak was studying her shrewdly. "And if the wolf gets your hand in his jaws, you must not try to pull it free. If you do, you lose your fingers."

"What do you do?"

He attempted a careless tone. "You push your hand all the way down the wolf's throat and squeeze. And you use the knife in the other hand quickly."

Penelope loped along, her breath making clouds in the clear air. Her mission seemed very distant. There was only this sparkling white wonderland, fringed here and there by stunted trees, stretching on in barren grandeur. Time did not exist—not when the sun shone at midnight in summer and never appeared at all in winter. Somewhere in that vast glistening expanse was her prey —wolves and man. First the wolves, with a magnificent primitive creature like Vana as her hunting partner. She resolved to do it the way Aslak had described it to her, with a knife and a stick.

She glanced backward without breaking her stride. The two big Russian wolfhounds were bounding along happily behind the sledge, their tongues lolling. She'd give them a treat, let them do what they were made for.

There was someone coming up from behind, overtaking them with a burst of speed. It was Vana.

He jogged along beside them, his face showing no effort. Like the hunter he was, he could run all day, with oiled automatic strides, never out of breath.

For that matter, so could she.

"Mita kuuluu," she said. "Aslak's been entertaining me with wolf-hunting stories."

"Aslak talks too much," Vana said.

"When will we see some wolves?" she said.

He sniffed the air like an animal. "There is a pack following the herd now. They are keeping their distance so far."

"Are they dangerous?"

"There is something more dangerous—for you."

"Oh?"

Vana said nothing. Penelope suddenly realized that Aslak had faded from sight. She hadn't noticed him drop back. There had been that flash of something obscure between him and his brother.

Vana turned his face toward her again. "Where you are going, there is a man more savage than a wolf. The Lapps tell stories about him. Mothers use his name to frighten their children when they are bad."

There was a click of wariness in Penelope's brain. *Where you are going,* Vana had said. What did he know? Or what had he guessed?

His next words left her in no doubt. "His name is Penkin," Vana said. "Sometimes he crosses the Mezen Bay to the Kola Peninsula. When that happens, word passes among the Lapps. We stay far away from him."

She spoke lightly. "And this Penkin? Is he on the Kola Peninsula now?"

"No. Word has passed among the *sitas* that he remains on Kanin."

Penelope digested that. "This bad man, Penkin, what does he do?"

"He hunts Lapps, the way Lapps hunt wolves."

"How can that be, Vana? The Soviet government wouldn't permit it. The Small Peoples, as they call them, are protected."

He sprinted along beside her. "Lapps, Khanti, Mansi, Nenets—all of the northern tribes who follow the reindeer—here and in Russia. They know about Penkin. He is lord of a castle in the ice. Let a man get lost in a blizzard and wander too close, and Penkin hunts him."

Penelope thought. Penkin had to be a Russian security man. And the castle in the ice must be the biological laboratory on Kanin.

"So this Penkin hunts the reindeer people? And takes them prisoner? Shoots them?"

Vana's expression was unreadable. "No. The man is a troll. A monster. Some say he can turn himself into a wolf. When he catches some lost Khanti or Nenet, he stakes him out in the snow. He sprinkles blood around him. The wolves can smell the blood for miles. They come. They eat the man alive."

Penelope shivered at the story.

"We're heading east, Vana," she said. "Don't you fear this Penkin?"

"I have nothing to fear, Penelope," he said. It was the first time he'd used her name. "But you do."

Fiona hung up the phone. "That was my greasy little friend, Gorev. He's breaking our date tonight. Something came up, he said."

Yvette looked up quickly, concern showing on her smooth, milk-chocolate face. "What else did he say?" she said.

"Something about winter sports. And flying to Ivalo."

Fiona was a stunning redhead, with an abundant figure and the high cheekbones of a model. She was quick and sharp and bitchy, and she liked to sleep late. But she'd never let the Baroness down yet—either as a fashion beauty for International Models, Inc., or as an agent. She could kill a man with a nail file, or coax information out of him that he didn't realize he was giving. She didn't much care which.

"I don't like it," Paul said. He stood up and walked over to the window. His handsome black features tightened. "This Gorev cat had the hots for you. He ain't gonna break a date for nothing. And Ivalo—that's less'n forty miles from the hunting lodge where the Baroness is meeting the Lapps. Too close for coincidence."

Fiona said, "I guess it paid off, cultivating the resident KGB agents the way the Baroness told us to."

"You think they have a line on the Baroness?" Yvette said.

"It has to be. Gorev is a talkative little creep. I got the idea that the Helsinki KGB office is fat and lazy. They don't stir from their comforts easily. Desk men. And suddenly—on an hour's notice—they're getting off their asses and taking a plane for Ivalo!"

"But how could they find out about the Baroness?"

"I don't know. An informer."

Yvette turned to Paul. "We'd better warn the Baroness that she might have company."

"Right on," Paul said.

He took Fiona's makeup case from her and opened the lid. Inside was an assortment of creams and lotions and cosmetics. They were all real, able to pass customs examinations, secret searches and chemical analysis. The components of the long-range transceiver were imbedded in the molded plastic of the case itself. There were fingernail-thin integrated circuits, and sandwiched capacitors, and four special-purpose minicomputers the size of poker chips. He pried at a rivet on the catch and pulled out twelve feet of antenna.

"I can't believe that thing works," Fiona said.

"Oh it works all right," Paul said. He plugged Fiona's hair dryer into the hotel current. It was the transformer. The end of the hose, with a concealed electrical contact, screwed conveniently into the round socket that had held a jar of cold cream.

Paul twisted the handle of the case, tuning in the frequency that triggered the MESTAR satellite balanced overhead on its polar orbit. MESTAR would do the rest of the work, triggering the receiver that Tom Sumo was monitoring, more than 600 miles away.

"What if Tommy's not on station?" Fiona said.

"Tommy's *always* on station," Paul grinned. "He's got a transponder built into the fillings in his teeth. Sacrificed a couple of good teeth to do it, too. As long as he stays within a couple of hundred yards of his receiver, he's gonna get the message."

"That Tommy!" Yvette shook her head. "Imagine turning your head into a radio!"

Paul was tapping out his signal now, pressing the spring catch that served as a key. He cocked his head, listening for the transponder signal that would tell him he'd made contact.

"What's the matter, Paul?" Fiona said.

"I don't know. I can't seem to raise Tommy's receiver."

"Is your transmitter working all right? Or maybe ME-STAR is out of range."

Paul shook his head. "I'm getting feedback from ME-STAR. *Our* part of the link is working fine."

"Paul, you've got to get through. There are two KGB men on the way. And there's an informer."

He gave her a somber look. "No way. Whatever the matter is, it's up there. The Baroness is in trouble."

Sumo staggered over to the growing pile of equipment and added the heavy, fur-wrapped bundle containing the laser autoclave to it. He set it down very carefully.

"Keep an eye on this, will you?" he said to Skytop. "I'm going back for the radio."

Skytop grunted. He and Wharton were setting up the two reindeer skin tents the Lapps had loaned them, while Inga, like any Lapp woman, was building a fire with birch twigs and bark.

Sumo walked through the encampment, his bones aching. The Lapps had finally called a halt. All around him they were brewing coffee, throwing dried meat and frozen cubes of reindeer blood into pots to make soup, unhitching the draft reindeer. The animals were grazing as best they could, scraping at the snow with their sharp hooves to uncover lichen.

He found the sledge where he'd left it, near a clump of stunted birch. While he was gone, Vana had finished unhitching the reindeer and led the animal off to graze. There were four or five other sledges nearby, their empty harnesses dangling limply from their prows.

Sumo dug into the pile of furs and felt around for the radio. It had been silent so far, thank goodness. When he had a chance, he'd have to do something about adjusting the transponder in his bridgework. Every time it went off, it gave him a toothache.

The receiver wasn't there where he'd left it. It had been moved several inches in the pile of goods. Sumo pulled it out into the light.

The wrappings had been disturbed. Sumo glanced around to make sure nobody was within sight. He untied the leather thongs and opened the package.

The radio receiver was still inside.

What was left of it.

Whoever had done it had been deliberate and thorough. The receiver was completely, hopelessly smashed.

Chapter 7

Penkin squinted at the sky, using an enormous gaunt-leted paw to shield his eyes against the Arctic dawn.

"Naprahva," he rumbled. "Here it comes now."

He was a giant of a man, with a skull like a bent boiler plate and a face like a crag. He wore the fur hood of his parka pushed back, heedless of the cold, showing thick blue-black hair that curled down low on his forehead.

"I see it, Evgeny Ivanovich," Viktor said. The little hunchback shivered, his nose and cheeks blue with cold. He raised a pair of binoculars to the sky.

There was a bright red dot high in the frozen sky. It

grew larger, resolving itself into a striped parachute with a blackened something swaying beneath it.

Together they watched it come down, a towering figure in furs and a little gnome of a man in a peaked hood, standing next to the squarish bulk of the *vezdekhod,* the big-tracked snow vehicle that Penkin roamed the peninsula in.

"Look at them, Viktor," Penkin said. "Like dogs after a bone."

A line of men and vehicles was spread across the snowy plain. They were already moving toward the probable point of impact. There was the recovery team that Moscow had transferred from the space center at Baikonur, towing a huge cushioned cradle on runners behind their tractor. Penkin's lip curled. They'd been a problem, those four dozen strangers with their Baikonur security clearances descending on his domain without warning. He was still checking them out. And crawling along beside them were the vehicles containing the biologists from the laboratory, who were going to supervise the handling of the spacecraft and its contents. Penkin could see the big yellow construction cranes mounted on tractor treads that were four feet wide; the scientists were very nervous about the transfer.

Scientists! Penkin spat into the snow. A bunch of troublesome schoolboys who had to have their noses wiped for them! If you spoke roughly to them, they complained to Moscow!

"Shall we go down and have a look?" Viktor said.

The spacecraft had landed. The striped parachute was collapsing, spilling over the snow. An advance man on a snowmobile was already cutting the shrouds.

"Let the children play with their toy," Penkin said. "I smell a Nenet."

A malevolent joy spread over Viktor's shriveled face. "No, Evgeny Ivanovich," he whined. "No Nenet would dare approach within fifty *versts* of here."

"Let's look around anyway," Penkin said.

He swung himself up into the cabin of the *vezdekhod.* The little hunchback followed him, moving sideways like a crab, pulling himself through the door with mittened hands. The cabin stank of diesel fumes and grease and garlic sausage from Penkin's lunch the day before. The floor was as littered as a wild animal's den: scraps of greasy paper and empty wine bottles and, over in the corner, the remains of a gnawed bone.

Penkin opened the twin throttles and the snow vehicle roared into life. They lurched forward. Penkin deliberately aimed it toward a group of technicians on foot, smiling as they scrambled to get out of his way.

He made a wide circle around the returned spacecraft. The big cradle on runners had been maneuvered into position beside it, and they were moving the yellow cranes into place. The craft was a stubby cylinder, as big around as a woodcutter's hut. It had to be, to contain the Lunokhod.

"Think of it, Evgeny Ivanovich," Viktor said, "it has come back from the moon."

"They're making enough of a fuss about it," Penkin growled. "Moscow's been shitting in its pants, plaguing me about tightening security here." He gave a short laugh. "Me!"

"The moon germs," Viktor said. "The Americans are afraid. They don't want us to have them. They want to keep them for themselves."

Penkin looked back through the narrow rear slot. Technicians in white protective garb with plastic face shields were spraying disinfectant over the burned and blackened space capsule. More technicians stood by with massive hooks to attach it to the cranes.

"Bugger the Americans!" Penkin said. "And those learned fools back there, too!"

His mood improved when they were out on the tundra. Here on the snowy steppes he was in his element. The red tape and the paper work were forgotten. He scanned the frozen immensity, white and bare as far as the eye could see, except for the long dawn shadows of the scraggly trees here and there. He cracked the side window and sniffed the fresh clear air. Beside him Viktor shivered.

For an hour he moved the big-tracked vehicle in a

growing spiral around the recovery site until one wide circle intersected the first security perimeter.

He braked to an abrupt stop beside a wooden kiosk, the treads of the *vezdekhod* sending up a spray of snow. A fur-capped soldier came out, a submachine gun slung negligently over his shoulder.

"*Dobray ootra, Direktor,*" he said.

"See anything, Lutsky?" Penkin said.

Lutsky's face worked with the effort of speech. He wasn't very bright. But he was a good sentry. He'd shoot anything that moved.

"I saw the parachute, Direktor," he said.

"Anything alive, you lout!" Penkin roared.

"No, Direktor."

"All right, Lutsky, carry on." He patted the man on the cheek. "Good man."

Lutsky squirmed with pleasure. He was loyal to Penkin, as all his security force were. They were loyal as dogs; he could kick them, beat them, rail at them, but they'd give their lives for a kind word from him. Lutsky was all right in the outer perimeter; he didn't have the brains for anything more complicated. He was unshaven, unkempt and never bathed. Penkin didn't care. He enjoyed seeing the discomfiture of the scientists when they got downwind of Lutsky.

He made several more stops, working inward through his security setup. There were the tripwires and the mines, buried under the snow; he didn't need a chart to tell him where they were; he maneuvered the *vezdekhod* through them by memory and blind instinct. There were the coffin-like concrete bunkers, unanchored, floating on the permafrost in slush generated by the heat of the men and stoves they contained, invisible till you tripped over them.

Then there was the outer fence.

Penkin pulled the *vezdekhod* to a stop, its twin diesels purring. The fence was twelve feet high, anchored on steel posts that sank another twelve feet into the permafrost. Even so, he had to pour new concrete every spring.

Inside that was another fence, topped by barbed wire. And beyond that, an electrified fence.

Between the two were the wolves.

Penkin had used the usual Alsatians and Dobermans during his first year as security director. The visiting officials from Moscow had noted that he kept his dogs more savage than guard dogs at any similar installations they'd inspected.

But the Soviet Arctic was full of wolves. A wasted natural resource.

He'd pulled every wire he could to call off the helicopter wolf patrol. He'd scared hell out of the bounty hunters on the Kanin Peninsula and the adjoining shores. Crippled one of them, in fact. Nobody hunted wolves for hundreds of miles around now.

They belonged to Penkin.

He'd captured a few wolves alive. Killed a couple of dams and raised the cubs. He'd put the wolves in with the Alsatians and the Dobermans.

They'd killed his guard dogs. He was overjoyed. He refused a shipment of replacements. Instead, he'd trapped more wolves.

His own personal wolf pack numbered over a hundred now. It took a lot of reindeer meat to feed them. But there were plenty of reindeer on the Kanin Peninsula too. And herdsmen to take them from.

He kept them hungry and mean. The kennel man didn't dare approach them. He threw them their food over the fence. The run was never cleaned. The sick animals were left to die, to be eaten by their pack mates. Only Penkin could enter the run. He'd raised the wolves from cubs. They accepted him. His physical size and strength kept him from being bowled over when they jumped up and put their paws on his shoulders. If he'd once fallen to the ground, it would have been the end of him; he knew that. They took his arms and legs in their jaws, not clamping down too hard, and he reciprocated by grasping their muzzles in his immense hands and shaking their heads; that was the way you greeted wolves when you didn't have jaws like theirs. On a couple of occasions, he'd been challenged by young males. He'd hooked his great arms around their necks, holding their teeth away from him, and broken their backs. He'd thrown the bodies to the pack. It was an object lesson. He was their leader.

The scientists and laboratory officials thought he was crazy. His own men worshiped him.

As he sat watching the fence through the windscreen, a wolf came trotting down the enclosure toward the *vezdekhod*. It was a big gray male. Penkin recognized him. The animal approached the wire, sniffing. He wagged his tail. Penkin laughed. The wolf sat down on his haunches and howled.

Penkin howled back. It was a good imitation. Viktor clapped his hands in glee. The howl set the rest of the pack off. There was an eerie chorus from the recesses of the run. A couple more wolves came loping out to investigate.

"They look hungry, eh, Viktor?" Penkin said. "Maybe they need a snack. You're about the right size."

He grasped the crooked little man by the belt and the nape of the head and lifted him off the seat. He kicked open the door and made as if to throw Viktor out.

Victor squealed in terror. "Please, Evgeny Ivanovich!"

Penkin roared with laughter. "Dog meat, Viktor, that's all you're good for!"

The little man was rigid with terror. "Please, Evgeny Ivanovich. By your father!"

Penkin scowled. He released the hunchback. After a moment he laughed again. He patted Viktor on the shoulder. "Had you worried, didn't I, Viktor?"

A crooked smile spread across Viktor's knobby features. "Worried? Me? *S'kakeekh por!* Not on your life!"

"Let's go."

He took a last look at the installation. Past the triple fences, mounted on immense pylons sunk deep into the permafrost, were the glittering steel and concrete buildings of the laboratory. It looked like an ice castle, from some half-remembered childhood fairytale, with the angular sugar-cube shapes of the research buildings and the tall slabs of the administrative headquarters and the round gleaming watch towers like chessmen at the corners.

It was his.

He shoved the left throttle and the *vezdekhod* spun

around on one tread. He cut in the other clutch, and the snow vehicle leaped forward, moving parallel to the fence toward the open tundra.

About thirty miles out from the laboratory, Penkin suddenly brought the snow vehicle to a halt. He slid open the side window all the way, stuck his head out and sniffed.

"Wolves, Viktor," he said. "Do you smell them?"

He climbed out of the cab and stood, wide-legged, on the broad caterpillar tread. Viktor scuttled out after him.

Penkin's nostrils twitched. "A large pack," he said. "Hundreds of them. No more than a dozen *versts* away."

Even Viktor could detect the scent in the clear air. It was a stench of wet fur and rotten breath.

"I'm glad the wind isn't blowing the other way," Viktor said.

Penkin laughed good humoredly. "Viktor, you are a coward."

The misshapen little man jumped up and down on the tread. "A coward, a coward!" he chortled. "Viktor is a coward!"

"Don't fall off, Viktor," Penkin said. "I might drive off and leave you."

The hunchback cowered in mock terror. "No, Evgeny Ivanovich," he said. "You wouldn't do that. For who would look after you then?"

"Viktor, you're also a fool."

"A fool, a fool . . ."

"Shove it!" Penkin said harshly. "Let's go!"

They found the Nenets a few miles farther on. They appeared as a cluster of black specks in the distance. Penkin spun the *vezdekhod* on its treads and glided toward them. There was a lazy smile on his lips.

There were two of them, a man and his woman, leading a reindeer on a long leather rope. When they saw the *vezdekhod,* they looked up and waved. Penkin could see the smile on the man's face.

He sat looking down at them through the windscreen. They were just a pair of primitive *inorodzi*—"other breeds," as people used to call them in his boyhood, though it was supposed to be *nyekulturny* to use the word these days. They grinned stupidly at him with their flat Mongol faces and slitted eyes, looking round and chubby in their hand-sewn furs. The reindeer had taken the opportunity to nuzzle at the snow, looking for lichen.

Penkin picked the submachine gun up from the seat beside him and climbed down. Viktor followed.

"*Zdrahstvooite,* Honored Sir," the Nenet began in broken Russian.

Penkin looked him up and down. "What are you doing this side of the Ob?" he said.

The Nenet seemed not to understand the import of the question, or to have noticed the submachine gun tucked under Penkin's arm. "We look for our stray animals," he said. "The wolves are very bad this year."

"Where is the rest of your tribe?"

The Nenet pointed south. "Many *versts.* We have been wandering for two days."

Viktor sniggered. "He wants you to give him a ride, Evgeny Ivanovich."

The Nenet nodded vigorously, looking pleased.

"I thought all you *inorodzi* herders were supposed to have been put in reindeer collectives," Penkin said.

"Our tribe follows the old ways," the Nenet said. "The government . . ."

"The government says you're not supposed to be here. This is a restricted area. *Agraneecheevatny!* You are spies!"

The Nenet stood there, still grinning stupidly.

"Don't you understand me, Nenet?"

Viktor said, "Perhaps he's wondering if the reindeer will fit inside the *vezdekhod.*"

"Is that what you're wondering, Nenet?" Penkin said.

The grin faded from the Nenet's face. He looked puzzled.

Penkin swung the submachine gun upward and fired one-handed. There was a short ugly rattle of automatic fire. The reindeer toppled into the snow, its flesh ripped and tattered. A red stain spread into the snow around the carcass.

The Nenet's wife was still holding the leather rope. She stared, stunned, at the dead reindeer.

The Nenet looked frightened. He had a knife at his belt, but he was smart enough not to put his hands anywhere near it. His wife began to wail.

Penkin reversed the submachine gun and hit the Nenet on the side of the head with the butt. The nomad slumped to the ground.

The woman whirled and sprinted like a startled deer. Penkin fired a burst over her head. She stopped.

Viktor, grinning broadly, limped after her and led her back. His eyes were pleading.

"So the dog wants a bone, eh, Viktor?" Penkin said.

"Please, Evgeny Ivanovich," Victor said reproachfully. "It is not nice to say such things."

"All right. Go ahead. If you want to freeze your *saseesky* off, that's your affair."

Viktor stripped the woman at knife point. Beneath the furs, she was broad and muscular, with a firm rounded belly and blubbery globes of breasts. He opened his pants, fishing for his thing underneath six layers of Arctic clothing. The woman shivered, naked, in the subzero cold. Viktor wasn't impressed; he'd seen others like her last an hour or more in colder weather than this.

He motioned her to lie down and crawled on top of her, a twisted hobgoblin shape with a lump on his back and a chin and nose that curved toward one another like a lobster's claw. His hand grew busy between his legs. Penkin squatted down beside Viktor and the woman for a closer look.

Viktor was having trouble. The woman moaned in humiliation and fear. Viktor slapped her across the face. Penkin laughed.

Viktor rubbed his implement frantically against the woman's belly, and slowly, reluctantly, it came to life. It stood out like a twig, as gnarled and twisted as he was, with a network of purple veins and a blue acorn tip. He pushed it into her body. She began to weep.

Two or three spasmodic jerks, and it was all over. He pulled it out of her, oozing a yellowish ichor. He wiped the thing on her discarded furs and stuffed it back inside his clothing.

Tears of laughter were pouring from Penkin's eyes. "Like a dog," he said. "Just like a dog!"

Viktor's lobster claw of a face twisted. "Please, Evgeny Ivanovich!"

The woman was crawling over toward the pile of furs that Viktor had stripped from her. Viktor kicked her in the head. She fell over on her back again, staring at him with dazed apprehension.

"There was no pleasure in you," he said. He took out a little knife and pushed the point of it into her navel.

"Not too deep, Viktor," Penkin said.

A little pool of blood welled up in the woman's belly button. She stared at it and cried, *"Ai, ai, ai!"*

"Get the spikes, Viktor," Penkin said.

The little man swarmed up the side of the *vezdekhod* like a rat going up a wall. He came back with a bundle of spikes and ropes, and a small sledgehammer.

He drove the spikes into the frozen ground, a troll with a hammer, and tied the unconscious Nenet's ankles and wrists to them. When he finished, the reindeer man was spread out like a starfish. The woman was making rhythmic noises that sounded almost like a chant.

She offered no resistance when Viktor staked her out too. He spread the furs out beneath her back to keep her from freezing too quickly.

"Well," Viktor said, looking up, bright-eyed. "Well."

"Put your knife away, Viktor," Penkin said. "This will be enough."

He nudged the dead reindeer with one boot, pushing it over closer to the two Nenets. He pondered awhile, then sprinkled some reindeer blood over them. The man stirred.

"The wind's changing, Evgeny Ivanovich," Viktor said.

In the distance, a wolf howled.

Penkin raised his head and sniffed. "Get into the *vezdekhod*," he said.

Viktor obeyed with alacrity. Penkin heaved himself into the driver's seat and backed the vehicle up forty feet, far enough from the two Nenets so as not to distract the wolves. They sat there and waited.

The wolves appeared in less than half an hour. It was a huge pack, running like one single liquid creature, twisting and wheeling in instant response to the direction of the leader.

"Look at that old fellow," Penkin said. "He's a big one."

The pack stopped at a good distance from the *vezdek-hod* and the two staked-out Nenets. They sat on their haunches and watched, like some satanic audience. Penkin could hear the young ones whimpering.

The Nenet regained consciousness. He raised his head and looked in the direction of the wolves. Penkin could see the expression on the man's face. He laughed and got out a pair of binoculars.

Some of the wolves became bolder. They started to drift over toward the two Nenets, giving the *vezdekhod* a wide berth. The man began to struggle against the ropes, then thought better of it when he saw that he was attracting the attention of the wolves.

One great gray beast gathered its courage and darted in toward the reindeer carcass. It tore a piece out of the animal's flank and began gulping it down. That was too much for the rest of the pack. In a moment, the reindeer was covered with a carpet of gray bodies, fighting and snarling over the meat. There wasn't enough to go around.

The leader of the pack began walking around the two helpless people, sniffing. He sat down on his haunches a couple of times, then resumed pacing. A young wolf sidled over toward the Nenets, its tail tucked between its legs. The pack leader lunged at him, snapping. The young wolf slunk off a few yards and sat down.

The pack waited. The woman began struggling. The man said something to her sharply, and she stopped.

A change came over the demeanor of the wolves. The flattened ears pricked up, alert. The fangs were no longer bared. They looked almost friendly, like tame dogs.

"It won't be long now, Viktor," Penkin murmured.

The big gray leader got to his feet and licked his lips. He trotted over to the woman and sniffed at her.

She screamed.

Penkin watched, the saliva wet in his mouth. Beside him, Viktor was jumping up and down in his seat. Penkin didn't notice him.

The pack finished off the two Nenets in a few minutes. There was a slashing, snapping fury that spattered blood over the snow for yards. You could see nothing but a confusion of gray fur and white flashing teeth. A wolf darted from the mass carrying an arm. Another wolf leaped after him, and they began tugging at the morsel between them. More wolves joined the fracas.

When it was over, a few of the bigger wolves settled down to gnaw at the thighbones, surrounded by patient supplicants who wagged their tails and waited. The younger pups, still hungry, were licking at the blood in the snow.

There was nothing left of the Nenets. Nothing.

"Evgeny Ivanovich," Viktor said.

The big man made no response. He seemed in a trance.

"Evgeny Ivanovich." The little hunchback shook Penkin's arm. "Perhaps we should get back to the laboratory. They'll be bringing in the space vehicle. We ought to be there."

Penkin gave a great yawn. "Right you are, Viktor," he said. He pushed the throttles forward, and the big snow tank moved ahead. The wolves looked up curiously as it passed.

The two doors of the receiving bay yawned wide. The building had been used as a garage. When word had come from Moscow that the spacecraft's course had been changed and that it would land in the Arctic, the laboratory technicians had improvised brilliantly. The garage had been emptied of *bobyks* and *vezdekhods*. It had been made airtight, with an inner coating of plasticized concrete. Every crack had been sealed. It had been sterilized, inside and out, with flame throwers, then sprayed with disinfectant. Filters and air pumps had been installed. Air was pumped out, through a series of ultrafine filters that would trap any known virus down to a diameter of a few microns. The pressure inside the converted garage was several pounds below atmospheric pressure. If a leak developed, air had to go in, not out. The moon virus couldn't escape.

But the doors hadn't been closed yet.

The huge construction crane edged forward, its fifty-foot boom held level in front of it like a giant's spear. It lifted the lunar vehicle out of its enormous cradle and poked it, inch by inch, toward the barn-size doors. The stubby charred cylinder swayed at the end of its chains.

The crane operator pushed the lever that would lower the spaceship to the garage floor. There was a grinding, grating sound.

The spaceship dropped.

It hit the cement floor with a crash. Cracks spread through the floor from the point of impact. Four tons of spacecraft and Lunokhod sunk into the concrete.

"Zdjelajtee vydakh!" someone yelled.

The technicians on the floor milled around, their faces gone white behind their plastic masks.

"Close the doors!"

The big steel doors began to swing shut, creaking. It took a couple of minutes.

Cautiously, a team of three technicians approached the spacecraft. The seal on the hatch was broken. One of the men flashed a light inside. You could make out the bulky washtub shape of the Lunokhod inside, with the row of capsules containing rock samples strapped to its side.

The men looked at one another.

"Capsule number six," one of them whispered. "Do you think it's still intact?"

The first technician played his flashlight through the bent hatch.

"Looks all right. Hard to be sure until we get at it."

The third man was breaking out into a sweat. "It better be all right, Comrades," he said. "If it isn't—and if what the Americans say is true—then we're all dead men."

Chapter 8

"There's somebody following us," the Baroness said.

Wharton said, "Are you sure?"

She was sitting on a fur throw in her borrowed rein-deer-skin tent, stripped down to her long johns. Outside it was forty below zero, but inside the tent, toasted by a birch fire vented through a hole at the top, it was stifling hot.

"I've been picking up the sound of snowmobile engines in the distance whenever the wind is right. Two of them, I think. They've been staying at the same distance for the last day and a half."

"Is that unusual in these parts?" Inga said, over by the fire. She was wearing only her Lapp underfrock, a tunic-like garment of coarse cloth. "Snowmobiles are getting to be a way of life in Scandinavia."

"That's right," Eric said. "Even the Lapps use them now—if they can afford them."

Penelope's great luminous green eyes glinted in the firelight. She tossed her black mane. "We've crossed a lot of snowmobile tracks," she said impatiently. "And I've seen a few snowmobiles in the distance. But these are staying with us. And they're keeping out of sight."

Skytop spoke up. "The Baroness is right. I've heard the engines myself. They stop when we stop. And I've caught a flash of sun on glass. Binoculars."

"All right," Wharton said. He slapped the holstered forty-five at his side in an unconscious gesture. "The Chief and I will go back and take a look."

Penelope shook her head. "I'll do it. Alone."

"We'll go with you."

"No. Whoever those jokers are, they have a friend in camp. The one who smashed Sumo's receiver. I don't want him seeing an *expedition* going out. I have a better chance of slipping out myself without being noticed."

"I don't like it," Wharton said unhappily.

"When will you go?" Sumo said.

Penelope twisted to face him. Under the clinging fabric of the long johns, her torso billowed. "In an hour or so. As soon as the Lapps settle down for the night."

Skytop cocked his head. "That won't be long. Sounds like they're getting themselves about all sung out."

From outside the tent, they could hear drunken voices raised in the primitive sounds of a *joik*—the strange-sounding chant that was the Lapps' way of singing. Penelope could make out a few words: something about "blood on the knife." She recognized it as a reference to the now legendary massacre at Kautokeino little more than a century earlier. No wonder the Lapps still stayed aloof from the Scandinavian society around them!

She shooed everybody out of the tent except Inga. "Unpack my hotsuit, will you?" she said.

Inga rummaged through the pile of gear against the tent wall. "The batteries are only good for sixty hours. You'll be using up survival time you might need on the Russian side."

"I'll try to conserve power."

Inga looked worried. "It's forty below. No wind, but if one comes up . . ."

"Then I'll use up some more survival time."

Inga handed her the hotsuit. It looked as flimsy as a body stocking: a smooth silky thing that you could have squeezed into a fist. But it wedded NASA's space age technology to the Air Force's survival research. There was an inner layer that somehow managed to be fluffy, despite the fact that it was thinner than a silk kerchief. The trick was a superdense mat of synthetic pressed fiber with thousands of microscopic air pockets and projecting cilia per square inch. There was a metallic middle layer that reflected back body heat. And another layer that trapped heat. And a tough, smooth, waterproof outer layer with an oddly structured cross section that had been developed, at a cost of millions, for a new type of skin-

tight space suit. The polymer material acted as an imper-
meable membrane for anything—gases or liquid—trying
to get in. But it let the wearer's body breathe, passing
through moisture, carbon dioxide and—through pinpoint
valves that became flaccid past a certain temperature—
excessive body heat.

Penelope shucked off the long johns and stood naked in
the firelight. The flames played ruddy highlights on her
smooth long limbs and rippling musculature. Her body
was as taut and functional as any hunting animal's. She
reached for the synthetic pelt that modern technology
had made for her.

It was all one piece. She pushed her feet into the boots,
soft and flexible as suede slippers, and pulled the hotsuit
up her legs. It fit like a second skin, showing the powerful
calf muscles and long line of the thigh. The upper part
had built-in support; nothing, not even a bra, could be
allowed to interfere with the efficient thermal design. The
top held her breasts firmly but comfortably, allowing
them to move without hindering her capacity for violent
action. There were thin, sensitive gloves of the same
space age materials, with extra heating wires for the
fingers, and an attached hood and face mask, with two
flaring, tip-up goggles that looked like cat's eyes.

The battery, a flat, flexible package of plastic elec-
trolites, fit into a pocket at the thigh. It fed a network
of fine platinum wires embedded in the suit.

"You look like the Snow Maiden," Inga said with a
trace of awe.

It was a good description. The white clinging garment
gave her the appearance of a naked woman, sculptured
in snow, with a spectral featureless face out of some
northern myth.

Penelope's laugh was muffled by the mask. "Good camouflage," she said.

Inga held out one of the *Galil* automatic rifles. "Here."

"I'll stick with the Bernardelli," Penelope said. "I'm
taking no luggage this trip."

She checked the clip of the little gold-plated automatic
and slipped it into the pocket on her left wrist. It hardly

showed. Only four inches long and as thin as a Ronson lighter, it was the smallest .25 pistol ever made.

"It has no range."

"I'll work close," Penelope said.

"At least take a couple of grenades," Inga pleaded.

Penelope thought it over. "All right." She slipped two of the plastic grenades into the hotsuit's exterior pockets, molding the pliable material along the contours of her body. The grenades were sandwiched in flexible fabric, with detonators no larger than a lipstick. You could mold them like a snowball for accurate throwing.

Penelope picked up the belt kit and the book-sized package containing the telescoping skis and poked her head out the tent flap. Around her, the Lapp encampment was silvery in the starlight. The cone-shaped tents, like fur teepees, were scattered at intervals over the snowfield, the owners' sledges parked outside them. She could smell the smoke of cooking fires and the pungent aroma of dung and wet reindeer fur. Somewhere a dog barked, warning a stray deer back to the main body of the herd.

She slithered out of the tent on her belly, almost invisible against the snow. In a series of quick acrobatic turns, she rolled like a log, going a good fifty feet without leaving a recognizable track.

She stopped. Sitting in front of one tent was a drunken elderly Lapp, crooning to himself with an aquavit bottle in his hand. He raised it to his lips and took a swig.

She made sure no one else was about, then ran at a crouch until she was over a low rise that put her out of sight of the encampment. She pulled the telescoping segments of the skis out to their six-foot lengths and locked them in place. They had teflon-coated bottoms, and were light as feathers. Her feet went into sock-like housings. Gas from a little aerosol can inflated the ingenious bladders, holding her feet as firmly as any Strolz binding.

She opened out the telescoping aluminum poles and twisted them to lock them. With a shove, she was on her way, gliding like a white wraith over the ghostly snowscape.

The little chemical detector on her wrist was about ten

thousand times more sensitive than a bloodhound's nose. It could recognize as few as a hundred molecules in a cubic meter of air. The needle snapped westward, toward the source of gasoline fumes.

An hour later, the concentration of gasoline molecules had reached something like 200,000 per cubic meter. Penelope stopped.

The land here was a washboard of gentle undulations, dotted with Arctic scrub. There was nothing visible against the skyline.

Then she saw it. One of the stars in Orion was missing. It was Betelgeuse. It should have been just above the horizon. Something dark was hiding it.

She lifted the slanting goggles and squinted. There was a little dark shadow against the luminous sky that could have been the peak of a tent.

She deflated the bindings and took off the skis. She folded them into their flat book-shaped package and clipped it to her belt. She kept one of the poles to use as a staff.

She approached cautiously, taking whatever cover she could. From behind a skeletal stand of birch, she saw it from less than a hundred yards.

There were the fish-head shapes of two snowmobiles, rental plates on their hoods. Behind them stood a two-man pup-tent.

One man was dozing in front of a fire. He was bulky as a stuffed teddy bear in his snowmobile suit, his back propped against a knapsack. One gloved hand was flung out, close to a high-powered hunting rifle.

Penelope crouched, making herself small. Where was the other man?

As she watched, he came stooping out of the tent flap. He was taller and leaner than the dozing man, but the padded suit gave him a bolster-like shape too. He bent over his friend and said something. There was no response. He shook the other man, then turned around in disgust and went back into the tent.

The two of them were within the twenty-foot radius of

her grenades. She only had to get another hundred feet closer for an accurate toss.

She hesitated. They *could* be a couple of innocent hunters. Perhaps they were after wolves. In that case there might be a reason for them to trail a Lapp reindeer migration. Bait.

It was highly unlikely. But she didn't fancy blowing up a pair of vacationing businessmen just because she was nervous. She began working her way around the stand of birch for a closer look.

The hood and the mask were what betrayed her. She had the flaps up over the perforated earholes, but her own keen hearing was more than half muffled. She didn't hear the crunch of a footstep in the snow until it was too late.

She whirled, her right hand darting toward the gun in the other sleeve.

"Nyet!" a harsh voice shouted.

He was a round-faced, chubby man, shivering in a flannel shirt and sweater. He was pointing a formidable-looking Tikka over-under shotgun-rifle at the exact center of her belly.

"You speak English, I'm told," he said. "Don't move. Don't move one little bit."

She studied the muzzle brake of the Finnish weapon and decided he was giving her excellent advice. It was set for the twelve-gauge upper barrel. At this range, it would spill her guts out into the snow.

The chubby man lifted his head, not taking his eyes from her, and shouted.

"Karp, I've got her!"

The other man came out of the pop-tent. He picked up the rifle next to the stuffed figure by the fire and headed up the slope toward them.

"This tells the story, eh, Gorev?" he said when he arrived. "Look at her. She looks as if she's naked. Nobody has gear like that. Except the *gneeloi bagahtee* CIA and their gadgets."

"Are you warm enough, darling?" the chubby man said.

"Warmer than you are, *dvayooradnee*," she said.

His eyes strayed toward the stuffed snowmobile suit by the fire. "I believe it," he said. "I've been shivering out here for an hour. But it worked, didn't it?"

"How did you know I was coming?" Penelope said.

He grinned a sloppy grin. "Our primitive friend saw the Ice Queen head west out of camp. . . ."

"Gorev!" Karp snapped. "Shut up!"

Gorev looked sulky. He waved his twin-barreled weapon. "Let's get back down there. I'm freezing."

They herded her down toward the pop-tent. It was very professional the way they got her inside. Karp made her lie on her belly, the hunting rifle prodding the nape of her neck, her arms held behind her. She had to wriggle through the low flap with Karp stooping and straddling her. There wasn't a fraction of a second when she could have rolled over to an effective position and caught him coming through the entrance.

He was just as ingenious about immobilizing her without having to approach her frontally. He told her to insert her hands between the tent fabric and two of the umbrella struts that supported it. Only after she was sitting against the wall of the tent, her arms stretched horizontally outward, did he allow Gorev to lash her wrists to the struts.

Gorev peeled off her hood and face mask. His little eyes flickered when he saw the rich cascade of dark hair tumble free, and took in her flawless beauty.

"Exceptional, my dear Karp," he said with a sly expression.

Impatience showed on Karp's ascetic features. "Search her."

Gorev began patting her down from the armpits, sneaking his hands around for a good feel of her breasts. "She can't be concealing much in *this* outfit," he said.

He found the tiny automatic and the plastic grenades, and put them aside with her utility kit. The skis intrigued him.

"Everything with the Americans folds up," he said. "Chairs, beds, now even skis."

Penelope tugged at her ropes. They seemed firm. "Are

you two boys the KGB representatives at the Helsinki embassy?" she said.

"We'll ask the questions," Karp said sharply.

"You're on Finnish territory, you know."

"So are you. And planning to cross over into Russia."

"Who told you? Your primitive friend?"

Karp gave Gorev an annoyed look. Gorev looked resentful. The two men got on one another's nerves. Penelope filed the fact away for future reference.

"Why are you crossing over to the Kola Peninsula?" Karp said.

"I'm running a reindeer survey," Penelope said. "For Santa Claus."

Karp slapped her across the face, hard. Gorev looked pained.

"What interests you on Kola?" Karp shouted.

Penelope said nothing.

"Or maybe it isn't Kola," Karp said. "Maybe it's Kanin."

"That's right," Penelope said. "With this suit I can walk on water."

Karp slapped her again.

Gorev pursed his lips. "She may be telling the truth," he said. "My man went through the equipment on their sledges. There couldn't have been anything larger than a rubber raft. And you can't cross all that open Arctic water on a rubber raft."

Karp whirled on him. "We don't know what arrangements they may have made at the waterfront," he said. He turned back to Penelope. "What's going on across the bay?"

"Didn't they tell you?" Penelope said sweetly. She watched Karp's face. He was getting rattled. Her attitude wasn't what he expected.

"We'd better notify Penkin," Gorev sighed. "He can take care of it from here."

Penelope could have kissed the chubby man. He'd just told her that these two clowns hadn't gone any further with the information their Lapp agent had given them.

"No!" Karp said. "We'll get it out of her. Then we'll round up her friends with the regular security force on Kola. We'll wrap it up for Moscow ourselves."

"Who's your Lapp friend?" Penelope said. "Is it Vana?"

Karp was thumbing through a handbook. Penelope recognized the cover. She'd studied it herself during her training. It was the KGB manual of interrogation techniques.

"Here we are," Karp said. "Page 43. Women. Gorev, get me a razor blade from your shaving kit. And a pair of pliers." He turned a page. "And melt some paraffin in a tin cup. I'll need a small funnel—you'll find one with the extra fuel cans. And put the little crowbar in the fire to heat."

Penelope shuddered. She remembered page 43 vividly. But it didn't get really bad until page 46. That was where the permanent mutilation started.

Gorev spread out an assortment of improvised torture implements on the nylon tent floor in front of Penelope. It was an incredible array: needles and pins and tweezers and a cake of soap soaking in a cup of hot water and a shovel handle with a sheet of abrasive tacked around the end, and all the other makeshift devices the KGB handbook recommended when you couldn't get to a proper interrogation room.

They were laid out in strict order. Karp was going by the book.

"Open up her suit," Karp said.

Gorev obeyed eagerly. He unzipped the hotsuit from throat to crotch, looking disappointed when the built-in cups continued to hold her breasts on either side of the bare vee between them. He took the edges in his hands and pulled them further apart. Her breasts spilled out.

"Enjoying yourself?" Penelope said.

Gorev was staring the way a starving man stares at a feast. Karp was looking at Gorev in disgust.

Penelope arched her back, as if she were trying to squirm away. Her breasts rippled. Gorev grew more agitated. So did Karp.

She kept up her squirming. Their distraction increased. So far, so good.

"Gorev, can you get her the rest of the way out of that suit without untying her hands? I'll need access to her vagina." He said the word with a grimace of distaste.

"You'll have to help me," Gorev said.

Together they pulled and tugged until her legs were out of the hotsuit. She cooperated, while seeming to resist. It wouldn't have been possible without her agile acrobatics. When they finished, the hotsuit covered only her arms and shoulders, dangling behind her like a cape.

Her feet were bare. That was the important thing.

She picked up the razor blade in her toes. They were still busy, peeling the hotsuit up an extra inch or two. They didn't notice that her kicking feet had brushed the neat row of torture implements.

Still writhing and tossing to distract them, she made a long slit in the nylon floor of the tent. It was easy. During her training she'd put in long hours practicing the art of picking things up with her toes and manipulating tools with them.

She put the razor blade back where she'd found it. Her leg covered the slit in the floor and stayed there.

The two Russians moved back and studied her. Karp picked up the first object, a pin.

She gritted her teeth. She'd just have to endure it. She couldn't do anything while there were two of them in the tent.

An hour later, Karp squatted back on his heels for a rest. He was sweating. He surveyed her naked body, looking at the marks he'd left.

"You're very stubborn," he said.

Mentally, Penelope inventoried the damage herself. Not too bad, so far. Nothing that wouldn't heal. There were some pin punctures in her breasts, hurting like hell and making her feel sick. It was going to burn for a few days whenever she urinated. There were a few painful minor burns here and there. And one of her fingernails was turning black.

Karp studied the row of implements. The next object was a cigar.

He held it out to Gorev. "Light it," he said.

Karp was a non-smoker.

Gorev puffed at the cigar till its tip was a cherry red. He handed it back to Karp.

"Which eye?" Karp said. "The left or the right?"

Gorev looked sick.

Penelope felt a little sick herself. This was phase two. From here on it was downhill all the way.

Karp knelt in front of her with the cigar. "Last chance," he said.

She shook her head. She could feel the heat of the cigar on her cheek.

"Too bad," he said. He raised the cigar.

"Karp," she said.

He waited, the cigar poised in front of her eyes.

"Aren't you out of sequence?" she said. "The poker is next."

Karp looked startled. He picked up the KGB manual and flipped the page. He flushed with embarrassment.

"You're right," he said. "I forgot. It's heating outside."

Penelope held her breath. Thank God, Karp was compulsive!

"Gorev," Karp said, "go outside and get the crowbar. It should be white-hot by now." He turned back to Penelope. "You needn't congratulate yourself," he said. "If you know the handbook, you know what I'm going to do with the crowbar."

"It's the only way you *could* do it, Karp darling," Penelope said.

He flushed again. "Did you hear me, Gorev? Get the bar."

Gorev went outside. Penelope showed her teeth in a sneer. She had only a few seconds to get Karp mad enough to come close to her. It wouldn't work otherwise.

"Pravda glaza kolet!" she spat.

He walked on his knees toward her and slapped her face. She thrust both legs through the slit in the floor and stood up.

©Lorillard 1973

DELUXE LENGTH

KENT

WITH
THE FAMOUS MICRONITE FILTER

King Size
or Deluxe 100's.

Micronite filter.
Mild, smooth taste.
America's quality cigarette.
Kent.

Kings: 16 mg. "tar," 1.0 mg. nicotine; 100's: 19 mg. "tar," 1.2 mg. nicotine;
Menthol: 18 mg. "tar," 1.3 mg. nicotine; av. per cigarette, FTC Report Sept. '73.

Try the crisp, clean taste of Kent Menthol.

The only Menthol with the famous Micronite filter.

Warning: The Surgeon General Has Determined
That Cigarette Smoking Is Dangerous to Your Health

It took all her strength: a mighty heave that tightened her leg muscles and strained her arms and shoulders, bound to the tent struts. She could feel the snow, cold on her bare feet.

The entire pop-tent lifted, Karp and all. He looked startled.

Outside, Gorev turned around and stared in amazement. The tent was rising off the ground. Underneath the seven-foot dome was a pair of naked female legs. Very shapely. The thought filtered through his mind that it looked like a walking breast.

Then he recovered and ran toward the levitating tent with the hunting rifle in his hand.

Inside, Penelope, her arms crucified to the supports, tilted the tent. Karp tumbled backward in a pratfall, his feet high in the air.

She let the tent down, hard, and pulled both feet back inside. They shot forward like a double hammer straight into Karp's crotch. The heels crushed the spongy tissue between Karp's legs to jelly. He screamed.

There was no time to waste on him. Her right foot flashed toward the Tikka shotgun-rifle lying on the floor. She hooked her big toe into the trigger guard and pivoted the weapon on its butt so that it faced the tent flap.

Gorev poked his head into the tent just then. She curled her toe around the trigger and fired. The shotgun barrel went off with an earth-shaking blast. Gorev's head disappeared. His brain splattered against the tent fabric on either side of the flap like some kind of bloody Rorschach test.

Instantly she swung the gun back toward Karp, her other foot levering the release for the under barrel.

She needn't have bothered. Karp was dead. The karate kick she'd used could shatter pine planks or brick. She didn't want to think about what kind of mess was under Karp's pants.

She rummaged through the scattered implements with her foot until she found the razor blade again. Balanced on her bottom, she raised her foot above her head and sawed at the ropes on her wrists until she was free.

It was getting cold in the tent, with the open flap and the rent in the bottom. She shivered. She got back into the hot-suit, zipped it up, and turned the heating element to high.

Cleaning up wasn't too bad. The remnants of Gorev's head had mostly been contained within the tent. She tied a duffle bag over the stump of the neck, and dragged the two bodies outside.

She propped Karp and Gorev behind the handlebars of their snowmobiles and piled all their gear behind them. There was nothing except a trampled area in the snow and a dying fire to show that anyone had been there.

A few hundred yards away was a frozen lake. She'd noticed the dark patches, beginning of the spring thaw, out on the ice.

She set the snowmobile engines going and aimed the vehicles in low toward the lake. They glided in slow motion over the surface, the bodies bouncing behind the wind-screens. Gorev's body, with a duffle bag for a head, looked like some kind of Halloween goblin.

The snowmobiles sped over the ice, gathering momentum. They reached the dark patches. A moment later they were gone, plummeting like stones to the bottom of the lake. They'd never be found.

The Baroness found a stimulant in her belt kit and popped it into her mouth. She'd need it. Her burns and bruises and pinpricks ached abominably. With a sigh, she unfolded her skis and bent to put them on. It was going to be a long push back.

Chapter 9

The Russian border was unmarked. They crossed it at midnight, by the light of a sun that hung a few degrees above the western horizon. It wouldn't set at all for a couple of months now.

Penelope trudged beside Vana, clad in her Lapp clothes

again. Chances were that somewhere out there in the snowy wastes, a pair of Russian binoculars were trained on them. But the Russians wouldn't bother to investigate closely. Too many migrating Lapps had passed this way in the last week or two. They kept coming across vast avenues of reindeer-trampled snow and the remains of cooking fires and little garbage heaps of discarded fish bones and coffee grounds.

She and Vana were at the head of the herd. She was leading a buck with a bell around its neck by a long braided rope. Close behind was the reindeer they called Follower, drawing the rest of the herd behind him like a magnet.

Vana stopped abruptly. The vast throng of animals and people behind him straggled to a halt. Vana frowned at the sight that lay in their path.

Penelope advanced a few feet for a closer look. They were reindeer carcasses, at least half a dozen, though they were so torn and mangled that it was hard to be sure. Bits of frozen flesh and splintered bones lay strewn over the snow.

"Volk!" Vana spat.

He'd used the Russian word for wolf, probably without thinking. Like the other Lapps, Vana spoke a bastard mixture of the languages of the countries his tribe passed through, along with his own dialect. But she'd never heard him use the Russian term before. Always he'd used the Swedish word for wolf, *varg.*

She looked at him. His face showed nothing but anger.

"This is the same one," he said, pointing at an enormous paw print with his staff. "The devil wolf, the one who kills for pleasure."

She studied the carnage with him. They'd come across similar butchery several times in the last couple of days. Most of the carcasses were uneaten, just chewed up and played with.

"How big a pack does your devil wolf lead?" Penelope said.

He examined the circling tracks. "Forty, maybe fifty."

"We're catching up with them, aren't we?"

"Tomorrow, maybe the day after, they will catch our scent." He shook his head. "These are not wolves that will carry off a few sick animals, or pick off the strays. If they get in among the herd, they will kill and kill until they are too tired to lift their heads."

He began moving forward again on his skis, making a wide circle around the dead animals so as not to upset the herd that was following them.

The wolves began stalking them the next day. They stayed just out of sight: dim gray shadows in the distance that faded as you looked at them. The dogs were uneasy. A couple of wolf hunters, led by Aslak, picked up their rifles and went off on skis. They came back without having found anything.

"The wolf is clever," Vana said. He hadn't bothered to go out with Aslak and the others. He sat by the fire and sharpened his knife.

The wolves grew bolder. A count of stragglers the next day showed that a half-dozen reindeer had disappeared. And that night a pet calf, tethered outside one of the tents, was carried off. The wolf prints in the snow were eight inches across. The family dog lay nearby, its throat ripped out.

A delegation came to Vana. "Tomorrow," he said. They muttered and went off. Vana continued to sharpen his knife.

The next morning he came to Penelope's tent. "Don't feed your dogs today," he said, and turned to go.

Penelope got through the day in a fever of anticipation. She stayed close to Vana, looking for signs, the two borzois tied to her sledge. She didn't want them running off on their own.

The Lapps made camp about ten that evening. It was still light; the nighttime sun scudded in a low arc above the horizon, never setting, casting long goblin shadows over the snow.

Penelope ate with Vana and Aslak, a simple meal of reindeer cheese and dried meat and blood soup, with the inevitable strong coffee. Vana had loaned her a wooden staff and a *puuko*—the long knife that every Lapp carries.

Vana was stuffing sedge grass, the Lapp equivalent of thermal socks, into his reindeer-leather *skallers,* singing a *joik* to himself.

"Gumpi don ednak vahag lek dakekam. . . ."

I curse you, wolf, flee far away. Penelope smiled at the words.

Aslak looked up. "A woman. On a wolf hunt. I don't like it."

Vana went on singing. *"I'll kill you with my hunter's knife."*

Aslak stirred uneasily. "The wolves won't come tonight anyway," he said.

Vana kept singing, a small anticipatory smile playing about his lips.

Penelope stayed out of it. She sat cross-legged in her leggings and Lapp blouse, patting Stasya and Igor. Wharton had told her she was crazy to go after a pack of Arctic wolves with a knife and a stick. "The Lapps themselves use rifles," he'd said.

"There's no point in doing it at all if I do it the easy way," she'd said. Wharton didn't understand. A kill was a kill to him. Nobody understood, except Vana.

Igor lifted his narrow head and whined.

"Easy, boy," she said.

There was a commotion outside. A child's voice cried, *"Gumpi lae bottsuin!"*

Other voices took up the traditional warning. *The wolf is in the herd!*

Vana got up without haste. He put on his long embroidered *kofte* over his underfrock, and donned his wolf-skin coat over that. He nodded to Penelope and she got up too.

Aslak was already at the tent flap with his rifle. He looked at Vana and flushed. That strange look passed between them again. Aslak put the rifle down and went out with only his knife and staff.

The reindeer were milling around in panic. Through the teeming jam, Penelope caught the flesh of gray shapes. A Lapp raised his rifle, then lowered it in frustration, unable to fire.

Penelope waded into the herd with the other hunters. The wolves were clever, eluding them in the confused mass. They were as bold as if the hunters were not there, cutting frightened animals out of the herd one at a time and ripping the living flesh away. The wolves faded away whenever a Lapp approached and went after another reindeer, leaving their meat. It was a slaughter.

The borzois were pulling her left arm out of its socket. She held on to the chains grimly. It wasn't the time.

She caught a glimpse of Vana through the sea of reindeer. Somehow he was facing a wolf, the only Lapp who had got that close. The terrible staff lifted and rapped the wolf on the nose. Vana crouched, moving like a flash, his knife hand a blur. Then he and the wolf were separated. The big gray beast, eight feet from nose to tail, lay dead on the ground.

The Lapps had organized themselves into an advancing line that combed through the herd. A man screamed and went down. A wolf circled behind and got shot. The gray shapes flowed through the herd like quicksilver, getting out of the way, their long jaws snapping to take snacks of living reindeer flesh on the run.

The nightmare shadows broke from the far boundary of the herd, running across the flat white land, getting out of rifle range before the Lapps could get clear.

The great creature at the head of the pack was the one Vana called the devil wolf. With a shock of disbelief, Penelope saw that it was carrying a fawn in its jaws. The fawn must have weighed a hundred pounds, but the huge wolf was lifting it completely off the ground, his teeth in its throat, the body flung back across his shoulder. It didn't seem to slow him down at all.

A few of the hunters had broken free of the packed reindeer and were firing at the wolves. The range was too great. The wolves knew it. They were running at a leisurely lope now, contemptuous of their adversaries.

Vana was at her side.

"Quickly!" he said.

They put on their skis. The borzois were going wild,

making the incongruous high-pitched yelping sounds that gazehounds utter when they want to hunt.

Penelope unsnapped their leads. The big white wolf-hounds shot forward like arrows. They streaked over the snow, side by side, following their ancient instinct to run in pairs. A cheer went up from the Lapps.

Penelope pushed off with her skis, following them as quickly as she could. Vana was at her side. We make a fine brace of hunting animals too, she thought.

The two dogs were already out of hailing range, speeding over the tundra at a deceptively easy gallop that gulped distance at close to fifty miles an hour. The wolves looked curiously over their shoulders and continued running. They didn't seem worried.

Beside Penelope, Vana suddenly grinned. He increased his speed, and she drove her legs harder. They both were enjoying the sight, the tireless piston running of those two mindless machines for killing. Igor and Stasya didn't much resemble the aloof aristocrats that had posed with her in so many fashion photographs.

The wolfhounds were at the rear of the pack now. They'd picked out their first quarry. It was a big brindle male wolf, running a little apart from the others.

When the wolf saw them coming, he picked up his speed. But a wolf can't outrun a borzoi.

They bracketed him, running easily on either side. It looked like a game. The borzois didn't seem at all menacing. Tall and heavy as the huge white dogs were, the wolf outweighed them by a good seventy pounds.

He turned his head to the right to snap at Igor. Igor danced casually out of the way. Instantly, like a striking snake, Stasya fastened his teeth in the left side of the wolf's neck.

It would have been all over for any other breed of dog. The Siberian wolf has enormously powerful neck muscles that can toss a full-grown donkey over his shoulder. Even Stasya couldn't have held on if he'd been alone.

But when the wolf turned to deal with Stasya, Igor made the instinctive move that is bred into a borzoi's genes. Timing it to the split second, the big white dog grabbed the wolf by the other side of the neck.

They dragged the wolf to the ground. He couldn't move his head in either direction. He'd stopped struggling by the time Penelope and Vana caught up.

Igor wagged his tail.

Vana said, "He is yours."

Penelope drew the long Lapp knife and slid it expertly into the wolf. The two-hundred pound creature went limp, the fire dying in its eyes. The two dogs looked up for approval. Penelope patted them and praised them. They wagged their tails and took off again after the fleeing wolf pack.

They picked off another couple of wolves and held them for Penelope. Then the pack, getting worried, began to protect its own.

The borzois changed their tactics. Now they turned killers. They bracketed their chosen prey as before, but now, when the wolf whirled to snap at the dog that was grabbing its neck, the other dog darted in and ripped out its throat. It was done too swiftly for the wolf to react.

The two wolfhounds roamed through the running pack, killing swiftly, dancing out of reach of the snapping jaws that sought to bring them down. Penelope and Vana skied past dead wolf after dead wolf, straining to follow.

The pack was slowing down. The effort of trying to deal with the two borzois had cut its forward momentum. The pack drew closer for common self-defense, in effect being herded by the two terrible white dogs. A couple of wolves sat down on their haunches and howled.

It was like skiing toward a collection of demons from hell. But Penelope didn't feel at all frightened. It was exciting, the most exciting thing she'd ever done. She could smell the rank fur, see the dozens of baleful eyes glaring. She laughed with the sheer joy of anticipation.

A huge gray shape leaped at her. She swung the wooden staff the way she'd seen Vana do it. It thudded into the wolf's muzzle and knocked it to the ground, dazed. Before it could recover, she drew the sharp blade along its underside, splitting its belly in two. Another animal was after her. She whirled and hit it on the side of the head with the stick. She could hear the solid *thunk,* feel the blow jar her own spine. She slipped her hand under the snapping jaws and cut the beast's throat.

The other Lapps were coming up fast. She could hear shots. Beside her, Vana was doing yeoman's slaughter, killing wolves with his own knife and staff. His coat and leggings were ripped and bloody, but there was a joyous unholy light in his eyes. The borzois worked the pack with the two humans, darting and snapping and harrying.

Another wolf came at her. She swung the staff and missed. The wolf was still moving. One hundred and seventy-five pounds of solid flesh rammed into her legs and knocked her over. The wolf immediately went for her throat. She flung out her hand, and the wolf grabbed it in his jaws.

She remembered what Aslak had told her. Don't try to pull free. She pushed hard, and the wolf swallowed her hand.

She could feel the long fangs raking her arm. The arm was buried in the wolf's gullet to the elbow. The wolf was gagging. Her hand closed on something rubbery down there. She squeezed.

It had all taken only a second or two. She brought up her knife hand and plunged the blade deep into the wolf's belly. She dragged the blade upward, through the dense wolf flesh, until it grated against bone. Carefully she worked her arm out of the dead throat. Her sleeve was in tatters.

Around her, the Lapp hunters were mopping up the pack with club and gun and axe. The snow was littered with bloodstained gray bodies. The surviving wolves were taking off in all directions, forgetting to run as a pack.

Aslak came up to her, a bloody knife in his hand. He shook his head. "A woman! To kill the wolf in the ancient way!"

"Where's Vana?"

He gave her a strange look. "He is gone. After the devil wolf, the leader of the pack."

"I'm going after him."

"No. The devil wolf is his."

"You're right. He'd never forgive me."

Aslak said, "Vana will not stop until he has caught the wolf. I must follow him and collect his clothes."

"What are you talking about?" she said sharply.

"A Lapp on skis does not rest when he is after a wolf," Aslak said. "Even in freezing weather like this, he will sweat. It is dangerous. He must throw away his clothing, piece by piece. If there is no one to follow and give him back his clothes after he has killed the wolf, he will freeze to death."

The image came to her unbidden. Vana, the lean wiry body naked, gliding on skis in the killing cold, chasing a gaunt gray demon the size of a donkey.

"Go quickly," she told Aslak.

He set forth with another man, an elderly Lapp in a gay red and blue tunic.

The Lapps were all around her, grinning and touching her shyly, like children.

"Buurist, buurist!" they said. "God save you!"

They made a fuss over the two dogs. Penelope clipped their leads back on and gave them to a pair of overjoyed little boys to take back to the encampment. The Lapps were babbling at her. A couple of them were already singing, improvising a new *joik* about her hunting prowess. She sighed. It was going to be a long night of partying.

She was halfway back to the encampment when she felt something cold on her cheek.

She looked up. Another snowflake was falling. And another.

The Lapps were looking worried. *"Mika kauhea,"* one of them said.

Blizzard!

The snowflakes fell, thick and wet and heavy. The horizon began to disappear.

Vana! He was out there on skis. Aslak and the other man would lose his trail. They wouldn't be able to find Vana's discarded clothes. Vana would kill the wolf. She was as sure of that as anything. But then, violent activity over, he would be naked in a blizzard, soaking with sweat.

He'd die.

She hurried back to her tent and stuffed her pockets with the things she'd need. The Lapps were already talking about Vana as if he were a dead man. It would be useless and dangerous to go after him, they told her. Aslak and the other man would wait out the storm, return to the encampment when it was over. Then they'd all try to find Vana's body.

They pleaded with her not to go. She brushed them off and started out into the snowstorm on skis.

Maybe the Lapps couldn't find Vana. But she could. She had a trick up her sleeve. Literally.

She was Vana's only chance.

She traveled by compass at first, following the direction Vana had taken, unable to see more than a few yards in the swirling snow. The little chemical scent detector on her wrist showed nothing. Its needle swung at random.

Then it picked up a few molecules of scent. Butyric acid. It was a prime constituent of sweat.

She lost the trail. She fanned out in a broad zigzag. The needle quivered again. This time the indications were stronger. Dozens of butyric acid molecules triggering the chemical receptors.

She'd set the detector for human sweat because something like two hundred and fifty billion molecules of butyric acid pass through the sole of a shoe at each footstep. A dog can detect a millionth of that amount—a quarter of a million molecules. The Baroness' technological marvel responded to only eight molecules of any given scent. She'd put any bloodhound to shame.

She skied. There was nothing except the blinding snow and the illuminated dial on her wrist. She plodded up the rises and pushed herself gliding along the level stretches and slid down the shallow slopes. After a couple of hours she reached in her pocket and swallowed some energy rations, not stopping. It made her feel better. She plunged blindly into the swirling white fury.

Vana was dead. He must have caught up with his wolf long before now. It had killed him or he had killed it. Either way he was dead. Naked, he couldn't last more than a quarter hour in this.

The concentration of butyric acid was increasing. The digital indicator was counting thousands of molecules, even through the damping effect of the snow. She pushed herself along, following the needle.

There! There was something ahead. She brushed the snowflakes from her eyelids and hurled herself forward.

Two dark shapes showed patchily though the snow. Neither of them moving.

She reached the first one. It was in the shape of a wolf. But there was something wrong with it. It was a purplish red, like raw liver.

She skidded to a stop in front of the other shape. It was another purplish thing, a lumpy ball not much larger than a duffle bag.

It moved. She bent over it.

"Buurist," it said. God save you.

"Vana!" she sobbed with joy.

A head poked out of the bloody bundle. Vana's blue eyes crinkled at her. He grinned, showing even white teeth.

"You skinned the wolf and wrapped yourself in the hide!" she said. The thick fur, inside-out, and his own body heat, had kept him warm at forty below zero, in a howling storm.

"I did it once before," he said. "That's where I got my wolfskin coat. They sing a *joik* about it."

She knelt beside him and cradled the protruding head against her breast.

"How did you find me?" he said.

"Darling, I just followed your scent, like any bitch on a trail."

He let that pass. "You must stay here until the storm passes," he said. "Aslak will find me in the morning."

"I hadn't planned on leaving, darling."

"We can scoop out a hole in the snow. Perhaps we can keep one another warm enough to stay alive."

She laughed. "Darling, I can do better that that."

He watched in amazement as she reached under her tunic and took out a tight bundle of fabric the size of a folding umbrella. There were three metal prongs sticking out of the end. She pulled them out into pencil-thin rods about six feet long. They were hinged somewhere at the top. She spread the rods out into a squat pyramid shape with a seven-foot base and pushed the prongs into the snow. The skeletal pyramid wore a little fabric cap that she pulled down over the framework.

"A tent!" he said. "But it will blow away!"

"Not on your life, darling," she said. She attached the polymer cables to the metal feet and fired the explosive pitons. The icepick-size devices drove through the snow and buried themselves deep in the frozen soil beneath. The points spread and took a grip. Penelope tightened the cables.

She zipped the floor into place and said, "Get in."

He obeyed gratefully, moving at a crouch, the wolfskin wrapped around his shoulders. She caught a glimpse of the tight pouch of his scrotum, and above it a pathetic blue acorn, shriveled with cold. She smiled. Never mind! The warmth of the tent would take care of that! And she'd do the rest!

She let him keep the wolfskin while she adjusted the heater. It was a flat box the size of a transistor radio, fed by a pint bottle of gas. A microminiature thermostat and a space age combustion chamber that burned with the efficiency of a moon rocket engine would keep the tent warm for at least seventy-two hours.

"So warm!" Vana said wonderingly. "And yet the tent is thinner than the skin of a fish!"

She fed them both with energy rations and bouillon made with snow she scooped up by reaching through the tent flap and a couple of L. L. Bean dehydrated camping meals reconstituted in a folding saucepan. When they finished, Vana slapped his flat stomach and belched.

"A meal like that from an envelope as light as a piece of birch bark! It's magic! Truly you are the Ice Queen!"

Her nerves tingled in warning. The Ice Queen! Where had she heard that? She remembered. The Russian, Gorev, had made a slip: *Our primitive friend saw the Ice Queen head west out of camp. . . .*

"What's the matter?" Vana said, giving her an intent look.

"Nothing, darling. I don't feel like an Ice Queen."

"It's an old legend. A woman made of snow with a heart of ice. Nothing could melt it. Until she met her match in the mighty hunter." He gave her a veiled, sly glance.

The hell with it, she thought. She didn't care if he *was* a Russian agent! This savage creature was one of the most exciting men she'd ever met. There was a bond between them: they'd hunted the Arctic wolf together, armed only with staff and knife. They were two of a kind —hunter and huntress from out of the dawn of time, living in a world that didn't understand either of them. They'd each made a place for themselves on their own terms. Hunter's terms! He in his way, she in hers.

She might have to kill him tomorrow, but tonight they were going to enjoy one another.

He'd be a worthy adversary. She remembered the way he'd faced the wolves, taller than he was when they'd leaped upright at his throat. She shivered with excitement.

There was a growing warmth and wetness between her thighs. It was all swollen and throbbing down there.

Vana's keen nose detected the scent of a female in rut. Matter-of-factly he took off the wolfskin and spread it on the floor of the tent, furry side up. No longer was there a shrunken blue acorn between his legs. It was a shank of veined ivory, formidably large, standing out as straight and smooth as a narwhale's tusk.

She was pulling off her clothes, fingers trembling, making little whimpering sounds. She thought she'd never get the damned things off!

There were no preliminaries. Neither of them could have waited. Penelope lay on the wolfskin and spread her legs, knees up. Vana knelt between them. He put a hand under each buttock and lifted her up to impale her on that long tusk. She pushed herself forward on her elbows to meet him. His tool slid into her effortlessly, riding the buttery fluids of her desire. She groaned. His shaft was a radiating presence in there, filling her, spreading a hot tingle through the fleshy caverns of her body.

It was luminous inside the tent. The midnight sun was spreading a ghostly light through the snowstorm outside, a light that filtered, as the cold could not, through the thin translucent layers of the tent. It turned them both white, white as ivory. Vana's face hung above her like a triangular moon, pearly and phosphorescent, the meaningless grimace of lust spread across it. He thrust himself into her again and again, panting harshly.

She pushed against him, moaning, gasping with pleasure at each collision of her swollen vulva with his hard pubic ridge. The hard thing within her worked away, a sweet torment that was impossible to bear. There was an avalanche gathering within her, a massive irresistible weight building up to spill down a long ravishing slope of desire. She squirmed with bliss.

She could feel the fresh-killed wolfskin rubbing against her back and buttocks at each stroke, a rough bristly sensation like a scrub brush. The smell of wolf blood was in her nostrils. Once she'd made love, carelessly, on a $20,000 mink coat. It was nothing like this.

It was coming closer. She wrapped her legs around his waist and drove against him, riding on her elbows and working the powerful muscles of her thighs and calves. His hands were still under her buttocks, lifting, pushing. He bent forward and nipped her breast and throat.

With a mighty heave, she jackknifed upward and embraced him with arms as well as legs. Her sharp fingernails raked his back. They strove together, a swaying upright of intertwined flesh. His cheek was against hers, smooth and angular. Her breasts were crushed against his hard hairless chest. She sank her teeth into the side of his neck and tasted blood. He didn't notice. His animal force was concentrated in a region of mutual ecstasy down at their melted loins, pushing and pulling the hot slick post of flesh in and out of her feverish scabbard.

She slid a hand down his back and under the tight narrow cleft of his buttocks, and caught his scrotum in her hand. She could feel his body stiffen with surprise.

Bites he knew about, but none of the simple Lapp girls he'd known had ever done this. She manipulated the testicles within their sac. He growled, stirred to a new level of passion.

His balls writhed in her palm. She decided to give him something new to think about. She extended her long middle finger and stroked the tender flesh between his buttocks. He grunted and continued his accelerating mating rhythm.

Did Lapps kiss? Or did they rub noses like Eskimos? She fastened her mouth on his lips. His lips parted and his tongue thrust between her teeth. If Lapps didn't kiss, he was giving a damned good imitation.

His pelvis continued to gyrate, not missing a beat. She was fastened to him at two points now. There was a hot volcanic core stretching between, down the length of her body. In the milky white light of the tent, Penelope had the illusion that the two of them were glowing cherry red, like a stove. The avalanche poised within her was heating, a pile of incandescent stones. Between their pressed bodies was a sheen of sweat.

He was going at it like a jack hammer now, a vibrating high-speed violence that drove her frantic. She heard her voice, sounding strange and far away: "Uh, uh, uh . . ." She twisted and squirmed on the ivory shaft that impaled her. She clawed at his back, pressing her mons against him, trying to get all of him inside her. There was a vast dispersed loosening. One of the glowing rocks tumbled, then another. She shuddered as they hit bottom, willing with all her force that the others stay poised for just a moment, a fractionated eternity.

Then it was too much and she came: a great shivering paroxysm that wracked her entire body with blessed convulsions. The avalanche tumbled down her interior slopes, bubbling and steaming, releasing her from its poised weight. Somehow she was aware of Vana giving a huge shudder and cry at the same moment, triggered by her spasms, blending his own flooding joy with hers.

They clung to one another, panting. The tent swam

back into focus. He pulled his head back and looked into her face with an expression of wonderment.

He pulled himself out of her and immediately rolled over on his back, beside her on the wolfskin, taking great heaving gulps of air.

She leaned over him on her hands and knees, her breasts dangling over his face.

"You were fantastic, darling," she said.

He grinned at her shyly. Somehow he'd managed to drape a corner of the wolfskin over his crotch. Penelope smiled at the gesture of primitive reticence.

"Are you a sorceress?" he said.

"Just a warm-blooded girl with a heart of ice."

It was no joke to him. He looked at her with superstitious awe. "What magic did you work on me? Never before have I felt so powerful the *strast*."

"You had it in you all the time, darling. Bottled up. You just needed me to bring it all out."

She kept her face from showing anything. Vana had used another Russian word in an unguarded moment. *Strast*. The storm of passion. He could have expressed his meaning much more precisely in his own Lapp dialect.

He looked away from her breasts. "You should put on your clothes," he said.

She reached over and peeled the wolfskin away from his groin. She saw why he'd been shy. Already his penis was standing up, straight and firm, with their mixed juices not yet dry on the long smooth shaft. He lowered his eyelids in embarrassment.

"I don't think I'll bother," she said. "I'd just have to take them off again."

The long line of white snowmobiles sped across the shore ice, a ghostly procession with muffled engines. Some of them were pulling sledges that were loaded with equipment. The rearmost sledge carried something that looked like a boom: a long metal cylinder the size of a 20-foot length of telephone pole.

Chu Fei sat hunched behind the windscreen, his gloved hands on the steering bar. The automatic weapon slung across his back felt comforting. Everything had gone well so far, but he was nervously aware of being in Russian territory.

He squinted through his goggles at the bleak shoreline he was following. The ship with the false Norwegian identification had deposited them on an ice floe in the Barents Sea and continued on a fake course toward North Cape that would satisfy the Russian radar on Novaya Zemlya. It would wait out of radar range and sail back to pick him up when he was ready.

He had a hundred men with him—a big force, but the minimum he needed to penetrate the security at the Russian biological labs. He shrugged. One hundred or fifty or one—it was all the same if they got caught.

They'd drifted in on electric outboards, the miraculous device from the 29th Radio Factory camouflaging their metallic hardware against Russian radar. They'd come ashore at the tip of the finger of land that stretched into the Arctic waters between the Yamal Peninsula and Cape Kanin. Another two hundred miles of travel westward would carry him around the Cheshkaya Gulf to the base of Kanin.

No one had seen them. No one except a polar bear and a few seals.

Chu rounded a bend in the shoreline and saw a dark shape ahead. A man. On foot; there was no vehicle near him. Chu frowned. He slowed down a little.

It was a fisherman, dropping a line through a hole in the ice. He looked up and waved.

Chu pulled up about twenty meters from the fisherman and let the man come to him. The man's behavior suggested puzzlement rather than alarm. He was probably wondering why the column of snowmobiles had stopped short of him. It didn't seem friendly. And he was probably speculating on what kind of an expedition, for what reason, had bothered to come this far north to a barren stretch of Arctic shore that held nothing.

The man was close enough so that Chu could see the smile on his face. He was a snub-nosed Russian in his fifties or thereabouts, wearing a fur cap with earlaps. The smile wavered. He was close enough so that he could see that Chu's features were Chinese. You could tell that he was trying to puzzle it out.

Chu didn't give him a chance. He unslung the submachine gun and fired a quick burst. The man spun around and went skidding for a couple of meters along the ice.

Chu motioned to his wing man, an enormous round-faced Cantonese named Huang. Huang ponderously dismounted and walked over to the body. He poked it with his foot, then dragged it over to the hole in the ice. He stuffed the fisherman into the hole head first, then threw the man's gear in after him—a stool, a small camp heater and a duffle bag containing fishing equipment.

"He walked from somewhere nearby," Chu said.

Huang pointed. "There are his tracks."

"Someone may have heard the shots," Chu said.

He issued his orders swiftly, and the column of snowmobiles swung left, following the tracks. They topped a rise and saw the settlement.

It wasn't much—a dozen log cabins, chinked with mud and moss, laid out in a rough street. At the end was a somewhat bigger building, a trading post or some such. Chu couldn't imagine how the people lived. Hunting and fishing, perhaps, trading their catch of furs once a year for rubles.

He drove down the street and stopped at the end, the snowmobile caravan pulling up behind him. There were a couple of little boys, bundled in winter clothes, playing in the street. They looked up in astonished curiosity. They probably didn't see strangers for months on end.

He gave a signal, and his men dismounted. They split up into five-man squads and headed purposefully toward the log cabins.

Some of the squads met villagers at the door, coming out to see who the men on snowmobiles were. The automatic weapons lifted and spat fire. The Chinese pushed past the bodies and went inside. There was the sound of more firing.

Other squads were kicking in the doors that hadn't

opened. Timing was essential. There was a prolonged chatter of automatic weapons.

The two little boys were staring toward the cabins, openmouthed. A Chinese soldier came out of a door and saw them. He raised his gun and shot them.

Huang came over, picking his teeth. He'd found some food in one of the houses. *"Wan pi te,"* he said. "All finished."

Chu pointed at the bodies of the two children. "Take them inside, out of sight. I don't want anything visible from the air."

Huang lifted the little corpses, one over each shoulder, and carried them to the nearest cabin. He tossed them through the door like a couple of fireplace logs.

Chu went swiftly through the cabins, one by one, checking. There was an elderly couple that had been sitting down to a meal of potatoes and fish. The bullets had tumbled the woman backward; she lay on her back with her legs up, draped over the seat of the chair. Her husband had fallen over the table, his head resting in his plate. In the next cabin was a family of four. They were sprawled around the stove they had been staying near to keep warm. In one of the cabins, a man had gone for a shotgun. He must have been very quick. It lay close to his hand, where he'd dropped it when the steel-jacketed slugs had torn him apart.

In the next-to-last cabin, Chu heard a groan. A young blonde woman was stirring feebly on the floor, trying to lift her head. She was spattered with blood. One arm had almost been torn off by machine gun fire.

Chu drew his revolver and shot her once through the head. He turned to Huang, bulking large at his shoulder.

"Find out who the squad leader responsible is," Chu said. "Reprimand him."

He took a last look around and went outside. The village looked peaceful in the clear Arctic air. All around him, his men were mounting the saddles of their snowmobiles again.

Chu smiled. The guns his men used were of an American make. The squad leaders, as directed, had dropped a few bits of false evidence here and there. When the Russians got around to checking things out later, there would be hell to pay.

For the Americans.

He gave the signal and the cavalcade of snowmobiles moved on, their silenced engines almost inaudible. Ahead was Cape Kanin. And a container of germs that would give China an invincible power against the world.

Chapter 10

The bear festival was getting out of hand.

The Baroness stood by the entrance to her tent, watching. A strange frenzy had overtaken the Lapps. They were no longer the gentle, courteous people she'd been traveling with.

A man staggered by, stripped to the waist in the numbing cold, his body smeared with the blood of the bear Vana had killed. A naked woman stepped into his path. The man dropped to all fours, shaking his head from side to side in imitation of a bear.

"How long does this go on?" the Baroness said.

"Three days," Eric said. "The hunters can't sleep with their wives all that time. Then they have a purifying ceremony. The women throw hot ashes at them."

Skytop was watching the woman. "I thought Lapp women were modest."

"That's not sex," Eric said. "She's shaming the bear, so that it'll turn aside from the attack."

Sure enough, the blood-smeared man pawed the ground, turned and scrambled away on all fours.

The Baroness shook her head. "Three days. I don't like it. We can't afford the time."

She cast a worried glance toward the huge bonfire some distance away. The Lapps were gathered around it, drinking, eating the boiled bear meat, singing the ritual songs thanking the grandfather of the hill for not breaking their spears.

A party of hunters had discovered the den that morning, only a mile from the line of march. The sacred ritual was organized quickly. The old man who served as sorcerer made the ancient incantations at the den's entrance. Two poles were set up to slow the great beast's charge. They shouted and rattled pots and pans to wake the hibernating animal up.

Vana stood there, armed with a wooden spear that looked flimsy and ridiculous against the gigantic, ill-tempered creature that charged toward him. The bear reared on its hind legs, nine feet tall and weighing close to to a half-ton. Claws like steel hooks reached for him. Vana stood his ground. He slipped his spear expertly into the bear's chest and braced the end of the spear against the ground. The great claws stretched toward him, just a foot out of reach. The infuriated bear pushed itself into the spear in its frenzy to get to him. Vana couldn't let go. He shifted his grip further and further down the shaft, trying to keep out of reach. By the time the bear died, he had bare inches left.

It was tremendously exciting. Penelope had felt her juices flow, her skin flush hot. Vana's three-day ritual celibacy was going to be a problem. She'd just have to make it irresistible for him to break his vow. The sorcerer could purify him later.

Wharton broke into her thoughts. "We're halfway across the Kola Peninsula. And border security is two hundred miles behind us. Maybe we should take off on our own."

"Yeah," Skytop said. "That three days is bad news."

"We'll see," the Baroness said angrily. She stalked away.

She bumped into Sumo, hurrying toward her tent. She tried to brush past him, but he grabbed her arm.

"I've got a toothache," he said.

He looked miserable. The side of his face was swollen.

"Where?" she said, instantly alert.

"Vana's tent."

"When?"

"For the last hour, while everybody's been busy with the bear festival. Pretty sophisticated equipment for a Lapp. Directional. He's been trying to raise someone almost due west. His signals just stopped."

"His contacts. The two I killed, Gorev and Karp."

Sumo nodded. "That's what I figured."

She patted him on the cheek. He winced. "Look after your jaw, Tommy. I'll take care of it. And will you adjust that damned gadget when we get back? We can't have you taking novocain every time you detect a transmission."

She headed toward Vana's tent. Good old Tommy! Vana had smashed the long-range receiver in the sledge. But he hadn't been able to smash Sumo's bridgework.

She closed the familiar steel shutters over her brain, the ones that kept her from thinking too far ahead. She wasn't going to enjoy killing Vana.

The flap of Vana's tent was parting. Penelope ducked behind a snowbank. After a moment she raised her head cautiously. There he was, striding away from her, tall for a Lapp with his Scandinavian blood. He looked splendid and barbaric in his embroidered tribal colors, the fresh wolfskin over his shoulders.

He bent to put on the skis he was carrying. He was going to travel a distance. Penelope fumed. No time to go back and get hers. Next to her was a tent with one of the hearth logs outside—a sign that the owners were away. Penelope did the unforgivable. She stepped over the log and entered. She committed the second great crime in the Lapp lexicon—taking something from a tent. It was a pair of handmade skis, lovingly polished. She took the single long ski pole beside them and hurried out. No one saw her. Out of sight of the encampment, she put the skis on, fitting the turned-up toe of her Lapp boots into the simple loop of leather in front.

She followed his tracks at a careful distance. Vana was a hunter. He'd know when he was being trailed.

The sun was at the bottom of its nighttime loop, beginning to climb: just after midnight. It would be in Vana's eyes, narrowing his irises and dimming his vision if he looked back. Good!

It was a clear beautiful night, not too cold, with the temperature hovering at a positively tropical twenty above. She slid across the smooth white blanket covering the ground, trying not to think, concentrating on enjoying the skiing.

But she *had* to think. Vana had been trying to raise his Russian contacts. He'd given up. Now the only place he could be heading was toward some Russian security post or military installation here on the Kola Peninsula. He'd turn the problem of the American spies over to them.

A sob escaped her throat. She was going to have to kill that magnificent sinewy body that had given her so much pleasure. It wasn't fair! Vana was a wild, primitive creature, despite the education he'd received at the Lapp school run by the Norwegian government. What did politics have to do with the primeval bond they shared?

She took inventory. She had the Lapp knife. The staff. The little gold-plated automatic. And her terrible, deadly hands.

Vana had his staff and knife. He'd killed wolves with them, and a thousand-pound bear. But he'd be no match for a gun.

She caught up with him by a grove of evergreens. He'd stopped to fix his boots, smoothing the lumps out of the senna grass they were stuffed with. His back was toward her. She glided silently up behind him, stopping twenty feet away.

"Hello, Vana," she said softly.

He turned around.

It was Aslak. His height and build had fooled her. And the embroidered colors of the *sita*. And the wolfskin.

His face registered shock and surprise. She'd never have been able to sneak up on Vana that way.

"You're wearing something that doesn't belong to you," Penelope said.

His features contorted with hate. "Vana has another wolfskin!"

"He earned it. You didn't."

He spat. "Vana! Always Vana! He is a fool! He knows nothing of the world!"

"But you do, don't you? How long have you been working for the Russians?"

"Since I was a boy at the Kautokeino school. They tried to interest Vana, too. But the fool lives in his own world."

"And you live in the Russians' world!"

He sneered. "They pay me well. In another year I'll have enough to live in a house in Stockholm or Oslo and buy a business. No more dirty Lapp! No more stinking reindeer!"

"I don't think you have a year, Aslak," she said.

She kicked off her skis and stepped forward, the shiny little gun in her hand.

It was going to be hard. Putting a bullet between those blue eyes that reminded her of Vana.

There was a blur of motion in the air between them, and something hit her wrist. The gun fell spinning to the snow. Her wrist was numb. It felt broken.

Aslak had snaked out with the staff. It gave him a ten-foot reach. She'd underestimated him. He was a Lapp. And he was Vana's brother.

She'd leaped back, out of reach, at the moment of contact. He moved forward, stalking her. She backed up.

His staff whizzed through the air at her. She caught it with the ski pole in her left hand.

Quarter staves! It was one of the esoteric forms of hand-to-hand combat she'd learned during the long year at the secret schools. Aslak couldn't possibly know all the moves. Ordinarily she'd finish him off quickly.

But she couldn't use her right hand.

His stick came at her again, aimed at the side of her head. She ducked and it sailed over her. Her own pole poked at his solar plexus. It was damnably awkward, manipulating an eight-foot pole at one end, with one hand. But it drove the breath out of him. He looked surprised. Then cautious.

She could kill him with her left hand if she could get close enough. But that long staff of his was going to keep her at a distance. The fight would be on Aslak's terms.

He whipped the staff in an arc, a foot from the ground,

trying to knock her legs from under her. She leaped nimbly over it.

She lashed out at him again, a foot of the handle braced against her forearm to compensate for the other hand. It robbed her of twelve inches of reach, but it was the only way she could manage. Aslak twisted like a snake, avoiding the blow.

"Curse you for a devil!" he panted.

He swung, a powerful blow that would have smashed her collar bone if it had connected. She writhed out of the way, but the staff slid down the length of her arm, grazing her knuckles.

She dropped her pole. She stooped to pick it up, but his wicked staff came whirling at her again. She jumped back, just in time.

She faced him, her hands empty.

He came toward her, grinning, his knife in his left hand, the staff in his right.

"Vana kills wolves that way," she said. "I guess you're just about good enough to kill a woman."

He uttered a bellow of rage. The long staff swung toward her head. It was an unskillful blow, spoiled by his anger. But it carried enough force to crack her skull.

She let it hit her. It was her only hope.

She rode with the blow, whipping her head to the side, her body already in lateral motion before the staff connected with her skull. She looked as if she'd been knocked sideways. Almost, her move hadn't been enough. She lay on the ground, dazed, her vision blurred.

She tried to lift her arm. She couldn't. She couldn't raise her head, either. Nothing worked.

It was frightening. She couldn't think too clearly, but she knew . . . something . . . what was it? Oh, yes, if he plunged the knife into her before she was able to move again, then she was . . . she couldn't remember the word.

Aslak was standing over her. He rippled. The whole world behind him rippled.

He put a mittened hand casually on her chest, between her breasts, pressing her down. He held the knife up. Its blade glittered in the midnight sun.

"As . . . Aslak. . . ." she said.

The knife paused. He'd stopped rippling. She could feel the beginnings of strength flowing back into her body. But was it enough?

The knife lifted again. There was a pitiless light in his blue eyes. The knife flashed down, toward her throat.

And her hand streaked up to meet it.

She caught his wrist in her left hand and deflected its motion. She made no attempt to halt it. It wouldn't have been possible to hold his wrist for more than a few seconds in her present condition. Instead she took advantage of Aslak's own momentum, turning its aside: just barely enough.

The knife blade plunged into the snow, a bare inch from her cheek. Immediately he snatched his hand away and raised the knife again.

But her hand was already streaking from the side toward his neck, the edge held straight and flat in the killing position that was burned into her subconscious.

Her *right* hand!

It wasn't broken after all. It had just been numbed by the blow. She hadn't noticed that feeling had been returning to it while her dazed senses recovered.

It sliced into the side of Aslak's neck, palm up, the terrible edge as rigid as a board. The force of the blow crushed the jugular vein and ruptured the carotid artery running alongside of it before knocking loose the neck vertebra that finally brought it to a halt. -

Aslak's blue eyes flew open in astonishment. The knife dropped from his hand. He swayed on his knees, blood welling from his mouth. He tried to speak but couldn't.

He died on his knees. Only after the light went from his eyes did the effort of will that he was exerting disappear, letting the tendons and muscles grow flaccid. He folded backward, like a shut book.

Penelope picked herself up off the ground. She was dizzy for a moment, then felt all right. She hobbled over to her skis and put them on.

She'd gone no more than a hundred yards when she saw him. The embroidered tunic was bright and gaudy against the illuminated snow. He moved easily toward her, gliding like a creature out of northern myth.

"Vana!" she said.

He stopped, gazing at her out of remote blue eyes.

"Where is Aslak?"

She motioned backward along her path. He made no move to go there.

She said, "Why are you here?"

"To catch my brother. I followed his trail, then saw that someone else was following him." He looked at her stolen skis. "I did not know it was you."

"To catch Aslak? What do you mean?"

He gave her a somber look. "Aslak wanted me dead. The other man told me. He picked up my clothes the night I followed the devil wolf. But he did not try to find me."

"The blizzard . . ."

"He turned back before the blizzard struck."

Penelope studied Vana's face. "Would you have killed him?"

"Perhaps."

They stood facing one another on their skis for a moment. Then Vana spoke again.

"The she-wolf has made a kill," he said.

He meant her.

She didn't say anything. It wasn't necessary.

His face twisted in pain, and a more complicated emotion. "I must kill you, then."

"Aslak would have killed me, Vana."

"I know."

"He would have killed *you*."

"He was my brother."

She waited. After a moment he said. "Go, Penelope, go from my *sita*. If I see you, I must kill you."

"Or I you."

He acknowledged the truth of that with a nod. "One of us. One will kill the other. And part of himself."

It was the sweetest bouquet anyone had ever handed her. Penelope was touched.

"I won't come back, Vana. Tell my friends where I am. Tell them to meet me here."

He nodded again. He turned to go.

"Aslak has your wolfskin," she said.

The blue eyes were cold as ice. "Let him keep it," he said. "At long last."

He pushed off on his skis. He stopped, just within hailing distance, and called back over his shoulder:

"Mana derivan!"

Go in peace, he'd said.

She watched his dwindling figure until it disappeared into the frozen landscape. Then she went back to bury Aslak. She wrapped him in the stolen wolfskin before tumbling him into the shallow trench she'd scraped out with her knife. Then she sat back under a pine tree to wait for Wharton and the others.

Fiona plugged in her hair dryer. She turned to Paul. "All right, go ahead."

Paul fine-tuned the transceiver in the makeup case. A musical chord sounded: a D-major telling him that he'd made contact with MESTAR, a couple of hundred miles out in space. A moment later, a C-natural was added to the harmony, making it a seventh chord. That told him MESTAR had completed the link to Key in Washington.

"Come in, Key," he said into an open jar of face cream. The face cream was real. The heavy opaque jar itself contained a microphone and scrambler, fantastically microminiaturized through metal oxide-semiconductor circuitry.

A box of mascara cleared its throat and spoke in Key's voice. "How are things in Helsinki?" it said.

"Helsinki is war," Paul said. "What've you got for us?"

"Two things. Maybe they're both the same."

"Shoot."

"First—the phony CIA man Coin killed at the Doomsday briefing. He wasn't Russian."

"One of our other alphabet agencies?"

There was a pause. "He was Chinese."

"Chinese? I thought he was a blond, blue-eyed honkie!"

"He was altered surgically."

"But the pigment . . ."

"He was a Chinese albino. They micro-tattooed him all over to *add* enough pigment so he could pass as Caucasian. They injected the irises of his eyes with a blue dye."

"Whew!" Paul said.

Key continued. "He had a woven microphone in his necktie. Got past the security guards with it. And a surgically embedded transmitter with a range of a half-mile."

Paul said, "So the Chinese know all about what went on at the Doomsday briefing, right?"

"That's about the size of it."

"What's the other thing you've got to tell us?"

"Our ELINT teams have been monitoring some interesting transmissions from Peking. And the Arctic Ocean. And one very suggestive high-speed code blast from Cheshskaya Gulf, two hundred miles east of the Kanin Peninsula. They fed it all to the 7090 computer at Fort Meade. And the computer came up with a very interesting answer."

"What?" Paul said, his voice tense.

"The Chinese have landed some kind of an expeditionary force in Russia. They're after the moon virus too."

Paul, Yvette and Fiona all looked at one another in silence.

Key went on, "So you'd better get on the stick right away and warn Coin. She's got more problems than she bargained for."

Paul said nothing.

"Do you hear me?" the mascara box said. "The Baroness is on a collision course with the Chinese army. You've got to warn her."

Paul spoke, despair thick in his voice. "We can't. She's out of communication. Something happened to her radio."

Chapter 11

She was in a womb. A warm, soft, yielding womb that rocked gently in a vast mother sea.

It was an illusion, she knew. If the rubbery bag that enclosed her were to puncture, the Arctic water rushing in would shock her to numbness in seconds, kill her in minutes. Her present comfort depended upon the frail magic of technology.

The Baroness put her eyes to the little periscope and squinted. The black waters stretched before her, an unknowable vastness. She thumbed the serrated wheel of the little control in her hand, and felt the reassuring tug of the nylon line connecting the bag to the electrically controlled aqua-wing ahead. She veered, bobbing, a little to the left, avoiding the small ice floe she'd seen through the scope. There was another tug from behind, as slack was taken up on the line hauling Skytop and the others, spaced out in a long chain behind her.

Something bumped against her feet, and she stiffened.

She waited, but nothing more happened. She'd never know what it had been. She didn't particularly want to speculate. The Arctic waters teemed with life: fish and seals and whales and basking polar bears—all of them looking for a meal. If a thirty-foot killer whale chanced along and thought the wriggling sack hanging just under the surface was a tempting piece of bait, there wouldn't be much she could do about it.

She took another look through the periscope. There! She could see it now! A long streak of chalky white against the western horizon!

She grabbed a handful of white plastic and felt around for the hard shape of the ring holding the trailing nylon line. She tugged three times to signal Skytop, then turned her attention to the shoreline ahead.

Cape Kanin. A godforsaken finger of ice sticking into the Barents Sea. An infected finger, bearing the mutated germs that could rot an entire world. She thought of the films from Houston and shivered.

The shoreline moved visibly closer, as the aqua-wing chugged on at its steady ten knots. It was going to be tricky, making landfall here. A sharp boulder and a wave to scrape her against it, and it would all be over. There was another ice floe ahead. She thumbed the little control, and the electric propellers pulled her on a sidewise course. Not good enough! There was another ice floe. She couldn't risk going through the forty-foot gap between them. She might make it, but if the nylon line snagged, Skytop and Wharton, Sumo and Inga and Eric, might be left adrift in the cruel icy-cold sea.

Icy cold? No, it was colder than that. The dissolved brine dragged the temperature of these Arctic waters well below the freezing point.

She hung in the waterproof bag, drifting parallel to shore, until she saw a clear expanse of open water, then moved in closer.

She could hear it now: the terrifying sound of ice grinding in the frigid surf. Through the scope she could see the tumbled white blocks, some as big as barns, and beyond them, unbelievably, bare glistening rock. An iceberg drifted by, sculpted into fantastic pillared shapes by the spring thaw. Through its white arches the midnight sun winked at her, an inflamed red eye that cast streaks of light over the black water.

She moved in closer. There was something that looked like a beach ahead. She'd have to chance it. She cut speed to five knots and headed toward a stretch that looked less foamy than its surroundings.

The surf caught her thirty yards from shore. It tossed her around like an inflated beach toy. She shifted her feet as if she were on a trampoline, trying to keep her balance. The side of the bag bulged inward, and something hard struck her a glancing blow on the shoulder. A piece of floating ice. She hoped there weren't any bigger ones nearby.

She couldn't use the scope any more. It was jumping around too violently. She tumbled in blindly, holding her breath.

There was a brief warning: she felt the cessation of pull that meant that the aqua-wing had struck bottom. Now it was her turn. A wave picked her up and hurled her forward. She landed on her hands and knees inside the bag. Before she could do anything, she was picked up again. This time she came down harder. She wriggled like an eel inside her rubbery membrane. She could feel a sharp pebbly bottom under her hands and knees.

She dared not delay any longer. Filling her lungs, she pulled the drawstring and burst through the mouth of the bag. She emerged, blinded and choking, into a punishing spray. The frozen brine stung her cheeks. She struggled into the waist-deep water, trying to keep her footing.

The aqua-wing was in front of her, jumping around in the surf. She picked it up as she passed, hoping it hadn't been damaged. Slinging it over her shoulder, she staggered with it to the safety of the shore ice.

She paused a moment to catch her breath, then dug her heels into the ice and hauled at the line, pulling Skytop in. She was able to drag him halfway clear of the water's edge before he popped out of his bag, looking like a newly hatched sea monster in his wetsuit. He helped her pull in Wharton; then she let go and let them do the rest of the work.

One of the supply bags had been lost. "Mostly food," Wharton said.

Skytop grinned. "I'll shoot us a seal to make up for it."

They packed the rest of the gear on the inflatable toboggans and pulled everything a few hundred yards inland, away from the dangerous exposure of the shore.

"Any radar, Tommy?" the Baroness said.

He peered at his detector. "I'm getting some bounce from a shore installation—probably about twenty miles south. Nothing that'll pick us up."

A look of cheer spread over Skytop's face. "We can break out the snowmobiles, then?" he said hopefully.

The Baroness shook her head sweetly. "We walk," she said.

The delegation from Peking arrived unannounced. By the time the staff was able to locate the Director in Laboratory Three of the botulism section, and he'd spent the necessary half-hour undergoing decontamination procedures, they were shuffling around impatiently in the reception area.

There were five of them. Someone already had fitted them out with smocks and rubber gloves and surgical masks. The masks were about as much protection against the deadly microorganisms bred in the laboratories as a paper shield would be against a bullet. But the Institute always issued them to visiting VIPs to make them feel better.

The Director hurried forward, a smile on his lips. "Welcome, comrades," he said. "The Ten Beautiful Thoughts Biological Research Institute is honored by your presence."

The delegation's leader limped toward him. The Director recognized him despite the white mask. It was old Hsing, a People's Congress deputy. Party Central sent him out about twice a year to check on the Institute.

"Greetings, comrade," Hsing said, more brusquely than usual. He indicated the other four with an abrupt gesture. "You are directed to show the comrades from Peking the preparations you are making to receive the *yueh shih* virus from the moon."

The Director's face grew stiff beneath the smile. He studied the other four as casually as he could manage, and realized with a shock that the man with the thick shock of black hair was Vice Chairman Wang Hung-Wen, the youngest member of the Politburo. He was not yet forty, but he ranked third in the Party structure. It was speculated that one day Wang himself would become Chairman.

"Certainly, comrades," the Director said. "Follow me."

He led them through the airlock into the vast dome of the pulmonary anthrax section. The five men from Peking gaped with visible unease at the glassed-in cubicles spread out below the catwalk. Workmen in protective clothing were installing new seals and erecting a new partition that ran the length of the laboratory.

One of the Peking men was shaking his head, his hands up at his ears.

The Director smiled at him. "It's nothing, comrade," he said. "The negative pressure is affecting your ears, that's all. Just swallow hard to clear them."

Vice Chairman Wang spoke. "The depressurization is to keep the germs from escaping, is it not?" He'd done his homework.

"Correct, comrade. Anthrax spores, to be exact. We are adapting an area within the pulmonary anthrax section for the moon virus because the decontamination facilities are most advanced here."

"But we are *inside* the depressurized zone," Wang said. His eyes were studying the man with the ear problems with evident amusement.

"There's no real danger, unless we were to enter one of the individual cubicles. The agar badges you're all wearing would warn us almost immediately if you were exposed to any drifting spores."

The other four Peking men glanced down instinctively at their badges. Vice Chairman Wang still looked amused behind his mask.

"How soon is immediately?" he said.

"Less than a minute. There's a special chemical stain in the agar medium. The first thing you'd see would be a spreading blue dot. Plenty of time to get you out of here and treat you."

The Vice Chairman advanced a dozen steps along the catwalk. His companions followed unwillingly in his wake. The man with the ear problem stared fearfully at his badge.

Emboldened by the Vice Chairman's matter-of-fact attitude, the Director said: "I'm told that this new germ from the moon is more dangerous even than pulmonary anthrax, comrade. Is it true?"

"It's true that the Americans are trying to frighten the

Russians with fairy tales about it," Wang said. "But China is not frightened, eh, comrade?"

"We will take all reasonable precautions," the Director said.

"Good. China needs this weapon. We cannot allow the Russians to get ahead of us. Or the Americans."

The Director risked another degree of intimacy. "You are right when you say fairy tales, comrade," he said. "I am told that the Americans describe the moon germ as a virus. But a virus cannot grow and reproduce without the free nucleotides it steals from a living cell. So the moon germ must be a bacterium, or perhaps some sort of fungus."

"But you are preparing for both possibilities, are you not?"

"Indeed we are." The Director snorted. "The moon organism might be able to get through an American wall! But not a Chinese wall!"

The Vice Chairman fixed him with a penetrating glance. "I'm glad you're so confident, comrade," he said. "When the germ is delivered to you, you must proceed as quickly as possible. You must find a way to grow it in quantity, keep it stable in an aerosol spray . . . and develop a vaccine with which we can immunize the entire population of China."

The Director quailed behind his frozen smile. Eight hundred million doses of vaccine! The Vice Chairman couldn't possibly understand the vastness of the program that would be needed to grow the quantities of killed or attenuated germs required.

"How long?" the Director said shakily.

"A year."

"A year?" the Director's knees went weak. "But . . ."

The Vice Chairman's voice was stern. "The Central Committee is aware of the difficulties. You will be given everything you need in the way of materials and people. China will strain every resource to develop this weapon." His eyes glittered with fervor above the mask. "When all of China is immune to this new germ, the rest of the world will have to listen to what we say, eh, comrade? The

Americans and Russians will have to accede to our demands, whatever they are. Their nuclear weapons won't help them if they're dead, will they, comrade?"

"How . . . how soon will I have the samples I need for seed stock?"

"Very soon, comrade," the Vice Chairman said jovially. "We will snatch the moon germ from under the noses of the Russians in no more than a day or two."

The Senior Pathologist looked frightened.

He was a weedy, carrot-topped man named McWhirter, and his freckles were stark against his blanched skin as he hurried toward the Secretary of Defense.

"Thank God you're here, Mr. Secretary, but they wouldn't let me talk about it on the phone!"

"I've established a command center in Denver," the Secretary said. "I'm sticking close by Operation Doomsday until the crisis is over."

"Come this way, sir," McWhirter said. "The lab director is waiting for us in the computer room with Dr. Barth."

There was a cluster of technicians waiting outside the computer room, peering through the glass windows. Evidently they'd been sent outside. It wasn't certain they'd been cleared for the data they'd helped develop.

They moved out of the way as McWhirter and the Secretary went through the door into the hermetically sealed room. Dr. Barth and the lab director, a big round-faced man with colonel's rank, whose name was Dr. Lovejoy, were over by a row of color CRT displays near the wall. The displays were generating a related series of what looked like schematic views of molecular diagrams. One computer was moving a continuous series of equations across its screen while a teleprinter chattered away, spewing out a permanent record.

"What's this all about?" the Secretary said.

Dr. Barth turned to face him. The lean saintly face was lined with sleeplessness and worry.

"Nitrogen," he said.

"Nitrogen? What about nitrogen?"

Dr. Barth drew a deep breath. "The Russians are storing the moon virus in a capsule containing an inert gas. The gas is nitrogen, isn't it?"

"That's the assumption, yés."

"Assumption?"

The Secretary of Defense shrugged impatiently. "All right, certainty. At least that's what our analysts infer from the factory markings on the capsule we saw on TV. Now what in hell is all this about?"

Dr. Barth turned to the nearest computer console and punched the keys. A three-dimensional tinkertoy began to rotate on the screen. New components began to hook themselves into the diagram as the Secretary watched, while a flow of meaningless symbols marched across the bottom of the screen.

"We've got a pretty good computer model of the way the moon virus reproduces itself," Dr. Barth said. "More than twenty-thousand man-hours went into the programming alone, not counting all the preliminary work done by the biological and mathematical teams."

A chill went down the Secretary's spine. "The way the virus reproduces itself?" he said. "Does it have something to do with nitrogen?"

"The moon virus is made of DNA," Dr. Barth said. "The four nucleotides that compose DNA all have nitrogenous bases."

A dreadful comprehension began to dawn on the Secretary. "Go on," he said.

"Unlike ordinary viruses, the moon virus is able to use free nitrogen to assemble the purines and pyrimidines that the bases are composed of."

"Let me get this straight," the Secretary said. "The virus can feed on the inert gas that's supposed to *keep* it from reproducing?"

Dr. Lovejoy spoke for the first time. "Like letting a rat into a grain silo," he said.

Dr. Barth's face twitched. "It goes exploring," he said. "It eats its way through to the outside, picking up whatever trace elements it can find."

"How long?" the Secretary whispered. "How long before the virus eats its way through the Russians' capsule?"

"That's what we needed you for, Mr. Secretary," Dr. Lovejoy said. "We need information on the construction of the Russian capsule—thickness of the wall, and so forth."

The Secretary picked up a phone. He got through to his assistant in less than two minutes. He spoke rapidly into the mouthpiece, then listened for a moment. "I'll wait," he said.

He listened for another ten minutes, taking notes on a pad. When he was through, he handed the pad to Dr. Barth. "Here it is," he said.

"We've already got a program on tape," Dr. Barth said, taking the pad. He punched the console of a peripheral. The teleprinter began rolling out paper before he finished. He studied it and frowned.

"How long?" the Secretary said.

Dr. Barth glanced at the big clock on the wall. "The moon virus should eat its way through the capsule in something like forty-eight hours," he said.

The Secretary whirled and picked up the phone again. "Put me through to the director of the National Security Agency," he said.

There was a brief interval, and the Secretary's face suddenly went raw with anger. "Don't give me that crap, soldier!" he said. "Get me through to him, *now,* or you'll be breaking rock at a federal prison for the next twenty years!"

There was another wait. The Secretary's color slowly subsided. He nodded, and said:

"Hello, Sam. I've got some bad news. Your agent on the Kanin Peninsula has a deadline."

John Farnsworth nodded politely as his television set spoke to him. Marshal Dillon's face filled the screen, but the voice was the voice of the director of the NSA.

". . . so you see, Coin has a time limit," the set said. "If that capsule isn't destroyed inside of forty-eight hours, it's the end of the world anyway. It'll all have been for nothing."

Farnsworth gripped the glass of Scotch he was holding. The glass shattered, and blood mingled with the whiskey, but he didn't notice.

"We'll have to hope that Coin's able to complete the mission by then," he said.

"Hope?" the voice crackled. On the screen, Marshal Dillon smiled at Miss Kitty. "What the hell do you mean, *hope?* Get on the stick and tell Coin that he's *got* to do it by then. No matter what the cost. When that capsule is breached, the whole world goes down the drain—starting with the Kanin Peninsula and your agent. He's got to go in and snatch the capsule *now*—even if it's suicide." Marshal Dillon took off his hat and set it on the bar. "If he doesn't, your agent is dead anyway."

"There's a problem," Farnsworth said.

"Problem? What kind of a problem?"

"Coin's out of communication. I can't get through with your message."

Chapter 12

The Baroness flattened herself against the snow and listened. Somewhere nearby in this white and silent waste was another human being. The chemical scent detector on her wrist was going wild. The air was loaded with butyric acid molecules.

Human sweat.

She didn't need the detector now. There was a little breeze blowing her way from up ahead. She raised her head and sniffed cautiously. Whoever it was hadn't bathed or changed his socks for months, if ever.

She inched forward, a white wraith in her skintight hotsuit. It was high noon, and she was almost invisible in the bright glare. It was better than trying to penetrate the Russian defenses at night, when the low, never-setting sun cast long shadows.

Skytop and the others were dispersed several miles away, awaiting her signal. Reconnoitering the germ warfare laboratory was a one-man job. She'd get as far as she could, then call for help if she needed it.

She hoped she'd get all the way.

But even then, she'd probably need help getting out. Or a diversion.

The source of the smell was in view now, a bare forty feet away. It was a wooden sentry booth with a black stove pipe sticking out of its conical roof. As she watched, a soldier came out.

She stayed motionless as an Arctic hare, her face mask a featureless blank.

The soldier was a shambling ape in a fur cap, a submachine gun slung over his shoulder. He had a slack mouth and a week's worth of stubble. Penelope wondered why his commanding officer allowed it. She smiled. Perhaps this was the one they scraped the germ specimens from.

The soldier yawned, scratched and unbuttoned his trousers. A yellow stream spattered against the snow. It seemed to go on forever. Penelope held her breath and waited.

He finished, yawned again and took a long look around. He stared directly at her without seeming to see anything and then went back into the booth.

Penelope made a wide detour, crawling forward by inches, using the long telescoping brush to wipe out her trail behind her. She'd penetrated the first security ring. It had been easy. What lay ahead?

The scent detector saved her life. She'd set its pinhead electronic brain for a random scan of the two dozen or so scents she was most interested in. Now a red flag showed on the dial. She punched the stem to find out what she'd run into.

Lead azide. A high explosive detonator. And she was almost directly over it.

A mine. She was in a mine field.

What set it off? Pressure? Body heat? She couldn't be sure.

She backed off ten feet and tried again, ten feet to the right. There usually was some sort of a checkerboard grid to a mine field. If she could figure out the pattern, she could get through.

The red flag winked again. Parallel to the first mine. She crawled carefully backward and tried again, this time to the left.

Another mine! She began to worry.

Another fifteen minutes of crawling on her belly, and her worst suspicions were confirmed. There *was* no path through the mines. It was an overlapping barrier, stretching a deadly line that she could not cross. The Russians must get across at specific points, probably well guarded.

She fingered the butt of the Spyder in its holster. The powerful pistol-winch was useless to her. It could get her over a fifty foot wall, or let her down the sheer side of a cliff. But here, in this flat expanse of snow, there was nothing high enough to fire the piton-tipped plastic line at.

She thought it over. If she couldn't fly over the mine field, she'd have to go under.

She fumbled in a pocket of the hotsuit and got out the instant digital thermometer. She held it up and triggered it. It changed color along a portion of its length. Twelve degrees Fahrenheit. More than twenty degrees below freezing.

She unzipped the lifesaving garment and peeled it off. The freezing cold gripped her naked body like a fist of ice. She shivered, her teeth chattering uncontrollably.

She managed to get the hotsuit turned inside-out before her fingers turned numb. She spread it out in the snow and lay on top of it, stretching her arms along its sleeves. The cruel Arctic air still punished her back and paralyzed her toes and fingers, but enough of the blessed warmth wafted upward to keep her alive. She turned the heating element up to high and waited.

After a few moments she felt herself sinking. She melted her way downward through the fluffy snow, riding a raft of synthetic fibers and platinum wires.

In fifteen minutes, anyone who might have happened along would have seen a seven-foot shaft in the shape of a woman sunk in the snow, with a smooth white back and a pair of rounded buttocks shimmering at the bottom. Penelope twisted her head to look up the smooth sides of the shaft and decided she was deep enough. She picked herself up off the hotsuit and pressed it against the wall of snow in front of her.

She walked on her knees at the rate of almost a foot a minute, the accumulating warm slush getting her legs wet. It wasn't too bad once she'd made a few feet of tunnel. The overhead snow trapped the heat escaping from the hotsuit. By the time she'd gone a couple of yards, the temperature was almost comfortable.

Once her hand encountered something hard. She peeled the hotsuit away from the forward wall and saw the ugly metal bulge of a mine. This one had been planted deeper than the others, or she was underneath a declivity. She'd bumped it pretty hard, but it hadn't gone off.

That answered her question. The mines weren't set off by heat or vibration. It was the victim's weight that did it. Fortunately the detonator could only detect pressure from above.

All the same, she made a wide detour around it.

Now it was getting dark inside the tunnel. The air was stuffy. She judged she'd tunneled twenty or thirty feet. It was far enough. With a continuous perimeter of mines, there was no reason to plant them more than two rows deep.

She began melting herself upward at a forty-five degree angle. Rivulets of water trickled past her, down the shaft. After another quarter-hour, a translucent light appeared in front of her, and a moment later she broke through into the frigid air.

The first thing she saw was the startled face of a Russian soldier.

She shot out of her burrow like a striking cobra, giving him no time to think. They rolled around in the snow, his rough woolen greatcoat against her naked flesh. She had him by both wrists, trying to keep him from getting his hands on the submachine gun slung over one shoulder. She could feel the buttons of his coat digging into her tender breasts and bare belly. His breath was hot against her cheek.

She had the advantage of surprise. He must have been shocked as hell to see a naked woman suddenly pop out of the ground in front of him and clamp her body around his like a vise. It was all unreal. He still hadn't recovered.

She had to kill him soon, before he thought to shout, before the cold got to her. But she daren't let go of his wrists.

She inserted a bare knee between his legs and stabbed with it. But the heavy greatcoat protected his groin. He grunted with surprise. Now it had dawned on him that all this was serious. He strained with his right hand to reach his weapon.

She wrestled with him, looking longingly at his throat. If only she could afford to let go long enough to get her thumbs into it. There was no weapon except her teeth. She'd used them before. She didn't mind the taste of blood in her mouth, not when she was fighting for her life. But she couldn't get past the high military collar.

His mittened hand had reached the trigger guard now, despite her efforts. Her fingers were growing stiff. It was only a matter of time before they'd be too frozen to hold him. A couple of minutes' worth, at best.

She had one more weapon. Her head.

Tensing her powerful neck muscles, she drove the top of her skull like a pile driver upward into his nose. He cried aloud in pain. She was sure she'd broken his septum.

Before he had time to recover, she let go of his left wrist and sunk her fingers into his right biceps. She swung her body away from his and doubled up, getting her shin underneath his right elbow. She leaned on his arm with both hands, and heard the sharp crack of bone. He screamed.

She scrambled off him and tugged the submachine gun off his floppy arm. He had time to realize what she was going to do.

"*Nyet, nyet!*" he pleaded, his eyes popping, as he stared

uncomprehendingly at the naked woman standing over him, her breasts swinging and her long black hair tumbled over her white shoulders, the gun in her hands, butt forward.

It was the last thing he ever saw. Penelope swung the heavy stock into his skull and crushed it.

She dropped the gun and scrambled for the hotsuit, lying twenty feet away in the snow. It already had melted its way into a foot-deep bowl of slush. She fished it out with fingers that had ceased to feel. She thought she'd never get it turned right-side out. Her body was wracked with great uncontrollable shivers. The cold cut like a knife.

She got it on at last. It was sopping wet. It didn't matter. It was a warm wetness. With the heating element on high, the permeable membrane of the suit began to pass moisture through. In ten minutes, she was dry.

She turned the heater down to normal. She frowned when she read the gauge. In the last hour, she'd used up more than twelve hours of survival time.

It couldn't be helped. And after all, she'd survived.

She dragged the body of the Russian soldier over to the hole she'd come out of and pushed it inside. She dropped the gun in after him. Across the mine field, she could see the other hole, in the shape of an outstretched person. She hoped it wouldn't be recognizable for what it was from a flat angle at a moderate distance.

She found the soldier's lunch nearby in the snow. Garlic sausages and black bread, with a jar of tea. It was an encouraging sign. If he hadn't eaten yet, he still had more than half a shift to do. No one would miss him for a while. The tea was warm. That was even more encouraging. It meant he'd just come out.

She trudged onward. She could see something glittering in the distance. The glass of the laboratory windows. They looked like fragments of ice.

She didn't like it. There was a wide open expanse between her and that distant glitter. There had to be something on it. Another mine field? Sentries in camouflaged foxholes? A microwave detection field?

She plastered herself against the snow and looked it over very carefully. Nothing.

It was too good to be true. She lowered the flaring goggles and thumbed the little wheel that polarized them. There! She could see them now. Dark patches against the snow. There was one about a quarter-mile ahead of her, and she could see more of them stretching in a line at fifteen-hundred foot intervals. There was something exerting pressure, tons of it, on the underlying permafrost.

Bunkers. Buried under the surface.

Each would have two or three men in it, scanning the sector through periscopes, listening through earphones for the vibrations of anything larger than a lemming. This was as close as she could get without being detected.

The solution came with the sound of twin diesels. There was something coming almost directly toward her from outside the security perimeter, at an angle to the direction she herself had traveled. Whatever it was wouldn't run across whatever traces of trail she'd left, or the melted shaft with the dead soldier in it, but it would intersect her.

She burrowed into the snow and reached one hand upward to smooth the surface. The ground rumbled and there was a stink of diesel fuel.

Almost it crushed her. A big clanking track passed less than a foot from her head. The sky was suddenly blotted out by an enormous shadow. It looked as if a tank was passing over her.

A *vezdekhod!* Literally, a "go-anywhere." The Russians used them in Siberia and the frozen north.

Her hands scrabbled upward, groping for something to hold. But the underside was smooth as ice, a slippery belly that would help the *vezdekhod* keep from getting stuck if the treads sank too low.

It kept going, and as the rear deck passed over her head, she saw the metal tow bar, like the stump of a dragon's tail, sticking out behind.

She grabbed it with both hands and swung herself upward. The big snow tank was traveling about fifteen miles an hour, and she felt as if her arms were being wrenched from their sockets. But she straddled the dragon tail and worked her way forward.

She lay at full length crosswise, flattened to keep below the level of the narrow slot of the rear window. The steel surface vibrated boneshakingly from the engines. The huge tracked monster bore her toward the line of buried bunkers.

Scooping snow from the surface of the rear deck, she arranged it around herself to break her outline. By the time the angle of sight allowed the sunken observers to see above the rim of the deck, she'd be far enough away to pass scrutiny.

The snow vehicle lumbered onward. Once she thought she saw a face like a lobster's claw appear at the rear window, but it disappeared almost immediately. The distant installation grew in size. There was a collection of frosty cubes, sparkling in the sunlight. A somber brooding structure the color of lead towered over them: some kind of administration building. And at each corner, a round watch tower topped with battlements.

Here, riding the broad back of the *vezdekhod,* she'd be invisible to the watch towers.

A bloodcurdling chorus of howls filled the air as she approached. Dogs? No. No dogs howled like that. Wolves!

She could see them as the *vezdekhod* veered toward the triple fence: gray demoniac shapes that paced restlessly behind the wire mesh. They were huge. One of them stood up on his hind legs, wagging his tail, as the *vezdekhod* came close. He was taller than a man.

She tried to fathom the quality of a mind that would pen a pack of wolves in a dog run like that. It had to be the mysterious Penkin, the security officer Vana had warned her about. What had Vana called him? A monster. A troll. A man more savage than a wolf. A sadist who staked living people in the snow to be devoured by animals. She looked at the pack and shivered. She could believe it.

The *vezdekhod* lurched, turning on a course parallel to the fence. It was heading toward the main gate.

Penelope looked up over her shoulder at the watch

tower behind her. This was the dangerous part. If anybody happened to be looking at the *vezdekhod* at this moment, they'd see her sprawled across its rear deck.

And she couldn't ride in with the *vezdekhod*. She sighed. It would have been so easy that way! But she'd be in full view of the sentries at the gate house.

She rolled off sideways and hit the snow with a jarring crunch. One heavy steel-link tread crawled like a metal snake past her cheek, reeking of lubricating oil. By the time it was past her, she was safely burrowed into the snow, level with the surface, with only the white camouflage of the hotsuit showing.

A new problem started to develop.

A few of the wolves were drifting over to the part of the fence closest to her, sniffing. In a minute or two, their behavior was going to attract the attention of the guards in the watch tower.

Moving her arm carefully, she brought the dial of the scent detector into view. She punched a digital code into the stem. The pinhead electronic brain wrinkled its metal-oxide brow and set to work puzzling out the odor of the person who was wearing it. The answer appeared a couple of seconds later, in the form of a series of numbers on the dial.

Penelope found the little scent generator in the sleeve pocket of the hotsuit. It was a tiny box containing four bean-size phials filled with the volatile molecules of the four primary scents: fragrant, acid, rancid and burnt. By combining them in the right proportion, you could reproduce any odor on earth.

The scent generator had a little dice-size computer that could do just that.

She thumbed in the formula that glowed on the scent detector's dial. The scent generator mixed its molecular brew in a little chamber about the size of a cocktail onion, and released them into the air around Penelope.

They weren't Penelope's odor. They were exactly the opposite. They were her odor turned inside out. The complex molecules worked like antigens, locking into the structure of the individual molecules that comprised her distinctive scent, nullifying them.

Now she lacked what every living thing on earth had: an odor.

The wolves stopped, puzzled. The world of a wolf—like the world of a dog—is composed more of smells than of sights. Its nose is an incredible million times more sensitive than a man's. To the wolves, it was as if Penelope had suddenly flipped a switch that made her disappear.

As long as she didn't move, she'd be safe.

The wolves drifted away, losing interest. There was nothing outside the fence except an oddly shaped mound of snow. Their noses told them so.

She waited in her shallow trench until the midnight sun was low on the opposite side of the laboratory complex. Now the long shadows were working for her, not against her. Cautiously she lifted her head.

Lights were going on in the laboratories and the nearby barracks. A searchlight winked on at the top of the watchtower near her and began probing the field of snow beyond.

Now all she had to do was get over the fence, wade through a pack of wolves and cross an electrified barrier!

There was nothing on the other side of the fence in her vicinity except an empty expanse. Nothing she could fire the Spyder at.

It had to be the watch tower.

She'd seen the face of a soldier up there earlier, peering down at the wolves. He hadn't appeared for a while. She hoped he'd stay on the other side of the battlements for at least a minute or two. There was going to be some noise.

She drew the Spyder and aimed it at the top of the watch tower, the pistol-grip warm and comfortable in her hand. She thumbed a piton into the firing chamber. The piton's iris bore gripped the tip of the thread-fine plastic line and secreted a single drop of instant-drying epoxy that sealed it with a breaking strain of over a thousand pounds.

She pulled the trigger, and the Spyder spat. Up above

there was a faint pop as the explosive piton went off and gripped the wooden parapet with little steel claws.

Penelope gripped the Spyder with two hands and hit the clutch. The incredible little spring began winding in plastic line, and Penelope was suddenly yanked out of her burrow and into the air.

She flew almost twenty feet straight upward before the Spyder got tired and swung her like a pendulum toward the watch tower. Her heels hit the tower walls with a thud. She didn't pause to worry whether or not she'd been heard. She'd find out soon enough if she had.

She walked straight up the outside of the tower, the Spyder's spring pulling her along. There was a slight overhang at the top. She rested a moment in its shelter, holding on to a strut while she worked the piton loose and holstered the Spyder.

The tower was outside the triple fence. It was a jump of more than thirty feet across. It would take a human flea to do it.

She smiled to herself. That was exactly what she was going to become.

She reached down and massaged the heels of her boots. She could feel them getting lumpy and uncomfortable against her feet. She kept up the massage until the boot heels had become as tight and hard as they could get.

It was one of the minor technological miracles produced by NSA's Special Effects Department. Synthetic resilin protein. The same stuff that enables a flea to jump more than a hundred times its own length.

She rapped her heels sharply against the tower wall, and the resilin snapped like some extraordinarily powerful rubber band. Penelope shot forward like a cannonball, tumbling over and over, clearing the triple fences by a comfortable three feet. She caught a blurred glimpse of the faces of the wolves, turned upward toward the strange phenomenon.

She hit the snow like a circus acrobat, easing the force of impact by letting her body collapse and roll over. A couple of wolves made a yipping sound. She lay motionless.

The searchlight swung over and examined the wolves. They were milling around restlessly. The yellow beam moved and began dutifully to examine the snow outside the fence. Penelope almost laughed.

The searchlight lost interest after a minute or two and resumed its probing of the distant landscape. The wolves lost interest too. Their noses told them there was nothing lying in the snow, no matter what their eyes had seen.

Moving her head by inches so as not to attract the attention of the wolves, Penelope took a long and careful survey of the complex of buildings inside the triple fence. They were spread out over at least ten acres, dominoes of concrete and glass and prefabricated aluminum panels.

Somewhere, inside one of them, was a metal capsule about the size of a fire extinguisher. The fire it could extinguish was the fire of life. All life on earth.

Where? Which building was it in?

There was no gadget on earth that could tell her.

Except one.

Her brain.

She studied the jumbled complex of buildings carefully, her mind emptied of all thought, her consciousness arranged in the deep reverie of Samadhi meditation. The Yoga exercises began to alter her perceptions. The alpha-wave rhythm of her brain slowed, and its amplitude increased. Trains of theta-wave activity—even slower than the alpha-rhythm—began to appear. The world became an illusion. And as such, she mastered it.

There! The moon virus was in *that* building! She saw it as plainly as if red paint had been splashed on the door.

Her mind snapped back to reality. She shook her head to clear it.

She studied the building again, this time with cool attention. What clues had her subconscious picked up during her Samadhi reverie?

It was a squat, ugly, two-story garage, exactly the same as the half-dozen other garages that stood nearby. But there were no fresh tracks going into it. Nothing more recent than a blurred set of monstrous, four-foot-wide treadmarks that were at least two or three days old. Ergo, something *big* had gone into the garage two or three days ago, and nothing else had gone into it since.

There were other clues. Some sheet metal vents on the roof that looked newer than the blackened chimney stacks of the other garages. They *could* be part of a freshly installed air filtration system. And—she couldn't be sure at this distance—what might be fresh calking around the upstairs windows. And the big steel doors looked scorched, as if someone had played a flamethrower over them.

She grinned. She didn't need any *reasons* for knowing the moon capsule was in the building. She *knew!*

With imperceptible movements, she wormed her way on her belly toward the building, stopping whenever she thought she might be attracting the attention of the wolves in the enclosure behind her. A quarter-hour later, she'd put a safe distance between her and the animals. She found temporary shelter in a corrugated steel shed that held tools.

She peeked through the crack of the door at the building, a good two hundred yards away. How to get inside? There would be security—guards might see her approaching across that expanse of bare snow. And of course she'd never get through the door unchallenged.

There were people wandering about the grounds, hurrying along paths shoveled between buildings. The light, in this Arctic night, was dim. If she could become one of the strolling researchers! But the hotsuit was no longer good camouflage. Now it would make her conspicuous.

Two of the strollers were coming toward the shed. They were holding hands. A man and a woman, both looking sexless in their bulky winter clothing.

The Baroness moved further inside, away from the door. It looked as if the path of the couple would take them past the shed. Could she drag them both inside, without one of them making a noise before being silenced, without anybody noticing?

She didn't have to. Their footsteps crunched closer through the snow. She could hear them talking.

"But your wife, Mikhail . . ." came a woman's breathless voice.

"The hell with my wife!"

The door opened. The pair of them groped their way into the dark interior.

Penelope struck with ruthless precision. First she clamped a hand over the woman's mouth, stuffing her fingers inside to stifle the scream. Holding the startled woman by the jaw, like a gaffed fish, she slammed her against the man's chest and held her there with all her strength.

That gave her purchase on both bodies for a few seconds. It would have to be enough. Her other hand came up and expertly found the man's carotid artery under the thick fur collar. Her thumb dug in.

He began to thrash about. He tried to raise his arms to tear away her hand, but he was made clumsy by his woman friend's body pressed against him. The two were fighting one another, getting in one another's way. By the time he got hold of Penelope's wrist, his blood-starved brain had made his movements feeble. Relentlessly she continued her pressure on the artery until she was sure he was unconscious.

The woman was wriggling away, making gagging sounds. Penelope let the man's body drop and found the Bernardelli automatic in its sleeve pocket. The little gun weighed only nine ounces, but she swung it with all her might against the side of the woman's head. The woman slumped to the ground, senseless.

She stood panting over the two bodies, listening for sounds from outside. There was nothing. She'd gotten away with the gamble. It would have been so much easier and safer simply to have killed the two of them. But she wasn't supposed to harm any of the Russian scientists. That was the word from Washington. Détente was a fragile thing. They didn't want an international incident if she got caught.

She made a little grimace of satisfaction. They hadn't seen her. Nobody would know that America was responsible. Or at least they wouldn't be able to prove it.

She lit a match and thumbed their eyeballs. She gave

both of them an additional tap on the head for safety's sake, ensuring they'd be out for at least an hour or two.

She bent over the Russian woman and stripped off her outer clothing—a fur-trimmed parka, boots and a white lab uniform. The sleeves were too short, but otherwise it made a loose fit over her hotsuit.

She looked dubiously at the snoring woman sprawled on the floor. The woman had been left with nothing on except her long underwear. She was wearing her lingerie —pink knee-length bloomers and a formidable satin brassiere—over the long johns rather than under them; probably to give her lover a treat. She'd freeze to death in that rig, in the unheated shed.

Penelope sighed. It was going to be a handicap, this taking care not to harm the Russian technical staff. But it had to be done. She found kindling and split logs in a woodbox and made a fire in the potbellied iron stove. It would keep the two of them alive until they were found.

Nobody was in the immediate vicinity. Wearing the parka and boots, Penelope walked confidently out of the shed and proceeded, with short sturdy strides, along the path toward the converted garage. Body language was everything; she *looked* as if she belonged there. Her posture was a correct imitation of a short, chubby, middle-aged Russian woman scientist. It would do, from a distance.

She passed a trio of technicians heading in the opposite direction and nodded brusquely at them. They barely looked up, continuing a conversation about potency titrations for bubonic plague germs. Penelope shuddered; it was a reminder of where she was and what she was here for.

She walked past the guards in front of the building, ignoring them. They were mere soldiers, beneath the notice of a woman scientist from Moscow. They stared resentfully at her back as she continued down the path. It wasn't their business to challenge anyone unless they actually tried to enter the building. Even then, some of these high-and-mighty scientists became difficult about showing their identification. You had to treat them with kid gloves!

She turned the corner of the building and continued down the shoveled path. The snowbank at her left was shoulder-high. There was another pair of sentries at a side door. She walked past them, her chin held high. Behind her, she heard one of them mutter and spit in the snow.

Without breaking stride, she crouched below the level of the snowbank as soon as she turned the next corner. It was a magician's trick. She was out of sight of the guard who'd spat. And from the point of view of anyone who might have been looking across the snow, she'd disappeared after a change of direction. Unless some observer had seriously been following her progress, her failure to re-emerge wouldn't be noticed.

She hoped!

There were no guards at the back side of the huge garage. There were no doors that would have made it necessary.

She shucked off the heavy coat, rolled it into a ball and shoved it into the snowbank. The color of the technician's uniform was a fair match for the snow and the concrete wall. She'd have to depend on speed and luck.

There were no lights showing along one stretch of second-floor windows. She fired the Spyder into the eaves above them. Agile as a monkey, she swarmed up the silken cord, the powerful spring and clutch of the pistol-winch reeling her in as she went. She was at the window in less than five seconds.

Her body plastered against the wall, she spent another second getting the suction cup out of her belt kit and attaching it to the window pane. The tiny ultrasonic generator was next. It was the size of a pair of fountain pens, hinged together at one end. She spread it into a vee, and ran the twin points around the edge of the pane. The two beams of high-intensity sound focused just below the surface of the glass and made a hairline path of molecular discontinuity. A square of glass came free. She held onto the suction cup to keep it from falling.

The window was triple-paned against the Arctic cold.

Penelope dangled the first square of glass from a cord attached to the suction cup, and pressed another suction cup against the next pane. She cut out another square of glass and repeated the process on the inner pane. This time she pushed the glass all the way inside and lowered it carefully to the floor.

She swung herself into the opening on the Spyder's line. She was out of sight of any outside watchers. The whole thing had taken less than fifteen seconds. Meticulously, she fit each of the triple panes back into place and fastened them at the corners and sides with squares of transparent sticky tape from her burglary kit. The window would pass casual inspection, from inside or out.

She was in a small cubicle containing a lab bench and a lot of glassware. There was a binocular microscope and a long row of glass bottles lying on their sides in a cradle of rollers that turned them slowly, like frankfurters on a motorized grill, spreading a film of trypsinized embryo cells in a culture medium evenly over the glass.

Penelope swore under her breath. The bloody fools! The Russians were actually making preparations to *grow* the moon virus. They didn't realize that it needed no help in multiplying.

There were footsteps outside in the darkened corridor. The door opened and the light went on. A big jowly man in a white lab coat stared at her in surprise.

She looked up at him, an annoyed expression on her face. That bought her a few seconds, while his mind struggled with the problem of why this woman in white technician's garb should be irritated at *him* entering his own laboratory.

She crossed the room swiftly, still looking annoyed, saying in fluent Russian: "Where the devil have you been? I've been looking all over for you!"

He opened his mouth to defend himself. It was still open when she hit him behind the ear with a piece of pipe she'd snatched from the bench.

She dragged his limp form over to the binocular microscope and propped him up behind it. He'd keep for an hour or so, she decided.

She gathered up a thick file folder to give herself a reason for wandering through the corridors, then stepped outside. She walked past rows of glass cubicles, some darkened, some occupied by late-working biologists.

There was no problem about finding the room she was looking for. It was at the end of the corridor, plastered with signs that read DANGER and CAUTION and NO ADMITTANCE. She could see the triple airlock, and the gaskets, and the jury-rigged air pumps that maintained negative pressure inside.

Through the glass she could see two men standing in the center of the chamber, having an argument over a report. One of them had his respiratory mask dangling down carelessly over his chest.

If he could live inside there, so could she.

She squared her shoulders and opened the outer lock. It made a slight pop. She closed it behind her and went through the next two doors.

The two scientists broke off their argument and looked up at her. She walked over to the one without the mask and kissed him on the lips, her hands lovingly cradling his face.

The other scientist raised his eyebrows. "This is not the place for such goings-on!" he said severely.

By that time, she had her thumbs pressed firmly into that convenient spot under the jaws where the carotids and jugulars cross bone. His hands came up instinctively. It looked as if he were affectionately gripping her wrists. His eyes glazed over. She kept him upright, her lips still fastened on his, her strong hands holding him by the neck.

"Here, here!" the other biologist clucked disapprovingly.

When Penelope was quite sure that her man was unconscious, she let him drop and, swiveling on the ball of one foot, delivered a roundhouse blow to the point of the other scientist's jaw. He crumpled to the floor.

She dragged the two of them behind a workbench, out of sight of the glass ports.

There was a sealed isolation unit against the far wall, the size and shape of a wine cask. A pair of rubber gloves for manipulating things inside the unit was mounted in the transparent end.

Penelope peered through the glass, a crawling sensation going down her spine. She'd never been afraid of anything in her life. But she was afraid of what she saw inside.

It was a dusty metal cylinder, not much bigger than a fire extinguisher. The resemblance was furthered by the wheel at one end that screwed the airtight lid down firmly over its gasket.

She thrust her hands into the rubber gloves and turned the capsule over, studying every square inch of its surface for cracks or dents. It was heavy—probably forty or fifty pounds. It seemed to be intact.

One of the unconscious biologists groaned. Penelope jumped.

There was no point in delaying. The thing looked all right. It was either the end of the world now, or in a day or two when the Russians got around to opening the isolation unit.

She undogged the hatch and opened the isolation unit. There was a hiss of air as pressure equalized.

She reached inside with her bare hands and dragged out the metal cylinder. She remembered the films from Houston. If she was going to die, she'd know it in less than an hour.

There was a soiled smock hanging on a peg. She wrapped the thing in it and carried it out into the corridor, closing the airlock behind her. She had to strain to carry the capsule's forty-plus pounds as if it were nothing heavier than a bundle of laundry. In one of the cubicles she passed, a round-faced young man looked up at her without interest, then bent over his work again. Sweating, she made it back to the room she'd started from. The man she'd knocked out was still lying on the floor.

She unreeled a few feet of plastic line from the Spyder and improvised a harness for the capsule. Slinging it crosswise over her back, she stepped to the window and looked out. There was nothing down below.

She peeled the transparent tape off the two inner window panes and set them carefully on the floor. She left the tape in place along the top edge of the outer pane, hinging it to swing outwards and fall back into place after she was outside. There would be a draft, but not one bad enough to raise an alarm.

The metal cylinder dragging at her shoulders, she swung herself out the window and slid down the line.

They were waiting for her at the bottom. They must have been hiding just around the corner of the building.

"Astanaveetes!" a harsh voice said below her. "Hold it!"

Dangling on her silken thread, she looked downward.

There were two of them. A great big fellow, bareheaded and barehanded in the freezing cold, cradling a submachine gun in one huge arm. And a little hunchbacked dwarf, a figure out of Grimm's fairytales, in a peaked hood and long red scarf, dancing excitedly around the other man.

If she could push outward from the wall, she might be able to drop directly on top of the bareheaded giant before he could swing his gun up and fire. She tensed her muscles.

"Don't try it," he said.

Chapter 13

The Baroness let all her muscles relax and hung, limp, against the side of the building. She recognized that tone of command. It meant the man who had spoken was a pro. It meant that he had noticed the imperceptible tightening of her body, had recognized her intention, and had no doubts whatever about his ability to swing the submachine gun upward and fire one-handed.

"Kharasho," the big man said. "Now come down. Slowly."

She slid down the plastic line and faced the two of them. Her captor grinned at her through stained teeth.

He had curly blue-black hair over a low simian forehead, and a big bent nose that stuck out of a face that was like battered granite.

"So far so good," he said. "Now put down the capsule. Carefully."

The Baroness hesitated. Even now she could hurl the capsule at him, try to get hold of the gun. But she didn't dare. Suppose she damaged the capsule? Suppose a wild bullet punctured a hole in it?

"Be careful, Evgeny Ivanovich," piped the little hunchback. "Watch her."

The bareheaded giant waited, picking his teeth with a fingernail, the heavy weapon pointing negligently in her general direction.

With a sigh, the Baroness set the metal cylinder down in the snow and backed away from it. The big man looked disappointed.

"You shouldn't have lighted the stove," he said.

She followed the direction of his nod and saw a bunch of snow-shoed medics and security guards bearing two blanket-wrapped forms on stretchers toward the main building.

"I couldn't let them freeze to death," she said in her best Russian.

"Ah, she's a tender one, eh, Evgeny Ivanovich?" the dwarf said with a wink.

The other looked at the little man shrewdly. "You want to play with her, Viktor?"

Viktor jumped up and down, the red scarf flapping. "Play with her, play with her! Viktor wants to play with her!"

The big man yawned. "I don't think so, Viktor. I think I'll just feed her to my wolves."

"But Evgeny Ivanovich, shouldn't we interrogate her first? She got past security. She stole the moon germs. Moscow will want to know *how*. Let's find out. *Then* we can feed her to the wolves."

"Viktor, Viktor," the giant said gently. "You're not thinking clearly. The last thing in the world I want to do is make out a report to Moscow. What, and have it be known that someone was able to get inside and steal the capsule? No, no, Viktor. We must get rid of her quickly."

Tears were in the dwarf's eyes. "But Evgeny Ivanovich, don't *you* want to know? At least let me have her for an hour or two. I'll make her talk, I will. I'll find out what flaws you have in your security. . . ."

Without taking his eyes off Penelope, the big man gave Viktor a backhanded swipe that knocked him flat.

"Shut up, Viktor!"

The little hunchback picked himself up and brushed the snow off his padded tunic. "That was not nice, Evgeny Ivanovich," he said reproachfully. "You should treat me with more respect. Who was it who took care of you, raised you after your poor father and mother. . . ."

"Shut up, I said! And don't mention my father and mother again." The giant's knuckles were blue on the trigger guard. "Maybe I ought to feed *you* to the wolves, too, little toad! Though you'd probably poison them!"

The dwarf backed off, looking frightened. "There, there, Evgeny Ivanovich," he said soothingly. "Of course we'll feed her to the wolves. Immediately."

Penelope listened to the sick little scene with disbelief. The big man must be Penkin, the Russian chief of security. People in such jobs tended to have unpleasant neuroses. Some of them were a little mad. But one expected a measure of ruthless efficiency along with the madness. She could only assume that Penkin's security measures had never been challenged as she had challenged them. He was reacting badly to her rape of his magic circle. That was why he wanted to get rid of her, forget her, as quickly as possible.

She shrugged under the stolen white uniform. At least Washington would be happy. Penkin would get rid of the evidence that it was America that had committed this diplomatic outrage.

They'd be happy. For a few days or weeks. Then they'd be dead.

"Get along!" Penkin growled.

He prodded her toward one of the adjoining garages. A mechanic in a fur cap and mittens opened the big doors for them and they filed inside.

"Get out!" Penkin roared at the half-dozen mechanics working at the rows of snow vehicles. They fled. He shut the doors after them.

"Lie down!" Penkin ordered.

Penelope lay down on the oily concrete floor. Penkin held the gun on her while Viktor bound her wrists and ankles with lengths of wire flex. Then, lifting her as easily as if she were a kitten, he climbed atop the steel tread of a *vezdekhod* and flung her through the door into the cramped cabin.

It was as untidy and smelly as an animal cage inside. There was half of an unfinished meat sandwich in one corner, growing rotten. A sour-smelling wine bottle with some sediment still sloshing around inside rolled about the floor. There was a little pile of dirty socks and underwear stuffed under a seat. The windshield was greasy.

She eyed the wine bottle longingly. It wouldn't be any good against wire flex.

She heard Penkin's voice outside.

"Watch her, Viktor. I'm going to have a talk with the guards, find out what other damage she may have done. Tell them to keep their mouths shut until we get back. Keep those scientists she roughed up under lock and key. We'll have to cook up some story to explain it all, eh, Viktor?"

"Right you are, Evgeny Ivanovich!" came a squeaky voice. "Maybe we can make it look like an inside job. Blame it all on those two turds, Blok and Ropatkin. You've been wanting to get rid of them for a long time. You can kill two birds with one stone."

She heard footsteps growing fainter, and the clang of an iron door. Then silence.

After a while there was a scrabbling sound, like rats, outside the cabin. The *vezdekhod* trembled slightly. She looked up. Viktor's head and shoulders were framed against the cabin door.

He swung himself through the opening, long-armed and misshapen, and crouched in front of her, looking like a puppet out of a Punch and Judy show with his curving chin and crescent nose.

"What's on your mind, Viktor?" she said.

He looked longingly at her. He sniffed and wiped his nose on his sleeve.

"So you brought Penkin up?" she said. "He doesn't seem very grateful. What happened to his mother and father?"

"Shut up, woman!" He unfastened a couple of buttons of her white lab blouse and thrust his hand inside. He seemed disappointed when he encountered the metalized material of the hotsuit. He opened the blouse all the way and looked for the hotsuit's zipper.

"Penkin told you not to play with me," she said. His little hand, rough as sandpaper, was under the hotsuit, pinching and squeezing her breast.

"Shut up, I said!" His other hand was between his legs, fumbling. His teeth were gritted.

"It doesn't work when the woman isn't afraid of you, does it, little man?"

He gave a sob of rage, and pinched her nipple so that it hurt. He reached into his pocket and came out with a wicked little knife.

"Let's see how cleverly you talk when I cut it off," he said.

Penelope stared at him with cool contempt. "Penkin won't like that," she said. "He'll feed you to the wolves."

Viktor gave a start as if he'd been slapped. The little knife clattered to the floor. He picked it up and put it back in his pocket. Tears were running down his bright red cheeks.

"Why is Penkin so obsessed with wolves?" Penelope said.

He made a choking sound. Then, unexpectedly, he gave her a foolish grin. He cocked his head to one side and said in a parrot's voice, "The wolves, the wolves, Viktor knows about the wolves!"

"Tell me, Viktor," she coaxed. "I'd really like to know. It doesn't matter, does it? Not if I'm going to be dead soon."

"Dead soon, dead soon," he cackled.

She raised herself as best she could with her bound arms and said, "I think Evgeny Ivanovich *should* treat you with more respect, Viktor, if you really did bring him up. Now stop playing the fool. It's not necessary with me."

He gave her a bright gnomelike glance. "We lived in the same village," he said. "A remote area in eastern Siberia, east of the Lena. The government hardly noticed us. We were never electrified. I was a woodcutter. Evgeny Ivanovich's father was the village blacksmith. We still used horses, even after the war with the Germans."

"Go on, Viktor." She favored him with a look of rapt attention. Surreptitiously she edged closer to the wine bottle on the floor.

"The army took our young men to fight the Germans." He gave a bitter laugh. "The hunchback was spared. Our village was without wolf hunters between 1941 and 1945."

She saw what was coming. "The same thing happened all over northern and eastern Europe," she said. "There was a postwar surge in the wolf population. The hunters were gone. And there was more game for the wolves, because the deer and the rabbits weren't getting shot either. It was so bad in Finland that the government organized a mass wolf hunt by the Finnish army in 1949."

He nodded. "For us, the worst year was 1947. The wolves were migrating in huge packs across the taiga, looking for food. They were hungry, and very bold. Day by day, we found their tracks closer and closer to the village. They killed livestock on the outlying farms. And they killed our watchdogs. Soon there were none left to warn us when wolves were near. The wolves began to take people. Children, playing near their homes. Women they caught alone, working in the barnyard or gathering firewood."

Penelope's hands closed around the neck of the wine bottle. She shifted it in her bound hands behind her back for a firmer grip.

"And the men?" she said. "Didn't they go out to hunt?"

"There was nothing they could do. The whole area was infested with wolves. Thousands and thousands of them. The packs were migrating from both east and west. There was no food for them. They were desperate. One day a hunting party was organized. Twenty men with guns. We heard shots in the woods. But they never came back."

Penelope shifted her weight and found a hard projection of metal she could shatter the wine bottle against when the right time came. With luck, she could twist around and drive the jagged edges into the dwarf's throat. Then what? Perhaps it would buy her enough time to work on the wire flex before Penkin returned.

Viktor moved closer to her, the little gnarled hands gesturing. She could smell the garlic on his breath. "Now there were no guns in the village. No guns and no dogs. When a wolf appeared in the streets, we could only run inside and bar the doors and windows. Soon they had us trapped in our own houses. We could hear the wolves outside, fighting over the horses and cattle. When they finished with our livestock, they started sniffing around our doors and windows. They broke through the weaker shutters and devoured whole families."

"In 1947? Surely . . ."

"We were isolated. A few days later an airplane making a survey flew over, and the pilot saw that the streets of the village were full of wolves. The army was sent in with grenades and machine guns. By that time, there were only a few people left alive. The wolves had broken into almost every house."

"And you, Viktor?"

The queer little barrel chest puffed out with pride. "My house was strong."

"And Penkin? He must have been a small boy at the time."

"His parents locked him in a heavy wooden cabinet when they heard the door starting to give way. Evgeny Ivanovich watched through the keyhole while the wolves ate his mother and father alive. The wolves tried to get in the cabinet, but they couldn't. They knocked it over and gnawed at it. Evgeny Ivanovich was inside the cabinet for two days before the soldiers came."

"How horrible!"

"Even today, he dreams about the wolves. He likes to have me sleep in a cot at the foot of his bed to wake him up when the nightmares come."

"So now he has to prove his mastery over wolves. . . ." Penelope made a grimace of distaste. What a casebook in abnormal psychology—the little boy who'd seen his mother and father devoured by wild animals while he was locked away in a dark place, then the two days of terror while the wolves tried to get at him, too!

The little hunchback went on, "I took care of him, raised him to a man. He was smart and strong, my little Evgeny. When he got his first important job in Moscow, he sent for me. I have been with him ever since."

Viktor rocked on his heels, his eyes far away. His knobby face was flushed and mottled. Penelope cracked the wine bottle smartly against the projecting metal and twisted her body around, whipping herself backward, the broken bottom of the bottle aimed squarely at Viktor's face.

The little man moved with startling speed. He hopped upward and sidewise, like a jack-in-the-box. The broken glass ripped at his sleeve. A second later, a thick-soled little boot kicked the bottle out of Penelope's hands.

He stood there, panting. "Bitch!" he spat.

"Little toad," she said.

He slapped her across the face, then reached in his pocket for the little knife. He was leaning over her with it when the *vezdekhod* shook and Penkin poked his head in through the door.

Penkin took it all in at a glance: the broken bottle, Viktor's ripped sleeve, Penelope's unbuttoned blouse.

"So, Viktor," he said. "You have been careless."

The little man was fighting down tears of rage. "She is dangerous," he said. "She charms you, then bites like a snake."

Penkin seated himself behind the controls and sent the

big snow vehicle crawling outward through the garage doors. "Let her charm the wolves," he said.

Penkin was quite jovial and conversational about it. "Wolves can smell blood for dozens of miles in the Arctic air," he said. "In fact, that's how the Lapps sometimes trap them. They'll smear some reindeer blood on a sharp knife and wedge the handle in the ice. The wolf will lick the blade and cut his tongue. But the frozen steel keeps him from feeling pain. His own blood will excite him further, and he'll keep on licking the blade until he bleeds to death."

They were forty or fifty miles from the biological laboratory. Penkin had explained that a migrating wolf pack was in the vicinity, heading west. In fact, he'd recently fed a Nenet herdsman and his wife to them. The wolves were getting used to taking their food this way.

Penelope felt herself lifted like a sack of potatoes and slung over Penkin's shoulder. He handled her easily as he jumped down from the *vezdekhod* and carried her over to the four spikes that Viktor had hammered into the frozen ground. He dumped her unceremoniously between them.

"Just a little blood is enough to attract them," Penkin went on. "I don't want you to bleed to death before they arrive. It's no fun that way, eh, Viktor?"

"You're a pair of sick bastards," Penelope said.

Penkin laughed. He wired one wrist and ankle to stakes before he separated her arms and legs to tie down the other wrist and ankle; he was taking no chances with her. She tried to break free, but it was impossible. He wrestled her wrist, with two hands, to the other stake while Viktor lashed more wire around it.

"Spread out like a Warsaw whore, isn't she, Viktor?" Penkin said.

He peeled the hotsuit off her like a banana skin, cutting through the compound fabric with a knife to get it past wrists and ankles. He frowned when his knife became entangled in the fine embedded wires, but sawed through them until it was free.

The cold gripped her body like a giant fist, shocking the breath from her. The day was relatively mild—only ten degrees below freezing—and there was no wind. But she could feel her fingers and toes already growing numb.

"Aren't you afraid I'll freeze to death before the wolves get here?" she said.

He grinned through yellow teeth. "It won't take them that long," he said.

He examined her body with clinical interest, then scored the point of his knife down the inside of her thigh. She felt nothing—Penkin had been right about that—but she could see a thin line of blood oozing out of her white flesh.

Viktor was dancing about, holding his crotch with both hands. "Please, Evgeny Ivanovich," he begged. "She looks so beautiful lying there in the snow. Like a fairytale princess. Just once, can't I have a woman like that?"

"All right, Viktor," Penkin said gruffly. "But be quick about it. I'll keep a watch for the wolves."

The gnome moved toward her and knelt between her legs. He dipped a finger in the blood on her thigh and tasted it. Then, a sly smile spreading like a crack over his lumpy features, he lifted his tunic like a curtain.

"See," he said.

There was the dull thwump of an explosion in the distance. Viktor's head jerked around.

Penkin was standing on the *vezdekhod*'s caterpillar tread, holding an earphone to his head. "It's the laboratory!" he shouted. "An armed force is moving in on it! They've just blown up a bunker!"

Viktor scrambled to his feet.

"Hurry up, you little worm!" Penkin yelled. "We've got to get back there right away!"

Viktor scuttled like a crab over the snow. Penkin reached down and plucked him off the ground by the coat. He threw the little man into the cabin and climbed in after him. A moment later, the *vezdekhod*'s twin engines roared, and the bulky vehicle lurched toward the laboratory, forty miles away.

Penelope turned her head to watch it dwindle into the

white waste. The sound of the engines grew fainter and faded away.

A few minutes later she heard another sound. It seemed to be coming from the opposite direction, a mile or two beyond a ridge. It was a low wail that ran up the scale as she listened to it, and was joined by other howls.

Wolves.

Skytop raised his head at the sound of the explosion. It almost cost him his life.

"Duck!" Wharton yelled.

The stream of slugs hosed past him, sending down a shower of ice chips from the vertical face at his back. He buried his cheek in the snow and waited until the machine gunner got tired.

"That explosion came from the Russian lab!" Skytop said.

Wharton, lying beside him in the snow, nodded. "Sounded like about forty pounds of pentolite, detonated just below ground level as a demolition charge. Somebody blew up a bunker."

"The Baroness?"

Before Wharton could answer, there was another explosion, bigger than the first.

"No," Wharton said. "She wasn't carrying anything like that."

A snowmobile charged out of the gloom at them. Wharton fired a burst from his *Galil* assault rifle to discourage it. The snowmobile veered and hid behind the crest of a low hill.

"Maybe she swiped the explosive, set it off as a diversion. Dan, she needs help getting out of there!"

"If she wanted a diversion, she would have set off a hell of a lot more than forty pounds. Besides, the second explosion sounded as if it was coming from the far side of the lab. There are at least two groups working. They're trying to get inside, not out."

There was a chatter of machine gun fire from the hill. Skytop and Wharton ignored it. It was just some trigger-happy bozo trying to rattle them.

"Same bunch as the ones shooting at us?"

"They have to be. I thought at first they were some kind of security patrol from the Russian lab. But it sounds like they're using American guns. M-16s."

"Jesus!" Skytop said. "Who are they?"

Wharton shrugged. "Maybe Washington got desperate. I don't think so."

Another burst of machine gun fire streaked over them, too high and too far to the left.

"Whoever they are, they've got us pinned down."

"They must think *we're* a Russian patrol."

Inga came wriggling through the snow, leaving a furrow behind her. "Eric and Tommy are circling around," she said. "They'll be able to dump mortar shells down on those bandits from that hill there."

Skytop shook his head. "That'll take a couple of hours, at least. And in the meantime we can't move."

Another one of the mysterious snowmobiles came swooping from cover, the man in the rear saddle pumping bullets in their direction. They drove it back with rifle fire.

"We'll just have to wait it out," Wharton said, frowning. "From the sound of things back there, the Russians are too busy to worry about gunfire out here."

"*We* can wait it out, Dan. The Baroness can't."

"Look, Chief, I know how you feel . . ." Pain wrenched Wharton's rugged face. Skytop pitied him for his hopeless fixation on the Baroness.

"She should have signaled us hours ago. Unless something happened."

Inga gripped Skytop's thick arm. "If she's still in there, there's nothing we can do. But if she made it outside, she'll be caught in the middle of this war. With nothing but a little boudoir gun."

"I'm going," Skytop rumbled. "Cover me, children."

Wharton grabbed him by the sleeve. "You can't find her in all those hundreds of square miles. Not without the sniffer. And the Baroness has that."

Skytop grinned. "We've got sniffers, too. Two of them. The organic kind."

Wharton got the idea immediately. "It might work. If you're lucky enough to cut across her trail." He let go of Skytop's sleeve. "You stay here, Chief, and help Inga keep our friends busy. Inga, where are the borzois?"

"In my tent, tied down. The gunfire's driving them crazy."

Wharton made a move to head toward Inga's tent, out of sight below surface level, as all of their equipment was.

"Hold it, Dan," Skytop said.

"Hands off, injun."

"Don't be dumb, Dan. The Baroness needs help, not heroics. You're the big military mind in this outfit. You can keep those snowmobilers busy better than I can. And I can track better than you . . ." A mocking expression came over his face. ". . . white man," he added.

A struggle showed on Wharton's features. Finally he gave a sober nod. "All right, Chief. Be careful."

Skytop rolled sidewise like a log, while Wharton and Inga sent up a maniacal fusillade of fire from their assault rifles. He hit a small declivity that gave him cover as he crawled backward from the shallow ridge that had sheltered the three of them. A snowmobile engine buzzed, as one of the machines made a sudden foray. But it was directed against the position he'd just left. He turned his head in time to see Wharton's arm flash upward. A black dot hurtled in the direction of the snowmobile—falling far too short, naturally, but still traveling an incredible distance for an object thrown from a prone position. Wharton's throwing arm was fantastic. The grenade burst with an ugly crack, and the snowmobile fled back to its hiding place.

Skytop squeezed his way into the tent. It was steamy with the breath of the two dogs. Stasya and Igor whined, wagging their tails. Their ears were flat back.

"Okay, fellas," Skytop said. "We're going for a little walk."

Stasya sobbed, sounding incredibly human, when Skytop untied the chains that were fastened to the big steel staple. They lunged and tried to get out of the tent, but

Skytop held on relentlessly. Their more than two hundred pounds of combined frenzy were almost too much, even for him, but he got a grip on their wide collars and wrestled them outside, forcing their heads down low. He crawled a couple of hundred yards with them, down a small slope, before he judged that it was safe to stand up.

He set off toward the Russian laboratory, fifteen long miles toward the southeast, festooned with grenades, the automatic rifle slung across his back and a spare machine gun in his right hand. The dogs' leads were wrapped around his wrist, pulling him along on his snowshoes.

With luck, he thought, he might reach the vicinity of the Russian laboratory in five or six hours.

He had no inkling whatever that he was heading in exactly the wrong direction.

Chapter 14

They were sitting in a circle around her, looking like a jury out of hell. They were gaunt, battle-scarred creatures with torn ears and patches of mange on their fur. They watched her with intelligent eyes, ears pricked forward and lips drawn back over white fangs in the horrible semblance of a smile.

The Baroness concentrated on her right wrist, working it back and forth, trying to loosen the iron spike in the frozen ground. She could feel the spike moving minutely, but she knew that the wolves would overcome their natural caution long before she worked herself loose.

So far they'd kept their distance, but the circle kept growing smaller and smaller. They were near enough for her to smell the dank fur, the rotten-meat stench of their breaths. A couple of them paced back and forth on the fringes of the circle, whining impatiently.

She remembered something she'd heard: an adult wolf

can eat thirty pounds of meat at a sitting. There wasn't going to be very much of her to go around.

She was freezing cold. The polar sun shone down on her naked body through the clear still air, starkly lighting the blue gooseflesh on her limbs, the puckered, shriveled knots of her nipples. It would be almost pleasant to freeze to death, compared to what was in store for her. But Penkin had been right; the wolves wouldn't wait that long.

She tugged again at the wire snaring her right wrist. The movement sent her breasts rippling, her legs straining. The wolves stirred. It was obvious that she was helpless. One great silvery beast got to his feet and shook himself. He yawned. He sniffed the air and whimpered. Penelope could see him drooling. Looking like a big, intelligent, friendly dog, the wolf trotted toward her.

Skytop slogged across the empty white plain, wrestling with the borzois, his snowshoes rising and falling automatically. The dogs were being unruly. They kept pulling to one side, trying to go at a tangent to his route.

"*This* way, goddammit!" he yelled, tugging them toward the distant glitter of the germ warfare installation. There had been more explosions. Smoke was rising in a dark greasy column, and now he could hear the faint rattle of automatic weapons fire.

The dogs lunged, almost pulling him off his feet, to sniff at the tracks of some large treaded vehicle. Cursing, Skytop hauled them onward toward his goal.

His keen ears heard the mosquito whine of the snowmobile engines in plenty of time. But there was no way he could have prevented what happened next. He was the only object on a vast flat field of white. There was no place to hide.

Far ahead, a line of tiny dots sped toward him. The line split into a vee when they caught sight of him, spreading out to ensnare him from either side.

Skytop let go of the dogs' leads and dropped to one knee, bringing up the muzzle of the automatic rifle, knowing in advance that it was hopeless. The dogs ran off immediately. Someone in one of the snowmobiles took a pot shot at them. There was the sharp crack of a long-range rifle, and one of the dogs yelped. The two borzois disappeared into the distance, their white fur almost invisible against the snow.

There were six snowmobiles, each carrying a driver and a man riding shotgun. They buzzed around him in a wide circle, out of effective range of his automatic rifle. He didn't bother to shoot. After a while, the anonymous marksman grew tired of his stupidity. There was another sharp crack, and a bullet whistled over Skytop's head. It wasn't intended to kill him. He thought it prudent not to try their patience any longer.

With a sigh, he threw the automatic rifle as far away from him as he could. He unslung the spare weapon from his back and threw that away too. Instantly the snowmobiles converged on him, sending up sprays of white crystals.

He was startled when he saw them up close. All the faces were Chinese, and they wore the red star insignia of People's Army regulars. So *that's* what all the shooting and explosions had been about!

The Chinese patrol leader dismounted and approached him warily, a pistol in his hand. He was a huge moon-faced man, his expression masked by goggles. He gestured with the pistol.

"*Vy menyah paneemah yete?*" he said in an abominable attempt at Russian.

Skytop shook his head.

The man studied Skytop through his goggles, evidently puzzled at his Cherokee features.

"English, then? Do you speak English?"

Skytop kept his mouth shut.

"You speak English," the man said with a show of confidence. "You come along now."

Skytop let himself be taken. The Chinese hadn't shot him out of hand because he represented a puzzle. They were a long way from home; they couldn't afford to make any mistakes. They wanted to question him first.

He submitted passively while they bound his hands

behind his back and seated him on one of the snow-mobiles. He was jammed between the driver and the heavy bulk of the rifleman, unable to move. The driver kicked his machine into life, and they started off with a jerk. They headed toward the battle at the laboratory, eager to dump him off for later interrogation and join the fighting. He was a nuisance right now, a helpless bundle that was slowing them down. Skytop grinned. He almost felt sorry for the poor bastards.

The Baroness felt the wolf's muzzle, warm and insistent, against her ribs. It poked hard, hard enough to leave a bruise. If she hadn't been tied down, it would have flipped her over.

Instantly the wolf backed off and studied her. She could see the rough fur on its face, bristly as a scrub-brush, and the knowing brown eyes. The long red tongue hung down over yellow teeth. Drool dripped down into the snow.

Satisfied at her helplessness, the huge silver beast gathered its courage to leap in and snap at her—a first bite that would tear some five pounds of flesh from her living body. Where would it be? Her thigh, her breast, her soft belly with the tempting entrails it contained? Hyenas usually went for the face.

The wolf wagged its tail, for all the world like a dog that has just had its supper bowl set down in front of it, and lunged.

And was knocked off its feet by a white streak that came out of nowhere and hit it in the side like a javelin.

Igor! The big borzoi must have been traveling at sixty miles an hour when he hit the wolf with his rapier nose. The impact had knocked him flat, too.

And there was Stasya, circling around, keeping be-tween Penelope and the rest of the wolves.

Igor scrambled to his feet before the silver wolf did and lunged at his opponent's throat. The wolf jerked its head around, snapping, and suddenly Stasya was at its throat from the other side, tearing out a great mouthful of flesh. Blood spurted on the snow, and the two wolf-hounds bounded away, light as feathers, and faced the rest of the pack.

There were about thirty of them, all trying to make up their minds about this new intrusion. A young wolf, bolder than the rest, darted at Stasya, contemptuous of the queer narrow dog that looked too light-bodied for its size.

Stasya's long face lifted in a blur too fast for the eye to follow, and the wolf slammed into the ground with its momentum, its throat torn out. The other wolves waited, evaluating the situation.

Penelope renewed her attempt to work the steel spike loose. She had an idea.

"Here, Igor," she cooed. "That's a good boy."

The big wolfhound trotted over to her, swaying on his long legs. He whined and licked her face, upset at her failure to pat him. Finally he nuzzled her right hand, demanding affection.

She caught hold of his collar. "At 'em, boy!" she commanded.

He needed no urging. Another wolf was edging too close. Igor surged with his hundred-plus pounds of strength. The Baroness added her own efforts. She thought she felt the spike give a little.

"Go, boy, go!" she said.

Igor tried once again to leap. His collar was torn out of Penelope's grasp. He stood there, tail wagging.

But the spike was loose now. She moved it back and forth a few times, and pulled it out of the ground.

The rest was easy. She worked at the spike holding her left wrist, two-handed, and when that came free she unfastened her legs.

The borzois were in the midst of the wolf pack now, slashing, snapping, darting in and out, faster than the heavier wolves could react. They worked in a deadly silence, playing out the ancient role that had been bred into their genes by generations of wolf-hunting Russian noblemen.

The Baroness got to her feet, shivering with cold, a

spike in her hand. She managed to coax one of the borzois over to her for a moment and slip the heavy chain
he was still dragging. She stood there, spike held ready
and a double length of chain dangling from her left hand.
It was a pretty good approximation of the dagger and
staff combination that the Lapps used for wolf killing.

A shaggy big-headed beast broke through the borzois'
defense and leaped at her throat. She sidestepped and
swung the chain. It cracked him across the face, stunning
him, and she drove the point of the spike into his throat.
He snapped at her futilely when she pulled the spike out,
then collapsed to the ground, arterial blood pumping out
of his neck. The Baroness whirled and rapped the chain
across the face of a wolf that had been trying to sneak
up behind her. She got the point of her spike into his
belly and ripped. He staggered sideways, his entrails
dragging on the snow.

The snow was littered with dead wolves now, at least
a dozen of them. The Baroness waded into the fight, taking her position beside Igor and Stasya. They accepted
her help as naturally as if she had been another wolfhound, instinctively positioning themselves to form a circle
that faced the wolves on three sides, here where there
was nothing they could get their backs against.

The wolves could only dart in one or two at a time.
The naked, wild-haired woman and the two tall white dogs
worked in concert, with fangs and snapping jaws, swinging chain and glittering stake. The Baroness' right hand
was sticky with wolf blood, past the wrist. Once a wolf
caught the iron spike in its teeth, but one of the borzois
slashed at its throat. Once a big gray animal sunk its
teeth into Stasya's shoulder, and Penelope was able to
kill it before Igor could go to his teammate's aid.

When it was over, she stood there, panting. There were
fewer than a dozen wolves left alive, and they slunk off,
breaking into a run when the two borzois began harrying
them.

"Igor, Stasya!" the Baroness called sharply. The two
dogs came reluctantly back to her. Ordinarily they'd never
have come back while there was a chance of prey, but

their blood-lust was partially slaked by the mass slaughter they'd just committed, and Stasya was hurt, and they were a little intimidated by the vast empty space that contained the comfort of just one human presence.

The Baroness surveyed the damage. Stasya's shoulder —just torn muscle. He wouldn't bleed to death. Multiple minor wounds that made red patches on Igor's white fur. And aside from one long slash down her forearm, where a dying wolf's fang had caught in her flesh, only surface scratches on her own body.

She wasn't cold for the moment. The heavy exertion had sent the blood pumping through her veins, overheating her body. She was covered all over with a thin sheen of sweat.

It began to freeze on her body as she stood there. The pain of the cold was worse than she'd imagined. There was no shelter, no clothing, no help for miles. She was naked in the Arctic.

She shivered violently. Little shards of ice fell from her quivering skin. Already, her bare feet could feel nothing.

If she had a knife, she could skin one of the dead wolves, the way Vana had. But she had no knife— nothing but the steel spikes. And they didn't have an edge.

She stared hopelessly at the carcasses of the dead wolves all around her. Without a knife, they were no good to her. No good at all.

Her body was growing numb rapidly. The pain diminished.

It wouldn't take long—ten or fifteen minutes at best. She would be dead.

Chapter 15

Skytop wedged his bound wrists down as far as he could into the space between the saddles. The soldier riding behind him didn't notice. It was hot down there from the heat-exchange fins of the air-cooled engine—hot enough to cook flesh.

Deliberately he pressed his wrist against the scorching metal. He gritted his teeth at the searing pain. He'd be a hell of an Indian if he couldn't take a little burned flesh. It wasn't half as bad as the burning coals the shaman had put on his chest during his manhood rites.

The line of snowmobiles roared across the tundra, bouncing and jolting, occasionally lifting straight up at some surface contour and slamming down hard again. Holding on with his knees was child's play to Skytop; it was a picnic compared to some of the ill-tempered broncos he'd ridden. But the man behind him was holding on for dear life, hugging Skytop like a long lost brother.

They were fifth in line. There were four snowmobiles ahead and only one behind, there to keep an eye on the prisoner. That was good; it would make things easier when the time came.

It took about forty seconds. He could smell the burnt hair of his wrist, the first suggestion of roasting meat.

And then there was something writhing like a serpent on his wrist. His watchband. It snapped straight out into a hard, rigid shape, eight inches long.

Memory plastic. A thermal-set resin that Wharton described as a neo-methylmethacrylate co-polymer. It was cast in the form of an eight-inch blade with a sharp point and a serrated cutting edge. Then it was softened and textured to masquerade as a leather watch strap.

But when you applied heat, the plastic "remembered"

its original shape. The molecules flowed, and the strap became thin-edged and sharp and rigid.

He twisted his right thumb and forefinger and caught the blade by the buckle end. He began sawing away at the rope around his wrists.

A minute later his hands were free. He reached behind him and caught the Chinese soldier by the family jewels.

Instinctively the man let go of Skytop's torso and clawed at the hand that had him between the legs. Skytop squeezed, and the man screamed in his ear. Skytop tugged the soldier sideways by the tender handful and the man tumbled off the rear saddle. Skytop grabbed the rifle slung across the man's shoulder as he fell.

In front of him, the driver turned his head to see what had happened. Skytop drove the plastic knife into his kidneys and pushed him off to join his mate. He caught the steering bar with a strong thumb and forefinger, his leftover fingers still gripping the knife, and spun the machine around.

Lifting the rifle one-handed, he fired without sighting, and caught the driver of the following snowmobile squarely in the chest. The buzzing machine tumbled over, spilling its two riders.

Skytop sprang from his own machine before it stopped moving and dived into a snowbank. The four machines ahead were making a sharp turn and coming back to see what had happened.

The rifle was a .300 Weatherby Magnum De Luxe with a scope—a strange weapon for a Chinese soldier to be carrying. Skytop got the driver of the first snowmobile in the crosshairs and let him come close. Then he squeezed the trigger.

The rifle butt slammed into his shoulder, and the driver flung his hands up to claw at the hole in his chest. Somehow the body remained in the saddle, a limp doll, while the snowmobile weaved out of control. The man in the rear saddle fired his submachine gun wildly at Skytop's general position. Skytop ignored him. There was small danger from an M-16 at this range. Instead he concentrated on the other three drivers.

He picked them off like targets in a shooting gallery, one by one. He snapped the three shots off in as many seconds. The high velocity bullets splintered windshields, tore through flesh. One of the snowmobiles tipped. The second slid to a stop, while its passengers jumped off and dived for cover. The third, its rider leaning forward to grab at the controls, turned and tried to get away. Skytop shot the survivor in the back.

One of the Chinese gunners was obviously dead, crushed under the tipped snowmobile. The one who'd been on the lead snowmobile had recovered and was shooting. The bullets, almost spent, spattered at Skytop's feet. Skytop raised the long-range rifle and shot the man through the head.

There was one more man out there to kill. Skytop couldn't see him. He'd burrowed into the snow, holding his fire. Skytop didn't dare walk away and leave him. He couldn't afford to let the Chinese hop on a snowmobile and get away.

Deliberately he stood up. Even an almost-spent slug could kill him. And if the Chinese kept his weapon on full automatic, he could spray him like a garden hose. Accuracy wouldn't count.

The temptation was too much for the Chinese. Up ahead a machine gun chattered. Snow and ice kicked up at Skytop's left, moving toward him. Coolly, Skytop lifted the Weatherby and fired three times at the movement against the snow. The firing stopped. Skytop could make out a twisted shape in a white camouflage outfit through the scope.

He turned around to see what had happened to the gunman who'd been riding the rearmost snowmobile. On the way back he found the soldier he'd yanked off the saddle behind him. The man was writhing in the snow, clutching at his crotch with both hands, his face a sickly yellow. Skytop bent over and sliced his throat open with the plastic knife.

The last man was lying in the snow with a broken leg. He tried to crawl for his automatic rifle, a few yards

away. Skytop kicked the gun further away and grabbed
the man by the hood of his parka.

"Who the hell are you, buster?" he said. "What's going
on at the Russky germ factory?" He tried to assemble a
few words of his primitive Chinese, frowning at the effort

But the man understood English. He stared at Skytop
and said defiantly "Long live the thoughts of Chairman
Mao!"

Skytop sighed. He never could stand bores. He drew
his blade across the man's throat and wiped the knife
on the white tunic. There wouldn't have been time
to question him, break him down, anyway. He had to
find the Baroness.

He loaded a few supplies on one of the intact snowmobiles, and took along the Weatherby and a couple of
automatic rifles. He started the engine and got going
backtracking to the place where the Chinese had captured
him.

He picked up the tracks of the borzois and started following them. Maybe they'd got onto the Baroness' trail
maybe not. But it was the best chance he had. Probably
the only chance.

Only it was going to take hours.

Igor's collar dangled from the Baroness' numb fingers
a broad limp strap, glittering with gems, useless to her
in its present form.

Memory plastic. All her team wore watchbands made
of it. It was colored and textured to look like leather
Apply heat and its complex molecules twitched and
flowed. It became a knife, rigid and sharp.

All she had to do was pass it through fire, and she'd
be able to skin a couple of wolves, wrap herself in th
fur that would save her life.

Penelope smiled wryly. If snow would burn, she'd hav
it made. If she had a match to ignite it.

There wasn't much time to lose. Her fingers had almos
stopped working from the paralyzing cold. She had on
shot at saving her life, and she had to be damned quic

about it. If it didn't work, her fingers would be too numb for her to try again.

Sobbing with cold, she used the point of the metal spike to pry the artificial gems out of the dog collar. The cold steel burned like a branding iron, and when she tried to put the spike down, it stuck to her palm. She pulled it loose, and a strip of skin came with it.

The jewels spilled out of her deadened fingers and scattered in the snow. She tried to pick them up, but she couldn't seem to make her fingers work. There! She had one between thumb and forefinger. Damn! She dropped it again.

The cold was like a knife now, piercing through to her bones. The two wolfhounds sat a little distance away, their heads cocked, watching the strange activities of their mistress with doggy curiosity.

The wolfhounds! A dog's body temperature is 101 degrees. She called them over to her and plunged her paralyzed fingers into their thick fur. Their bellies felt feverish with heat.

A little feeling returned to her fingers. But the rest of her was getting colder. It was excruciating.

She returned to the scattered gems and swept them into a little pile, on the flattish piece of bare rock poking out of the snow. Using the rounded head of the spike as a pestle, she pounded the jewels to powder.

Magnesium powder. The stuff used for photographic flash powder, signal flares, incendiary bombs. You could also cast paste jewels out of it. It was a handy way to get a bomb through Customs.

Now to set it on fire. She giggled: fire to make fire. . . . She brought herself up short. Her mind was growing fuzzy with the cold; this wasn't funny. With a supreme effort of will, she picked up the other dog collar.

There were two big glassy gems on opposite sides of the collar. They weren't paste. They were optical glass. With the buckle at *that* notch, just so, the focus was exactly correct.

She propped the collar in the snow, focusing a ray of sun through the two lenses to the little heap of incendiary

powder. She waited. A little curl of smoke appeared, an
then there was a bright hot flash that almost blinded he

The incendiary powder flared, hissing. She picked u
the first collar and thrust it into the flame.

The heat was as unbearable as the cold had been. Sh
felt it all the way up her forearms, thawing out the froze
flesh. Her face tingled. The returning circulation wa
agony.

But the dog collar was changing before her eyes.
writhed like a living thing. It lifted its point end an
became straight and hard. The edges flowed and becam
razor thin with little serrations. In seconds she was hold
ing a formidable-looking knife, a foot and a half long.

She toasted herself by the dying magnesium flare a
long as it continued to throw heat. Then she turned to th
carnage. Knife in hand, she set about to skin herself som
wolves.

It was good to be warm again. The Baroness jogged a
an easy gait over the snowy landscape, a strange appar
tion wrapped in wolfskin, two enormous white dogs lopin
at her heels.

The fur was soft and comforting against her naked ski
She'd wrapped the first layer around herself inside ou
the bloody hide facing outward. The second layer wa
pelt side out. The big floppy moccasins, fastened wi
pieces of the wire flex that had bound her, supported he
almost like snowshoes on the crunchy surface. She'd d
vised primitive-looking leggings, wrapped and tied wi
wire, and a pair of arm-length muffs, long enough to cu
her fingers into when she wasn't using them. There wa
a hood, and a mask for her lower face, and a poncho-lik
coat, belted with one of the borzoi's chains.

Her belly was full of raw wolf meat, giving her strengt
She pitied Penkin if she ever met him again.

She was following the tracks of the *vezdekhod*. They
lead her in the direction of the laboratory. She had to g
close enough to find out the meaning of those explosior
of the gunfire she could hear faintly when the wind w
right.

Could it be her own team? Had they become worried and gone in to get her?

It didn't seem likely. Wharton and Skytop would have waited a little longer before disobeying orders.

How many miles to go before she got within hailing distance of them? Twenty? Thirty? Perhaps another four hours of this steady mechanical pace, this dreamlike rhythm that made running seem effortless, as if she were watching someone else do it. She'd left her team in a small declivity, about fifteen miles on this side of the germ laboratory. Without the direction finder in the kit that Penkin had confiscated, she'd have to rely on her memory of the featureless landscape, and on the noses of the dogs. How had they found her? Traces of her scent must still have been clinging to the outside of the *vezdekhod*.

She bounded like a running deer over the barren wastes, her long legs rising and falling, a bobbing gray shadow against the dazzling snow. The dogs kept pace, occasionally darting ahead or running playful circles around her.

There was something else out there on the tundra keeping pace with her. The wolves. The tattered remnants of the pack that she and the borzois had decimated.

They were no longer a threat. They were wary of her now, and kept their distance. But they were hungry— ravenous. She'd seen their ribs. There was too much competition for too little game, here on this barren peninsula. The migrating wolf packs were close to starvation. So they kept her in sight, at a safe distance, in case she fell and became injured, or ran herself into helpless exhaustion. She was the only prospective source of meat for miles—too tempting to abandon entirely.

Something caught her eye—there on the fringes of her vision. She turned her head to scan the horizon. It was the wolves. They were making a wide circle around her, cutting ahead of her, yelping with excitement.

In a moment she saw why. Penkin's *vezdekhod*. He hadn't made it back to the laboratory after all.

The big snow vehicle had thrown a tread. She could see the deep circle it had gouged out of the snow as it went round and round helplessly, like some giant injured beetle, on its remaining tread.

She kept running toward it. She could make out two tiny figures struggling at the base of the titled machine. Penkin and Viktor. They were trying to jack the thrown tread back onto the drive gears. The tread sprawled like a scaly serpent across the snow. It would be hard work with a heavy wrench in the cold to fasten the severed ends back on their bolts and tighten the tread over the gears.

The larger of the two figures straightened his back and looked up. He hadn't seen her yet, but he could see the circling wolves.

He tapped the little hunchback on the shoulder, and they both scrambled for the safety of the enclosed cabin. The wolves surrounded the disabled machine, pacing restlessly.

Penelope drew closer. The wolves swung their heads toward her, respectful of her and the borzois, and turned back toward the *vezdekhod*. The leader threw back his head and howled.

A few moments later, the cabin door swung open. The dwarf clambered up onto the roof of the vehicle, a machine gun huge and unwieldy in his spindly arms. Penkin had sent the little man outside to deal with the wolves, too fearful to leave the safety of the cabin himself. Penelope was willing to lay odds that Penkin was remembering his childhood nightmare—the ghastly two days he'd spent locked in a wooden cabinet while the wolves who had eaten his parents tried to get inside.

Viktor braced himself against the kick of the weapon and fired a burst. It tore into one of the wolves, spattering blood and fur across the snow.

But the starving wolves were too desperate to be intimidated. They rushed in on their fallen mate and gobbled him up, fighting over scraps of flesh. Viktor fired another burst, but they refused to be driven away.

And then one wolf who had been circling around to the other side leaped for the roof of the *vezdekhod*, trying to get at the little man. He got his front paws over the edge and slipped back, falling ten feet to the snow. He picked himself up and leaped again.

Viktor's nerve broke. He dropped the gun and scrambled into the cabin, slamming the door behind him.

Unless Penkin had another gun in there, the two of them were helpless.

Penelope moved in among the wolves. They stood their ground, too hungry to be dislodged from their prey, still acknowledging the supremacy of this strange erect creature and her two deadly white-furred companions. The closer of the wolves assumed a submissive posture, lowering themselves on their front paws, tucking their tails between their legs and whining. Their ears were laid flat in deference. A few tails cautiously wagged.

It was a truce. They were accepting the Baroness as a member of the pack.

The submissive gestures worked on the borzois' own wolfish instincts. Igor advanced and touched noses with one of the wolves. Stasya followed. Their tails wagged. Dogs and wolves sniffed each other all over.

The wolves turned back to the *vezdekhod*. Some of them, impatient, flung themselves against the steel sides, making the machine shake.

A pair of frightened faces appeared at the window. Penelope let them see her. She stood among the snarling, snapping wolves and stared back at Penkin and Viktor. She showed her teeth in a gleaming smile.

She must have been an incomprehensible sight in her wrappings of wolf fur, still bloody from the skinning knife. They'd left her staked out and helpless, naked in the freezing cold, live bait for a howling pack of Arctic wolves. And here she was, in the middle of the nightmarish beasts besieging them.

Penkin's face was ashen behind the glass. The oversize lumpish jaw was trembling.

He must have gone berserk with panic then. His face disappeared from the side window, and the *vezdekhod*'s engines coughed. There was a grinding of gears, and the big machine spun round and round on its one intact tread, churning up the snow.

Penelope smiled coldly. Penkin wasn't going anywhere.

After a while, Penkin gave up. The *vezdekhod* ground to a stop, leaning over at an angle.

The door opened a crack. She could hear Viktor screaming.

"No, Evgeny Ivanovich, no! For the love of God, by the blood of your father, don't do it!"

And then the door was flung open and Viktor was pitched out. She caught a glimpse of Penkin, looking crazed, before he slammed the door shut again.

The twisted little man landed in the snow, among the wolves. They were on him in a flash, teeth slashing and snapping. There was one tiny high-pitched scream, choked off almost immediately, and then the wolves were pressed into a tight mass, feeding.

If Penkin had hoped to satisfy the wolves by feeding Viktor to them, he was disappointed. The little man was barely a snack. The wolves resumed their siege of the *vezdekhod,* leaping at its sides and snapping at steel. They were all over the machine now, pacing on the broad roof, flattening their noses against the glass of the windshield while Penkin cowered inside.

Penelope leaped for the cabin door and wrenched it open. She hurled herself inside, pulling the door shut after her to keep the wolves out.

It was dank and smelly inside, heavy with the stink of stale bodies and diesel oil. Penkin was a dim shape in the darkness. She slammed into his huge bulk, her hand reaching for the skinning knife. He whimpered with fear.

"*Nyet, nyet!*" he babbled at the touch of the wolfskins she was wearing.

His hysteria made him dangerous. A big arm, hard as a steel bar, jerked upward at random and knocked the plastic knife out of her hand. She grabbed for it, but his enormous clubs of fists were hammering at her. She got herself inside them, pressing herself against his bulky torso.

He was clawing at her, whimpering like a child.

She got her hands around his neck. It was like trying to throttle a tree stump.

He shook her off in his panic. She crashed painfully against the control levers. She picked herself up and leaped on his back. It was cramped in the cabin. He thrashed about slamming her against the steel walls.

She hung on, her fingers clawing at his chest. She couldn't let go, and it was impossible to reach a vital part of him with her knee. She sank her teeth into his neck.

He screamed.

He was unmanageable in the cramped interior, with his strength and his wild panic. He shook her off and made a dive for the cabin door. He's stopped thinking. His one object was to get out of this dark steel box, away from the terrifying thing in fur that was after him.

Penelope picked herself off the floor and poked her head out the door. Penkin was running across the snow, miraculously still on his feet. The wolves were after him, snapping at his heels. One great silvery beast that must have weighed two hundred pounds had its teeth in his shoulder. He shook it off and kept running.

He got a few more yards before they brought him down. They got him on the ground and tore him to pieces. Penelope could see the flailing arms and legs, flinging wolves off him like so many flour sacks, before they finally got the better of him.

They pulled the flesh off his body by the mouthful, fighting over the choice morsels. The body grew smaller. Soon there was nothing left except a red stain in the snow, and that disappeared too as the wolves, still hungry, licked every drop of blood off the ground. Penelope watched as the beasts continued to nose at the trampled snow.

"Give my regards to your father, Evgeny Ivanovich," she said.

She looked out over the terrain as a new sound cut through the air.

A snowmobile engine.

She found the submachine gun on the roof of the *vez-dekhod* where Viktor had dropped it, and inserted a fresh

clip. She hid behind the far side of the snow vehicle and
waited.

The snowmobile came into sight, a big heavy-duty
machine painted a camouflage white. It skidded to a stop
a few feet away, and a bulky, goggled figure dismounted
carrying a rifle as if he knew how to use it.

Penelope's heart leaped. "Joseph!" she said. "Joe
Skytop!"

He spun around, the rifle coming up, then relaxed. A
huge smile wreathed his ugly features. He said, "Crazy
outfit you're wearing."

The wolves had begun cautiously to stalk him. He
raised the rifle, deciding which one to shoot.

The Baroness joined Skytop and pushed the rifle away.
"You don't want to shoot them," she said. "They're
friends of mine."

Wharton and the others were waiting for them with
guns ready when they rode into camp. Skytop slowed the
snowmobile to a walking pace and waved a scarf at them,
signaling them not to shoot.

"Joe's told me about the Chinese," she said, as she
climbed down from behind him. "It seems we've got a
new hand in this poker game."

She brushed off their questions about the wolfskin outfit and her capture by Penkin. The firing at the germ
laboratory, ominously, had stopped.

"Tommy," she ordered, "get our transportation ready.
We're going to have to move fast."

As Sumo scurried off, she turned to Wharton. "The
snowmobile that Joe captured will hold three," she said.
"Were you able to salvage any of the machines that attacked the camp?"

"I'm afraid not," he said. "Eric and Tommy pretty well
clobbered them with grenades."

"All right," she said. "Break camp and gather up what
we'll need. We're traveling light."

She accepted a cup of hot soup from Inga, and warmed
herself with a swallow of bourbon from Skytop's flask.
Inga produced a spare hotsuit, and she climbed into it

quickly. Wharton brought her an automatic rifle and a new kit.

Sumo was busy unpacking his equipment. He pulled out three objects that looked like lumpy knapsacks.

"This better work," he said, pulling the release ring.

There was a hiss of pressurized foam escaping, and the fabric stirred and swelled. Within minutes, it had ballooned into something the size and shape of a snowmobile.

"Terrific job of engineering," Sumo said. "Notice how the two rollers holding the drive tread are stretched to proper tension? How the skis and handlebars and other rigid parts are locked into place?"

He poked a finger into the engine hood. It left a dimple in the fabric.

"Take a few more minutes for the plastic foam to harden inside those fabric layers," he said. He pulled the release rings on the other two inflatable snowmobiles.

The Baroness, Skytop and Wharton each took one of the collapsible machines, packing equipment on the rear saddles. Eric, Inga and Sumo doubled up on the big Chinese machine that Skytop had confiscated.

"I thought we'd just be using these to get away on," the Baroness said. "I figured we'd have used all this gear and thrown it away. It's a good thing we've got that extra machine."

Up ahead at the germ laboratory there was a string of explosions, one after the other.

The Baroness tilted her head and listened. "The Chinese are blowing the place up. They're going to get the hell out of there before the whole Russian army arrives on the Kanin Peninsula to see what's going on. We don't have much time, children."

She buckled on a handgun and pulled goggles down over her face. She kicked the starter, and hydrogen fuel ignited in the combustion chamber of the miniaturized spaceship engine that drove the snowmobile.

"You think the Chinese have the virus?" Wharton said.

She nodded impatiently. "That's what those demolition charges were all about. We've got to catch up with the Chinese before the Russians do."

"And before the Russians catch *us*," Wharton said with a wry grin.

She didn't bother to answer. She pushed the throttle, and the snowmobile shot ahead like the rocket it was. She didn't wait to see if they followed.

Chapter 16

They began to run across bodies a mile or two from the laboratory: the Russian guards and patrolling sentries who had been dispatched with ruthless efficiency by the Chinese. The concrete bunkers had been blown up or doused with napalm. An armored *vezdekhod* lay on its side, blackened corpses spilling out of the doors where they'd tried to claw their way to safety.

Mortar fire had pounded a path through the minefield. The guard towers, never intended to cope with a military force, had been demolished by rockets. Penkin's wolves, trapped between the wire fences, had been slaughtered by machine gun fire.

The Baroness had to admire the brilliance of it. It showed what a small, disciplined force could achieve when it had surprise, speed and planning going for it.

She smiled grimly behind her mask and goggles. The Chinese would find the rules had changed now. They were no longer the predators, materializing out of a snowy nothingness to strike at a sitting duck installation. Now they were a column on the move, strung out and vulnerable.

She gunned the engine, and her snowmobile leaped forward, kicked in the rear by the hellish exhaust of the liquid-hydrogen engine. The other snowmobiles followed in her track, with the big captured Chinese vehicle and its three riders bringing up the rear. The two wolfhounds ran alongside, their instincts adapting naturally to follow ing this new kind of sleigh that pulled itself along without the help of horses.

A man in a white lab coat popped out of the smoking ruins and took a pot shot at them with a handgun. The Baroness ignored him. There were dozens of disorganized survivors wandering around—scientists and office personnel, unused to coping with the kind of violence that had been visited on them.

She leaned over and scooped something off the ground as she sped by: a webbed ammunition belt with a stenciled *U.S.* Phony evidence dropped by the Chinese. The Baroness had no doubt that there'd be other planted items to implicate the United States. And Skytop had said that the Chinese were using American weapons and other equipment; the Soviet investigators would find plenty of shell casings and other debris.

She picked up the Chinese trail and followed it north. The Chinese were heading for the coast of the Barents Sea. She estimated from the tracks that they had a force of about eighty men, two to a vehicle. That was all they had left after their unlucky encounter with her people.

The wind whipped at her face, clawing at her even through the mask. She levered the throttle forward another notch. The borzois began to fall behind.

Up above, there was a droning sound through the clouds. Some kind of light aircraft: a Russian spotter plane. Russian troops would be pouring into the area before long.

She hurtled across another fifty miles of blurred white void before she caught up with the Chinese. She topped a shallow hill, and there they were, stretched out below her in a long straggling line, carrying their dead and wounded with them.

She leaned over for a sharp turn and got back behind the hill, sending up a spume of snow. She straddled her throbbing machine and waited for the others to close the gap. Then, with a bloodthirsty whoop, she swooped down on the Chinese column.

She shot past the startled Chinese on the left, steering one-handed, the *Galil* assault rifle braced against her right hip, firing sideways as she went. On the other side of the column, trailing her a little so as not to set up a crossfire, was Wharton raking the Chinese with his own automatic weapon. Skytop and Eric followed them, ten yards behind, taking a second crack at the column. Clinging to the rear saddle of the captured vehicle that Eric was driving, Tom Sumo happily dropped grenades behind him as fast as he could pull the pins.

It was bloody work. They caught the rearmost Chinese by surprise, stitching them with 5.56mm slugs before they were aware that anything was wrong. She could see the face of the first man she killed, his mouth open in astonishment just before his head exploded in a frothy pink cloud that rained down on the snow. His machine careened sideways, out of control, and behind her Skytop skillfully avoided it while he hefted his own automatic weapon into position.

By the time she was halfway up the column, heads had begun to turn around. The line of snowmobiles wavered and became ragged, and some of the soldiers with better reflexes were getting their own weapons out.

She could hear the popping of grenades behind her— Sumo tossing them into the Chinese path—and the short rough chatter of Wharton's *Galil* to her right. There were screams and curses, and the ugly metallic clash of snowmobile collisions.

The man leading the column was a cool one, twisting around in his saddle to fire at her with what looked like a pearl-handled Colt six-shooter. She swung the rifle against her hip and pulled the trigger, but the clip was empty. She veered off to the left for another pass at the column, reloading as she went.

She remembered the face: a thin, ascetic, intelligent one that had shot her a look of pure hate. She'd have to find him again. He'd be the one carrying the moon capsule.

She streaked toward the disorganized Chinese again from five hundred yards out, the automatic rifle resting on the handlebars this time. Skytop was riding parallel to her, twenty feet to one side. On the other side of the

Chinese convoy, Wharton and Eric were doing the same thing.

The Chinese snowmobiles were still crawling along, the line breaking up aimlessly. The slaughter had been terrific. More than half of the soldiers had been killed or wounded. The bodies lay on the snow, spilling over idling machines. One bullet-riddled snowmobile came sliding her way, a dead driver sprawled over the handlebars. Three of the machines were tipped, their metal jagged and twisted, caught by Sumo's grenades.

Bullets whistled past her. The Chinese were setting up a defense. But the gunners who should have been riding in the rear seats had been replaced by gear and the corpses and wounded they had carried away from the battle with the Russians; instead, they'd been pressed into service as drivers. That meant that they had to shoot while trying to control their machines, or stop and take aim. She and Skytop got through the hail of lead without being hit, and then they were opening up with their own guns.

She saw soldiers jerk and twist like puppets as she fired. She counted at least a half-dozen victims to her bullets and Skytop's, and then her clip was empty again, and she had to swerve off, tossing a grenade to give them something to think about.

When she returned for a third pass, the Chinese commander had managed to get his men drawn up in a defensive circle, wagon-train style. Skytop was amused. He pulled in beside her and yelled in her ear: "I have a feeling I've played this scene before!" Then he separated from her, hunched down over his steering bar, and charged the soldiers with a blood-curdling Cherokee whoop.

An explosion rocked her snowmobile sideways. She leaned in the opposite direction to compensate and bore in on the ring of Chinese. They were firing a mortar, the damned fools! It was one thing to lob mortar shells at a stationary position, like the Russians, but it wasn't a very useful way to defend yourself against a moving target.

She dodged bullets and tossed a grenade into the ring,

then sped off again before they could draw a bead on her. Beyond, she could see Wharton and Eric, charging in and out, punishing the other side of the circle. Sumo was covering each getaway with grenades, and Inga, riding behind Eric in the middle saddle, had an automatic rifle at her shoulder, drawing a line of fire across the Chinese position.

She was satisfied with what she'd seen on that last approach. There couldn't be more than fifteen or twenty able-bodied soldiers left out of the forty or fifty that had gotten away from the Russians. It was just going to be a mopping-up operation from here on out.

She charged on her bucking snowmobile once more toward the ragged circle, the big Indian riding at her side. He was firing one-handed, holding the heavy weapon in the crook of his arm as if it were a toy, getting off his high-spirited war whoops. He got a little ahead of her, speeding toward a weak spot he'd noticed in the circle.

And that was when she saw the big white snowmobile break out of the circle and speed away, heading north at top speed.

It was the Chinese officer. He knew the game was up. He was leaving his men behind to keep her busy, while he hightailed it to the coast, toward whatever pickup arrangements the Chinese had made.

Without hesitation she broke off her charge and swung after him. Skytop and the others could damned well finish the mopping up. She'd seen the long metal shape of the thing the Chinese officer had cradled in his lap.

The moon capsule.

The metal cylinder that contained the end of the world.

She rushed over the landscape in her light, shell-like machine, hatched out of plastic foam and propelled by a tail of fire that was hot enough to melt metal. The airspeed indicator told her she was going sixty, seventy, eighty miles an hour. The airstream whipped at her, stinging through the hotsuit. The saddle jolted her spine like a huge boot.

The gap between them narrowed. The Chinese machine, powerful as its engine was, was no match for the bomb she was riding.

And then she saw it hit a fault and spill its rider to the ground. Too late she tried to avoid the same trap. Her machine pitched her out, licking at her with its fiery dragon's tongue, and she rolled clear to avoid being incinerated. Helplessly she watched her snowmobile skitter off. It would be a mile before it came to rest, its titanium gullet gulping the last teaspoon of liquid hydrogen.

He was still alive, but it looked as if his leg were broken. The metal capsule was lying beside him in the snow. He crawled over to it and put a protective arm around it.

She was still holding her automatic rifle. Keeping it aimed at the injured Chinese, she advanced toward him.

He had his weapon too. He drew the pearl-handled revolver and snapped off a shot that sent her diving into the snow.

She couldn't get close to him. She raised the automatic rifle, then lowered it.

She couldn't shoot. Her bullets would puncture the moon capsule. She remembered what had happened in Houston when the virus had leaked.

What had Hans Kolbe said at the briefing? That if the capsule were breached, the virus would begin to spread itself around the world, floating on air currents, transported by birds and insects. Growing and multiplying. Turning every speck of life that it encountered into more virus. Plants, animals, bacteria, fungus, people. Everything. All eaten and transformed within—she shivered—fifty days.

The Chinese officer was crawling toward his snowmobile. It was still purring, a few yards away. The moon capsule was cradled in his arms. His leg stretched out at an unnatural angle.

But he'd be able to ride. If he reached the sea, he'd be picked up. The Chinese would have the virus to use as seed for a biological weapon. That would be bad enough. But it would be worse if, like the Russians, they'd underestimated the dangers of the strange new life form.

She fired a burst over his head to discourage him. Grimly he dragged himself onward. He wasn't going to be intimidated. She had to admire him.

Could she rush him? She picked herself off the ground and sprinted. His gun lifted in a flash and fired. She hit the ground fast. The bullet went through the space she'd occupied a half-second earlier.

He grinned at her and pulled himself up into the saddle. He knew what was going through her mind.

The Baroness leaped to her feet and sprinted toward him. The hell with it! If she was going to die, she'd rather be shot with a Colt .45 than be turned into spoiled jelly by a virus.

But he didn't waste time shooting at her. He got the big machine going and roared away, looking back once to see her standing there helplessly.

She threw away the automatic rifle and drew the Spyder. His back was a tempting target. The explosive piton would detonate in his spine, spreading its little steel claws, and she could reel him in like a fish.

But she mustn't. If he dropped the capsule, it might crack.

She aimed low and fired at the snowmobile's stubby rear. The plastic thread hissed across thirty feet of space. Instantly she was jerked off her feet. She held onto the Spyder's butt with both hands and went bouncing painfully over the snow at twenty miles an hour.

She was the fish. And now she was going to reel herself in.

She slid on her belly across the slick surface, going faster and faster. It was only a matter of time before she hit a rock or a tree stump that would kill her. She worked the Spyder's clutch like a deep-sea fisherman, gaining an inch of line here, a foot there, every time there was some slack.

The Chinese bent over his handlebars, oblivious to her presence.

She was getting closer. By God, her body was bruised all over, but she was pulling herself closer and closer to the runaway vehicle!

Her body slammed into a little hollow, knocking the breath out of her. She almost lost consciousness, but she hung on. A little more! Ten feet! A yard! A foot! And then her fingers were clawing at the snowmobile's rear trim, and she was pulling herself up over the whirring rubber tread.

He looked over his shoulder when her weight settled in the rear saddle. His mouth gaped in shock. He reached for his gun, dropping the capsule.

She grabbed for the capsule. The hell with the gun! She caught it and hugged it to her, holding herself on the leather perch with her strong thighs.

He was fumbling with his holster, having an awkward time of it. He got the revolver in his hand and twisted in his seat, trying to see the target riding behind him. She embraced him with her free arm, squeezing as close to him as she could get. His arm, clumsy in the heavy quilted sleeve, crossed his chest to fire over his left shoulder. She leaned to the right, and the bullet whistled past her cheek. She got her right arm further around his torso and grabbed the revolver by its cylinder. He pulled the trigger again, and she felt the cylinder trying to revolve under her fingers.

The snowmobile was zigzagging erratically, slowing down and swaying from side to side as they wrestled for the gun. His broken leg dangled inches from the ground. She kicked at it, where she thought the broken edges of the bone would be.

He didn't utter a sound. She had to give him credit for that. But she could feel his body jerk in a spasm of pain. He let go of the revolver and she plucked the revolver from his hand.

He grabbed for her forearm, but she had already shifted her grip to the handle of the Colt. She put the long barrel to his head, cocked the hammer, closed her eyes and squeezed. There was a deafening explosion, and she could feel the powder burns on her forehead and eyelids. She opened her eyes in time to see the side of his head fly away.

The snowmobile lurched to a stop. She dismounted and

propped the heavy moon capsule in his arms for safe keeping. He looked as if he were cradling a baby. Bloo from his ruined head dripped down over the dull metal giving the cylinder a darker cap.

The firing had stopped back there at the scene of th battle with the Chinese. Skytop and the others had finishe mopping up. They'd be coming after her soon, followin the track of her snowmobile. There was a clump c stunted birches about fifty yards away. Wearily, sh walked over and rested her bruised back against one c the trunks.

Sumo arrived about ten minutes later, riding by himse on a captured Chinese snowmobile.

"Eric and Inga are chasing after your machine's track I thought I'd branch off in this direction. Dan and th Chief will be along as soon as they tidy things up bac there."

Sumo untied a bulky squarish parcel from the back sea With an effort he set it down on the ground and un wrapped it. It was the laser autoclave.

"I thought you'd want to cook some virus," he sai with a grin.

Together they assembled the panels into the miniatur coffin shape that would hold the moon capsule. Sum adjusted the cylindrical laser housing at one end an turned on the switch.

"We're pumping photons," he said. "It'll take abou five minutes for this thing to warm up."

"I'll get the moon capsule," the Baroness said.

She started toward the Chinese snowmobile with i grisly burden. There was a strangled cry from Sumo.

"Stop!" he choked.

She stopped and looked at the corpse of the Chine officer she'd killed.

It was moving. Moving in a queer, unnatural way. boneless flow, like some soft-bodied sea creature, as inside the quilted jacket, tissues were slumping. As sh watched, the body slipped off the saddle to the groun holding the moon capsule in an abnormal embrace.

"The virus," she whispered. "It must have eaten through the capsule."

She and Sumo could see the head of the corpse growing softer. It sagged like jelly. It was a viscous blob that began visibly to flatten and spread over the snow. And now the upper torso of the body was growing shapeless.

Sumo turned to her, horror on his face. "Did any of that stuff get on you?" he said.

"I don't think so. I'd be feeling *something* by now. The virus must have broken through after I came over here."

Instinctively they both backed away a few more feet.

"Not much wind," Sumo said. "And it's blowing away from us, thank God! The virus must be working fast, with all that blood and those open wounds to gobble up."

The corpse was bubbling now as a fermenting mass forced its way through the fabric of the clothing. There was a brownish foam over the quilted jacket.

"Get back," the Baroness said. "I don't know how fast the contaminated circle is growing, but I don't want to be within a hundred yards of that thing. An hour from now I don't want to be within a mile."

Sumo faced her, the pupils of his eyes wide with dread. "I'll do it," he said in a small voice. "What the hell, I'm dead anyway. I might as well put the capsule in the autoclave. Fifty million degrees Centigrade. Even the virus can't survive in that."

He started walking toward the corpse. The Baroness pulled him back.

"Forget it, Tommy," she said. "It's too late. We were supposed to vaporize a sealed container. You can't put that body in the autoclave. You can't fit *yourself* inside."

His slight body went rigid. "It's the end of everything, then. Man. Plants. Animals. Life itself."

She faced the thought. It was a big one. It took a while to get adjusted to it.

"That's about it, Tommy," she said. She gave him a pale smile. "We made a nice try, though."

Chapter 17

Wharton was the first to arrive. He was driving one of the big Chinese machines. It was towing a long sledge that carried a twenty-foot metal pole with a red flag flapping from its rear.

Sumo ran toward him, waving his arms. "Back!" he cried, "back!"

Wharton jerked to a stop. The sledge, continuing on its own momentum, banged into the snowmobile's rear.

"What's up, Tommy?" he said.

They told him.

Wharton looked at them without saying anything. Then he turned toward the corpse, lying fifty yards away. The disintegration of the body was continuing. It looked flat inside its uniform, like a giant gingerbread man. There was a foul brown leakage from the sleeves and collar, staining the snow. The deadly cylinder had sunk deep into the chest, a pair of empty-looking sleeves wrapped around it.

"Jesus!" Wharton said.

The Baroness touched his arm. "We'd better get out of here, Dan," she said. "We can't outrun the virus forever, but for now we'd better put some distance between us and it."

"Maybe we can still lick it," he said.

"What do you mean?"

He jerked a thumb toward the sledge with its metal boom. "I found something interesting among the Chinese equipment. I thought I'd better bring it along for Tommy to look at."

They went over to examine it. Up close they could see that it was some kind of steel casing, its sections riveted together, with little service hatches spaced along its sides. Chinese characters were stenciled on each hatch. Sumo read one of the groups, his eyes widening. He looked up at Wharton and the Baroness.

"A nuclear bomb," he said. "The Chinese brought a nuclear bomb with them."

"They probably planned to blow up the piece of peninsula with the Russian laboratory on it, if they couldn't get inside," Wharton said. "If they couldn't have the virus, the Russians couldn't either. Or maybe they wanted to set off a nuclear explosion to cover their getaway. Leave the bomb behind at the coast to blow up a couple of square miles of Russian troops."

The Baroness leaned forward, her eyes gleaming. "Tommy, can you make that thing work?"

"I think so. The arming mechanism seems pretty straightforward. And here's the timer."

"What class bomb would you guess we've got here?"

He pondered. "Probably twenty megatons."

"That's my guess, too. The radius of total destruction will be on the order of eight miles. How hot is it going to get here at the center?"

He grinned. "About three hundred million degrees Centigrade."

"Hot enough to vaporize our virus, wouldn't you say?"

"*And* any of the landscape it may have contaminated."

"Get to work, Tommy. And hurry!"

It took Sumo about a half-hour to arm the bomb. He worked quickly, deftly, blowing on his fingers to keep them warm, glancing nervously over his shoulder from time to time. Skytop and Eric arrived and were warned from the immediate area. Inga pulled up shortly afterward, driving the Baroness' snowmobile, which she'd retrieved.

Sumo straightened up and put his gloves back on. "Let's get the hell out of here," he said.

They stood on the barren shore of the Kanin Peninsula's northern tip, gazing past the tumbled ice floes toward the sea. Somewhere out there was the nuclear submarine that was going to pick them up.

"We have to get in these rubber laundry bags again, huh?" Skytop said.

"Unless you want to swim the whole twenty miles," the Baroness said dryly.

Inga was coaxing one of the borzois into her waterproof sack. Eric would take the other dog. It was going to be easier this time, without the load of weapons and equipment they'd had to struggle with before.

Sumo made a last-minute inspection of the laser signal device. They couldn't risk any kind of radio this close to the Russian defenses—not even a high-speed burst. But the submarine was equipped to detect a laser flash in the invisible part of the spectrum. It would surface just long enough to pick up six bags of people and dogs. It had been waiting out there, raising periscope twice a day at a predetermined time, for a week. It had been told to wait out there until the end of the world, if necessary.

But the end of the world didn't seem so close any more.

"Something's bothering me," Eric said. "When that hydrogen bomb goes off, it's going to destroy a sixteen-mile circle of Russian territory. Including the bodies of all those Chinese soldiers and their equipment. But they planted all that false evidence at the germ lab which made it seem that America was responsible for their raid. And now a nuclear explosion. We may have saved the world from the moon virus. But haven't we risked starting World War Three?"

The Baroness shook her head. "We're planting some evidence of our own. The Chinese will get the blame."

"What do you mean?"

"Hydrogen bombs leave fingerprints."

"Yes, but . . ."

"This one's going to leave Chinese fingerprints. Russia's been keeping tabs on the fallout from the Chinese tests, just as we have. When they make their radio-chemical analysis of the debris from the explosion, they'll be able to tell what kind of bomb went off, the size, the design —and what country made it. The United States will be off the hook."

"Besides," Sumo grinned, "sooner or later somebody's

going to come across these Chinese snowmobiles we're leaving on the beach."

Joe Skytop was pacing restlessly, casting nervous glances southward.

"Why doesn't that damn bomb go off?" he said.

Sumo glanced at his watch. "Any minute now. And you'd better not look in that direction. You don't want to take a chance on burning your retinas."

They hunkered down among the immense jagged blocks of ice that the spring thaw had thrown up on the beach, and waited. Inga and Eric had tied scarves around the borzois' eyes and were patting them and soothing them. Sumo had found some dark glasses among the stolen Chinese equipment, and now he passed them out.

The Baroness strained to see through the lenses. They seemed to be solid black. She couldn't see a thing.

And then there was a brilliant flash through the opaque glass, bright as the sun. Even through the protective lenses, the Baroness was temporarily blinded.

She waited a few seconds, tears running from her eyes, then snatched off the glasses. Far away to the south, a gigantic column of smoke was shooting high into the sky. As she watched, it widened at the top into a mushroom cloud.

The shock wave hit them three minutes later. The ground trembled under their feet. There was a prolonged rumbling, like thunder. A wind buffeted them.

She turned to the members of her team. Unabashed awe showed on their faces.

"Don't look so gloomy," she said. "We've just cured a virus."

Operation Doomsday had taken over the Underground War Room. It would take all the resources of the Defense Department to get the plan rolling, now that the final deadline had passed. America was closing up shop forever. Army trucks and military transport planes would be needed to ferry supplies and key personnel to the secret underground caverns. The Marines would have to move in to guard vital communications links, take over television stations, put potential troublemakers under arrest. Troops would have to be deployed to keep the civilian population under control.

The President turned weary eyes toward his Secretary of Defense. Neither of them had slept for forty-eight hours.

"I never thought when I took my oath of office that I'd be the President who'd go down in history for ending two hundred years of American democracy," he said.

"Look at it this way, Mr. President," said the Secretary of Defense. "There isn't going to *be* any history."

The Majority Leader spoke from the vantage point they'd given him in the corner of the glass-walled observation booth.

"You've done your best, Mr. President," he said. "No one's going to blame you. This is your last responsibility —an ugly one. Doing what you have to do to save a little seed stock to start over again." He and the President had been political enemies for more than two decades, but now his voice was soft and gentle.

"Thank you, Senator," the President said. "I appreciate the way you've kept your people quiet so far." He shook his head. "But in the next few hours, all hell's going to break loose."

"It's a gamble anyway," said the Secretary of Defense. "Dr. Kolbe doesn't guarantee that we'll be safe from the virus even in the underground shelters. One speck—two or three molecules of virus DNA getting through an air filter—and . . ." He broke off and stared glumly at the scene below.

The enormous chamber was as busy as an anthill that has been poked with a stick. Couriers scurried back and forth, handing sealed messages to the men working at pushbutton consoles, or to the shirtsleeved Action Groups huddled together at their tables. The Joint Chiefs of Staff were in another observation booth, across the floor. Here and there, on the floor itself, were various command posts for the military services and government agencies.

Dr. Kolbe pushed his way past the guard and came into the booth. "I've rechecked the computer figures as you requested, Mr. President," he said. "There's no mistake."

"The virus is loose, then?"

The thick-bodied epidemiologist consulted his watch. "The virus would have eaten its way through the capsule about four hours ago. By now, the area of prime contamination should be approximately a mile in diameter. I would expect that birds and other wildlife would begin to accelerate the spread at this point."

The President looked at his Defense Secretary. "And no word from Coin?"

"I'll get Sam. He's on the floor somewhere." The Secretary picked up a phone.

The NSA Director had just shouldered his way into the booth when the CriCon alarm went off. The President looked at the Secretary and leaned past the technician on duty to punch a button on the console.

"Yes?" he said.

The map on the President's private screen faded. It had been showing the location of supply routes and Marine checkpoints throughout the country as they were established. Now the earnest face of the DIRNSA duty officer appeared.

"Mr. President?" The duty officer squinted at something off-screen: his own TV monitor, as he made sure of his identification.

The NSA Director poked his head into the monitor camera's field of view. "It's all right, Hotchkiss," he said. "You've really got the President. And I'm here."

"Yes sir. We've got a report of an aboveground nuclear explosion. Russia, on the Kanin Peninsula. About twenty megatons, from the seismograph readings. No other information yet."

The President turned to the Secretary of Defense. "What do you know about this?"

The Secretary was sweating. "It's not one of ours. I swear it. It couldn't be!"

The President stared at the NSA Director, his face dark with foreboding. "What the hell has your Coin been up to?"

NSA leaned toward the screen. "Stay on it, Hotchkiss. I want all the raw data from the VELA Nuclear Test Detection Satellite as soon as it comes in. And get a plane with a nose scoop into that cloud of fallout right away, and I don't care *how* close to the Russian coast it has to fly!" He turned to the President, visibly shaken. "Coin *wasn't* carrying any kind of nuclear device, Mr. President. You know we'd have to go through the AEC and the Defense Department, and it would have come to you for review."

The President turned abruptly to leave the booth. He paused at the door and said, "I'll be on the Hot Line, trying to sweet-talk the Soviet Premier. Christ! All we need at this point is a nuclear war! When I come back, you'd better have an answer!"

They sweated it out for the next two hours. Word had begun to leak to the War Room below. They could see it in the ripple of excitement that was sparked by a sudden increase in the foot traffic between the command posts and Action Group tables. At one point the Secretary picked up a buzzing phone and said peevishly: "No, I *don't* have anything to tell you yet. Try to hold things down, will you?"

The NSA Director was trying to patch through a link to Key through the President's console and the IBM 7090 computer at Fort Meade. The acknowledgment signal came through as the President re-entered the booth.

"The Russians say they'll keep their fingers off the button—for now," he said, mopping his brow with a handkerchief. "But they say the answers damn well better come out *right*."

"Mr. President," NSA said, "here's Key."

The image on the screen rippled. Hotchkiss's face was replaced by the strong, rugged features of a television Western star.

"What the hell *is* this?" the Secretary of Defense said.

Looking embarrassed, the NSA Director said, "It's Key's way of protecting his identity. *And* maintaining security. He's riding piggy-back on a network television program. He's modulating the carrier wave—just sneaking in a wave with an altered shape a few hundred times per second, in a randomized pattern. No one else could possibly pick it up. But the big computer at Fort Meade is programmed to take all the pieces and make sense out of them."

The U.S. Marshal on the screen moved his lips. "Coin just reported in," he said. "The virus is destroyed. And there's nothing, repeat, nothing, to tie the U.S. to an invasion of Soviet territory."

He gave the rest of his report in a few terse sentences. Marshal Dillon's face disappeared from the screen, to be replaced by the duty officer, who evidently didn't realize he'd been out of communication.

". . . and preliminary analysis indicates that the hydrogen bomb that exploded was of Chinese origin. There is reason to believe that the Russians have verified this independently. . . ."

The NSA Director looked smug. He leaned back in his chair, his hands folded, twirling his thumbs. "We're home free, gentlemen," he said. "Coin's done it. It wasn't possible, but Coin's done it. Destroyed the moon virus. Managed somehow to take out the Soviet Union's prime biological warfare facility, with whatever else they were cooking up there. Kept the United States out of it. And driven another wedge between Russia and China."

Everybody was smiling, slapping backs, shaking hands. The Senator took a flask out of his pocket and offered a drink to Dr. Kolbe. Two of the President's aides were scrambling for telephones.

The President looked through the glass wall at the milling throng below. Some of the color had returned to his face. He looked almost relaxed.

"Those people deserve some rest," he said. "I'm going to get some sleep myself."

He walked over to the door and paused. He turned to look at the Secretary of Defense.

"Cancel Doomsday," he said.

The Baroness Penelope St. John-Orsini floated on her back in the yacht's swimming pool, wearing just a pair of sunglasses and the bottom half of a bikini. The hot Mediterranean sun caressed her lithe, tawny body, baking out the memory of Arctic cold. It was glorious.

A head popped out of the water next to her and shook itself dry. It was Helena Pontarelli, the opera star, a bright chatterbox who was known to make a point of never having an affair with any man who was worth less than fifty million dollars.

"Penny!" Helena squealed. "How *marvelous!* Andreas and I never dared *hope* you'd accept the invitation to this cruise! You just dropped out of *sight!* Where in the world have you *been?*"

"Getting rid of a virus," the Baroness said.

"Oh you poor thing!" Helena gushed. "Are you feeling better now?"

"Much better," the Baroness said.

There was a lot of activity around the pool. White-jacketed waiters were serving drinks to guests in bathing suits, sitting at the poolside tables. A few people, early as it was, were dancing to the music of the five-piece combo that had come aboard at Monte Carlo. A famous American movie actress, naked as a jelly bean, was riding on the back of France's pet novelist, down on his hands and knees playing horse while she slapped at him with a big straw sun hat. A sweet young thing in a bikini had a busy hand under a beach towel that was draped across the lap of a famous film director who was reclining in a deck chair; the two were holding an animated conversation. A Texas oil millionaire was having a political argument with a notoriously gay television personality. And Penelope's host, looking sturdy and pugnacious in shorts and a faded tee shirt, was dressing down the yacht's first officer for some tarnished brass he'd discovered around one of the portholes in a stateroom.

The Baroness trailed a hand lazily in the water. "Helena darling," she said, "is there anybody *interesting* on board?"

"Of course! Isn't there always? There's Rex, and Lennie, and Truman, and of course the Prince, and Clint, only he's mad at me. . . ."

"I mean *interesting*."

"Oh. Well there's this marvelous South American. Only thirty-two, with a face like an angel, but he owns cattle ranches and oil wells and coffee plantations and a string of race horses that are the envy of the Keeneland set. . . . Perhaps you've met him. Hector Castillo."

"Does he have any brains?"

"I don't know, but he has a *beautiful* body. Oh, there he is! Hector!"

She waved at someone poised at the end of the diving board. Penelope looked up. He was a stunning sight, a rich golden bronze against the deep blue sky, with smoothly muscled shoulders and arms and a deep chest and flat hard belly and a white smile gleaming out of a classic face. He waved at Helena, recovered his balance, and dove with graceful economy into the pool. He reached them in a few powerful strokes. He spoke to Helena, but his eyes rested with frank admiration on Penelope's bare breasts.

"Hello, little one, and what is our dear host stocking his pool with these days?"

"Hector, this is my dearest friend, the Baroness Penelope St. John-Orsini. Watch out for her, she's an American."

Hector lifted his eyes to Penelope's face. His expression was serious. "I saw what you did at the Monaco Grand Prix," he said. "It was very brave of you. Sorry you lost the race."

"There'll be other races."

"True." He smiled. "Race you to the end of the pool!"

She rolled off the air mattress and shot like a minnow toward the pool's edge, without giving him a chance.

"Not fair!" he shouted, and plunged after her.

Helena yelled, "I should have warned you, the Baroness likes to win!" But his head was under water, and he didn't hear her.

He caught up with her and caught her around the waist, drawing her close to him. "I lost," he said. "How about another chance?"

She slipped a hand between his legs. Everything was satisfactory down there.

"I've got Stateroom D," she said.

He threw back his head and laughed. "Don't you know that's the one with the one-way mirror? Our host likes a little peep show once in a while. Why don't you come to *my* stateroom. I'm in G. No mirror, but there's a marvelous Vermeer on the wall."

She took his hand. "Then what are we waiting for?" she said, and pulled him through the crowd toward Stateroom G. The Vermeer was exquisite.